Winds Love

Winds of Love

Rebecca J. Hammond

AMBASSADOR INTERNATIONAL
Greenville, South Carolina • Belfast, Northern Ireland

Winds Cove

Cover design & page layout by A & E Media — Paula Shepherd

ISBN 1 932307 00 1

Published by the Ambassador Group

Ambassador Emerald International
427 Wade Hampton Blvd.
Greenville, SC 29609
USA
www. emeraldhouse.com

and

Ambassador Publications Ltd.
Providence House
Ardenlee Street
Belfast BT6 8QJ
Northern Ireland
www. ambassador-productions.com

The colophon is a trademark of Ambassador

To all the friends, family, teachers and mentors who have encouraged, prodded, pushed and praised. I am forever grateful.

chapter one

Secrets.

So many secrets.

Willow boughs trailed long fingers across the water's surface, sliding back and forth with the current in solemn contemplation... remembering. Remembering what? She wished she knew.

Jackie peered through the half-light of early morning and tossed another pebble into the waters of the cove. The stone vanished into murky depths. The wind rushed past her where she perched on the boulder, spraying her with seawater until her pale green eyes began to sting from the salt. She brushed the briny moisture away and listened to the wind.

"What secrets do you hold, wind?" she asked.

The wind only whistled louder and whirled away into the trees. The wind always had secrets, Jackie thought. It saw things no one else saw and heard things no one else heard. It whistled and whispered and whined. But it never told. Your secret was always safe with the wind.

She sighed and wrapped her arms tightly around her knees. Not much longer now. Her sister would be expecting her back soon for breakfast. Then there was school.

She wished she didn't have to go. She had tried a zillion times to convince Shonda she should home-school. But her sister always said no. Jackie flinched as a wave sent up a geyser of icy spray.

She couldn't help it if she wasn't like the other kids. Just because she liked to read and write and daydream and stay by herself, they called her a snob and a creep. It had been like that ever since she had moved to Kilree, Maine, six years ago. They thought it was weird, too, that she lived with her sister and brother-in-law.

Her brother-in-law, Kyle, told her life was like a dance. He said she was waltzing through her years while everyone else was doing the can-can. She had been flattered at first. Now she wasn't entirely sure who had come out on the short end of that one.

The sun peeked over the horizon and washed the sky with color. The waves scintillated with light, and a long finger of gold stretched from the distant skyline to the water that splashed her toes, pointing at her accusingly.

Jackie sighed and slowly climbed to her feet. "I know. I'm going."

She slipped and skidded over the treacherous rocks until she reached the trees. Vine draperies shielded the cove from the forest.

Jackie glanced back.

The sun began its climb, setting the ocean on fire. The blazing waves surged forward, spreading the dawn in a great golden flood. But the light seemed to fade when it came to the cove, drowning in the lingering shadows and leaving the rocks sheathed in darkness. She turned away. Winds Cove had its own secrets to hide.

"Good morning! Just in time for breakfast," Shonda said. The smile on her pretty face faded when she turned around. She sighed. "Oh, Jackie, just look at you!"

Jackie glanced down at her sodden clothes. She hadn't even noticed.

"Can you ever stay dry? And clean? Every time you go to the ocean, you come back looking like you took a mud bath!"

Jackie shrugged. It was no big deal to her. She was wet. So what?

"Morning, Jax," her brother-in-law's deep voice boomed from behind her. He tousled her long damp curls as he walked by. "Just got back, huh?"

"Isn't it obvious?" Shonda asked.

Kyle Lainson grinned at his wife, his brown eyes twinkling. He winked at Jackie.

"I don't see what's so horrifying about being wet," Jackie said. She started across the kitchen.

"Shoes," Shonda said. She pointed a long, slender finger at Jackie's muddy sneakers.

Jackie stepped back and quickly removed them, then went to the sink. "I mean, really, Shonda, water is a basic element, just like fire, earth, and air."

"But when the elements of earth and water mix they form a new element called mud that dirties up my clean floor." Shonda gestured to the trail Jackie had left. "You're dripping."

"Sorry."

"Not to mention the stains they leave on clothes."

Jackie shrugged. "Clothes are just coverings we wear to conform to society's idea of modesty."

"But I'm the one who cleans your coverings, so you might want to consider that next time you go out and get dirty."

Jackie sighed. "I'm sorry. I'll go change before we eat."

She hurried to her tiny room at the end of the hall and changed out of her wet clothes. She washed up in the bathroom and then pulled on a long flowing skirt of soft gray and a loose fitting top. She brushed out her long dark curls and swept them back from her face into a barrette.

Shonda was just putting scrambled eggs onto Kyle's plate when Jackie slid into her seat.

Shonda smiled, her blue eyes twinkling. "That's much better."
She filled Jackie's plate and then fixed her own.

Kyle said a quick blessing for the food and they began to eat.

"We must have the only fourteen-year-old in the state of Maine
that gets up before dawn seven days a week by choice," Kyle said
between bites.

"Mama always got up early, didn't she?" Jackie asked.

A shadow flitted across Shonda's face. "Yes… she loved to watch
the sunrise."

Jackie felt a pang at the sight of her sister's saddened face and
wished she hadn't mentioned their mother. She ate the rest of her
breakfast in silence.

When they were all finished, she loaded the dishes into the
dishwasher and then grabbed her backpack and headed off for
school.

Kilree Christian Academy was less than two miles from home,
so Jackie usually chose to walk. It was a pleasant stroll. It also put off
having to face her classmates.

The road stretched away before her, following the coastline in a
narrow, winding trek. The trees were already beginning to change
their emerald dresses for gowns of crimson, rust, and gold. Fallen
leaves rustled beneath her feet. Another month and the leaves would
all be gone. Two months and the ground would be cold and white.

A patch of goldenrod by the side of the road beckoned to her.
Yellow was such a happy color.

The school bus whizzed by. A boy shouted something out the
window. She let the words blow by her. They couldn't hurt her with
words. Shonda had told her that. They couldn't hurt her just as long
as she didn't let them.

A few minutes later the Academy loomed before her, its sturdy
brick structure rising up against the October blue sky. Her homeroom
classroom buzzed with the usual activity, the girls exchanging gossip

and teen magazines and the boys throwing paper airplanes and footballs. When she slipped into her seat, no one even looked her way.

Several minutes before the bell rang, the classroom door opened and Mrs. Cox, their homeroom, history, and English teacher, stepped inside followed by a couple who looked to be in their late thirties and a boy about Jackie's age. A hush fell over the room. Mrs. Cox smiled at the curious silence and introduced the strangers.

"This is Mr. and Mrs. Dawson and their son Montgomery. The Dawsons have just moved to Kilree."

The students murmured amongst themselves while Mrs. Cox spoke quietly for a moment with the couple. Kilree was a small town. It had been years since anyone had moved there. Most people moved away. Jackie remembered all too well the stares from the Kilree townspeople when she had arrived. She turned a sympathetic gaze upon the newcomers.

Jackie was instantly captivated by Mrs. Dawson. Slender and stately in a fashionable business suit, not a lock of her smooth dark hair out of place, she looked positively elegant. And Mr. Dawson, tall and imposing, had the look of someone important, like a senator or a governor. They must have moved from the city, she thought. Such elegant people would never live in the country! No, they would live in New York City and go to the ballet and the opera.

Her gaze came to rest on the boy. Montgomery Dawson, she thought, trying out the sound of the name in her mind. How marvelous! Just exactly the sort of name she would pick for a boy. His platinum blond hair fell forward across his forehead. Under the fluorescent lights it looked almost silver. And his eyes! So dark, almost black! His gaze, dark and challenging, shifted from face to face, and he stood tall and straight, as if ready to take on the world.

When his parents left, he relaxed a bit and shoved his hands deep into the pockets of his baggy cargo pants.

"Just pick an empty seat," Mrs. Cox told him.

He nodded and sauntered to the back of the room.

Jackie frowned. He walked like he owned the wide world itself. Cocky, she decided, and looked away.

"Why don't we all introduce ourselves to Montgomery," Mrs. Cox said. "Just say your name and something interesting about yourself."

Jackie turned her gaze to the trees beyond the window. She hated these name games. She could never decide what to say about herself. All the things she thought were interesting, everybody else thought were weird. She frowned and looked at the carpet. It looked like the goldenrod she had admired that morning. She could say that she loved Shakespeare. Or that her favorite painter was Monet. She let her hair fall forward in a curtain that shielded her face and blocked out the rest of the world. The curls cascaded over her cheeks in a waterfall of ringlets—not black, not brown, but somewhere in between. Just like me, she thought. There was something about being fourteen that made the world all topsy-turvy. You weren't a child. You weren't an adult. So what were you?

"Randall! Hey, you in the hair! Wake-up!"

The class snickered.

"Kris," Mrs. Cox said, a reproving tone in her voice.

Jackie glanced up, pushing her hair back out of her face. Everyone was staring at her. Kris Cappencella, sitting in the seat in front of her, rolled his eyes and turned back around.

"It's your turn, Jackie," Mrs. Cox said, a little too patiently.

"Um, I'm Jacqueline Randall and I—um…" she hesitated, racking her brain. Shakespeare? Monet?

"Don't have any parents," one of the boys said.

"Brent!" Mrs. Cox looked horrified.

Jackie felt her stomach tighten. Yes. She supposed that was interesting. She looked at the carpet again, thinking what an ugly color it was, more like brown mustard than goldenrod.

Brent muttered an insincere apology. She ignored him. Her gaze wandered about the room. The students weren't looking at her now.

Except Montgomery.

His dark gaze was fixed on her. What was he thinking? She met his eyes for a moment, so dark and strange. Eyes that knew many secrets, she thought. She wondered if he was so cocky after all.

"How was school?" Shonda asked as soon as Jackie walked through the door.

"Insufferable."

Shonda smiled as she peeled potatoes. "I'm sure it wasn't all that bad."

Jackie shrugged. She grabbed a carrot from the pile of vegetables on the sideboard and pulled a chair up next to her sister's. "A new student came today." She liked the way carrots crunched between her teeth.

"Really? Who?"

"Montgomery Dawson. Isn't that a beautiful name?"

"I suppose. Is he nice?"

"I don't know. He walks like some of the boys walk. You know, like he owns the whole world. And he dresses like the other boys too. Everything's baggy. Baggy cargos, tee-shirt, baggy flannel shirt all open and untucked."

"They'll be bringing the dress code back soon enough," Shonda said with a shake of her head. "The school board is discussing the possibility of uniforms." She handed Jackie a potato and a knife.

"He's beautiful, though." Jackie swallowed the rest of her carrot and began peeling the potato.

"Beautiful?" Shonda raised her eyebrows.

"Yes. His hair is silver and his eyes are black."

"Silver hair and black eyes?"

"Who's got black eyes?" Kyle suddenly appeared in the doorway.

"You're home early," Shonda said.

"Computers went down so we closed up for the day." Kyle snatched a carrot and began munching. "So who's the guy with the black eyes? Have you been beating up the boys again, Jax?"

"No, no! Not big repulsive bruises, but very dark *irises.*"

"Oh."

Shonda and Kyle exchanged amused glances.

"So what's his name?" Kyle asked.

"Montgomery Dawson."

"Dawson. Yeah, I heard a family was moving up here."

"It sounds like they might be a Christian family then," Shonda said, "if they've enrolled their son in KCA."

Kyle nodded. "It would be good to have another Christian family in town."

"Maybe we'll see them at church. Jackie, would you do me a favor and please baste the turkey?"

Jackie finished peeling her potato and then handed the knife to Kyle. She opened the oven door and slid the rack out. "Mr. and Mrs. Dawson are so refined!" She dipped the little basting brush into a small pan and began painting melted butter onto the turkey. "I'll bet they love the ballet. What I wouldn't give to see a ballet!'"

"Just go down to Mrs. Kendrick's," Kyle said. "Her kindergarten students are giving a recital at the end of the month."

"Very funny. Someday I'm going to a real ballet!"

"You go for it," Kyle said.

"And maybe I'll even invite you guys."

Kyle grimaced. "Thanks, but that won't be necessary. I'm not big on tights."

"Oh, Kyle, you have no appreciation of art and beauty!"

"Sure, I do. I married your sister." He winked at his wife.

Jackie made a face, halfway between a grimace and a grin. "I guess I can't argue that point."

"It's okay, Jax," Kyle said with a grin. "It's good that we have one idealist in the family. You keep us from getting too practical."

Jackie smiled. "Shonda, do you need help with anything else?" she asked.

"No," Shonda said. "I think I'm all set. Thank you, though. Supper at six."

Jackie nodded and went to her room. She changed into a pair of jeans, grabbed her Shakespeare, and headed outside. She paused for a moment on the back step, breathing in the autumn air. Her sister and brother-in-law's snug little single-story house sat back from the road in a sheltering grove of maples. She crossed the backyard to a huge maple tree and nimbly climbed up, settling herself into her favorite thinking place. Her room seemed to stifle the creative process, but out here in the midst of leaves, branches, and old birds' nests her imagination could run free.

She opened her book to Shakespeare's sonnets but didn't read. Her gaze wandered over the russet leaves. Sometimes she wished that she had a brother or sister close to her own age. Or it would even be nice if Shonda and Kyle had children. Her sister and brother-in-law were really her only friends. There had been a girl at school last year, Alison, who had been nice to her and eaten lunch with her sometimes. But she had moved away during the summer. And she wasn't really a friend, Jackie had to admit to herself, though she was probably the closest to a real friend Jackie had ever come.

She supposed that most girls were close to their mothers. She would have been close to her mother. She was sure of that. She just wished she could remember her better.

Each year it got harder to recall her face. Jackie squeezed her eyes shut and tried to remember. She could still see her mother's hair. It looked like Shonda's—all red and orange and gold. Like fire. Her eyes were like Shonda's too. Blue and sparkly. But she couldn't remember her voice. Or how she laughed. Jackie wanted more than anything to know what her mother had been like. But whenever she asked Shonda, her sister got really sad. Shonda didn't talk to anyone about either one of their parents. Not even to Kyle. Jackie tried to picture her father, but she couldn't remember him at all.

At supper she was unusually quiet, her mind still clouded with her thoughts. After the dishes had been done she went to her room and spent the evening with her volume of Shakespeare. She had no idea how long she'd been reading when Shonda knocked at her door.

"What are you doing still awake?" Shonda asked.

Jackie glanced at the clock beside her bed. It was almost midnight. "I didn't realize it was so late. I was just reading."

Shonda sat down on the edge of her bed. "What are you reading?"

"I just finished *Hamlet,* and I was going to start *The Comedy of Errors.* I don't like to go to bed on a tragedy."

Shonda smiled. "I think you would be a marvelous Shakespearean actress."

"Really?" Jackie sat up. Her heart fluttered at the thought. "It wouldn't be a practical way to make a living unless I made it big."

"Which I'm sure you would."

"But I would need to be strikingly beautiful."

"You are."

"My nose is too turned up, and I have *freckles.*"

"Your nose is just right for your face. And your freckles add allure."

"Allure?" Jackie raised her eyebrows.

"Sure. You know what Kyle told me after he first met you?"

"What?"

"That you had a pixie face and an agile mind."

"Really?"

"Uh-huh."

"I still think I'd blend in with the floor boards. I'd do better if I looked like you."

"Like me?"

"Your hair is golden. People in the theater would be entranced by your golden red hair."

Shonda laughed softly. "If you say so. But I think you'll do best sticking with your own face and hair."

"I'm too puny!"

Shonda leaned forward and kissed her on her forehead. "You look like a faerie princess. Good night."

"Good night, Shonda."

Jackie turned out her light and rolled onto her side, gazing out her tiny window at the stars winking at her above the trees. ☺

chapter two

Jackie fixed her eyes on the treetops visible through the classroom window. In her tree at home she sometimes let her hair fall loose and free past her waist and imagined she was Rapunzel letting down her hair. She wondered if her prince would ever come like in the fairytale. Or perhaps she would never marry. She could be a silver-haired, dignified old maid with many stories to tell about her illustrious career on the stage.

"Jackie. Jacqueline." The words dimly penetrated her imaginative shield.

Mrs. Cox gave her a reproving glance. "It's your turn to share your report."

Report? Jackie stared at her teacher. *What report?*

"The history project reports are due today, Jackie. Did you finish yours?"

The project was due today? Jackie just shook her head. "I'm sorry, Mrs. Cox. I—I guess I forgot."

Mrs. Cox frowned and shook her head.

Jackie shut out the sounds of her classmates snickering. Oh well. There was nothing she could do about it now.

Mrs. Cox called on someone else.

Jackie felt someone's gaze on her and looked over to meet Montgomery Dawson's dark eyes. Was he mocking her too?

She looked away.

At lunch break she wandered out under a small grove of trees and sat down on the grass. A group of boys were playing soccer nearby. Montgomery was with them. She watched for a while. Sports were so peculiar. Interesting. And fun she supposed. But really... running back and forth, trying to kick a ball into a large net? Human entertainment was such an odd thing. Montgomery must be very good, she decided. He seemed to have the ball most of the time and none of the boys could take it away from him. The boys seemed to like him well enough, and she'd seen more than one girl staring at him in class. He didn't talk much, but there were always people around him. Jackie shook her head. Every person was a mystery when it came right down to it. She opened her journal and began to write. The sunrise had been spectacular that morning, and she had managed to stay a little dryer for Shonda's sake.

"Look out!"

Her heart thudded against her chest as a ball hurtled by her, only inches from her nose. The soccer ball bounced off a tree and then rolled to a stop a few feet away from her. One of the boys quickly retrieved it and headed back to the field.

"Sorry about that," someone said.

Jackie looked up. Montgomery Dawson stood before her, an apologetic look on his face. His eyes looked blue in the brilliant sunlight. "You okay?"

Jackie nodded.

"Hey c'mon, Dawson! Let's go!"

"Yeah, leave the creep alone!"

Jackie stared at Montgomery's feet. His sneakers looked expensive. She realized they weren't moving. Why was he still standing there? She looked up.

"Sorry," he said again.

"Dawson, come on!"

He shrugged apologetically and jogged away. She watched him thoughtfully for a while, then returned to her journal.

The rest of the afternoon dragged by until at last the final bell rang. Jackie packed up her book bag and was heading toward the door when Mrs. Cox called her name.

"Jackie, would you wait a moment, please? I'd like to speak with you."

Jackie swallowed hard and nodded. It must be about the report.

The rest of the class filed out of the classroom and she was left alone with the teacher. She stood awkwardly at the front of the room, waiting. Mrs. Cox sat on the edge of her desk and sighed. "Jackie, I've spoken with the other teachers. We're all concerned. You don't pay attention, you're constantly forgetting homework, and your grades are falling lower and lower." She sighed. "I've seen you in English class, so I know you're a very gifted student, but you're not using your talents to their full potential." She paused for a moment. "Jackie, I realize that your background was... difficult. Do you think that's why you're having problems in school?"

"No, Mrs. Cox."

"Are you sure? Because if you think that's even part of the problem, I'm sure we could arrange for some type of counseling—"

Jackie shook her head. "It would be easy to say that I have learning difficulties because I come from a dysfunctional family, but I don't think it's fair to blame my parents for my own problems."

Mrs. Cox studied her for a moment. "All right. What do *you* think you need?"

Jackie shifted her weight from one foot to the other. "I don't know."

"I know the other students give you a hard time, and I want you to know that I'm here to help you."

"Yes, Mrs. Cox." Jackie studied the tops of her shoes. A couple of scuffmarks marred the left one.

"I also want you to know that I'm praying for you. All the teachers are. If you ever need someone to talk to or if you have a prayer request that you would like us to remember, all you need to do is ask."

"Thank you, Mrs. Cox," Jackie said woodenly.

Mrs. Cox sighed. "Please take this to your sister and have her sign it. Bring it back tomorrow."

Jackie tucked the note into her pocket. "Is that all, Mrs. Cox?"

The teacher studied her for a brief moment, then nodded. "Yes, Jackie, that's all. You may go."

Jackie quickly left the room.

She took a long time to walk home.

Shonda set the note on the table.

Jackie waited.

"We go through this every year."

"I know."

"When I was in school, I never had a problem with forgetting homework or paying attention."

"I know."

"It's a matter of self-discipline. You need to *make* yourself pay attention. From now on as soon as you get home, you work on your homework. Understood?"

"Yes, Shonda. I'm sorry."

That evening Kyle asked her to take a walk with him. The crisp air lifted her spirits, and she felt some of her natural buoyancy return. She jumped from one patch of dry leaves to another, reveling in the satisfying sound of them crunching beneath her feet.

Kyle remained silent, watching her with his typical half-amused, half-solemn expression.

"I'm not Shonda," Jackie finally said.

"I know you're not."

"But she doesn't. Every time I mess up, she's there telling me when she was my age, she did it right." Jackie jumped into a small pile of dusty brown leaves. *Crunch.*

Kyle was silent.

"I mean, I know she's perfect and I'm hopeless, but I don't need her to constantly rub it in my face. I know I always disappoint her. And I know she probably wishes she hadn't been stuck with me."

Jackie glanced up at her brother-in-law. He didn't say anything. He just looked at her with his knowing brown eyes.

She sighed. "Well, maybe that's taking it a little too far."

She squirmed a little under his gaze. "Okay, okay, you're right. I'm just throwing myself a pity-party. I know Shonda loves me. She shows me every day. I know she just wants me to do my best."

Kyle remained silent.

Jackie threw her hands up in the air and started walking again. "And I'll try harder in school."

Kyle slung his arm loosely around her shoulders. "I just love these little brother-sister chats."

Jackie sighed. "I just wish I didn't have to bother with school at all."

"Being 'refined' requires education beyond ninth grade."

Jackie frowned and kicked a stone in her path. Why did Kyle always have to make so much sense?

"Besides, don't you enjoy knowing things?" he asked. "About what things are made of and where we all came from and how to spell artichoke?"

Jackie smiled. "I do like learning. But sometimes I'll be paying attention and then suddenly these great ideas will come and just sweep me away! It's the most exhilarating feeling in the world!"

"But how much more exhilarating to have true knowledge about life, than to live in a daydream. There's nothing wrong with trying to decorate reality with some imagination. But when imagination becomes your reality—that's where it gets dangerous."

They passed by a patch of goldenrod. Jackie studied the ground. "My daydreams are so much more beautiful than my reality. What's wrong with just wanting to live in beauty?"

Kyle was quiet for a moment. "Nothing," he said at last. "Did I ever tell you I was a nerd in school?"

"What?"

He nodded. "A complete geek. Pocket-protectors, you name it."

Jackie giggled at a sudden vision of her cool brother-in-law with taped glasses and high-water pants.

"The kids picked on me all the time."

She stopped giggling. "Really?"

"Uh-huh."

"But you're so cool! What happened?"

"I got contacts."

"That's it?"

He chuckled. "Not entirely. But it helped. I could play sports without worrying about breaking my glasses. That was the beginning. Then I realized that as long as I was following God's Word and being who He wanted me to be, the rest really didn't matter. I remember I was reading through II Corinthians at the time, and a verse that really helped me was in chapter 10. 'For we dare not make ourselves of the number, or compare ourselves with some that commend themselves: but they, measuring themselves by themselves, and comparing themselves among themselves, are not wise.' I didn't need to compare myself to the other kids. They could call me whatever they wanted. What they thought about me didn't matter—just what God thought.

"Things weren't always rosy, of course. But once I stopped worrying about my classmates, I was able to focus more on my relationship with God. And on top of that, I had a lot more fun."

Jackie frowned at the ground. She knew it didn't matter what the other kids said or did. And most of the time she didn't let it bother her. But she couldn't help thinking how nice it would be to have friends at school to sit with at lunch and study with for tests. She glanced up at Kyle. "People don't treat you that way now. When did it stop?"

"I don't remember exactly. It was gradual, I think. I grew up. The other kids grew up too. Reading became more socially acceptable—and necessary in college. And being good at math and science became cool. Maturity wipes away a solid chunk of adolescent problems."

"So you're saying this will pass."

"Yeah. I think it will."

Jackie nodded and stomped on a curling brown leaf. College didn't promise a changed life, of course, but even if it did, four years seemed a long time to wait.

"And you know what else?" Kyle said.

She shook her head.

"I met the best friend of my life in college."

Jackie smiled. "Shonda."

"That's right. She brought a beauty to my life that I had never dreamed of. And so did you."

Jackie stared at him in surprise.

"You have the unique ability to make the world more beautiful. And to find beauty where none can be found. That's something God has really blessed you with. You have a gift, Jax. Use it. You've been making our lives more beautiful every year. Maybe it's time to widen your circle."

"How?"

"It doesn't take much. Sometimes it's the smallest things that can mean the most. For example... teachers."

"Teachers?"

"Yeah. They have a tough job."

"I suppose." She thought of Brent and Kris and the other boys who were always causing trouble.

"But a student who wants to learn—and who finishes her homework and pays attention in class—would be very rewarding to a teacher's profession."

Jackie furrowed her brow at his implication. She had never

thought of herself as a *problem* student. She looked at Kyle doubtfully. "So you're saying that just doing what I'm 'supposed' to be doing would make Mrs. Cox's world a more beautiful place?"

"That's exactly what I'm saying. Just like not tracking mud across Shonda's floor. Small things, Jax."

Jackie sighed. "Okay, I concede. You win. As usual."

"That's my favorite sister-in-law!"

"I'm your only sister-in-law." Jackie smiled as they turned back. Brothers-in-law were strange creatures. But they were kind of nice to have around.

When they got back to the house, Jackie went straight to her room and dug around under her bed for the plastic bag of library books she had checked out a week earlier. Each student had been assigned a different time and place to research, and the founding of Kilree had fallen to Jackie. She had meant to go back and check the microfiche for old newspaper articles, but as soon as she had stepped outside of the library, all thought of the history report had gone winging away with the seagulls soaring overhead.

Jackie sat cross-legged on her bed. There wasn't much published on the town of Kilree. Founded in 1847 by the Mulqueen family... Josef and Fiona... they immigrated from County Kerry, Ireland in 1846... that must have been around the time of the Potato Famine. She flipped through a skinny paperback written by a local author. It was more about immigration than Kilree, but it mentioned the Mulqueens. The only thing published on the founding family was a little pamphlet the librarian had pulled from a brochure wrack she kept by the desk for tourists. There was a picture of the old Mulqueen Estate, now the local inn, as well as a sepia tone photograph of Josef and Fiona Mulqueen. She opened the brochure and found more pictures—a drawing room, a stable, and another couple. The caption under their picture read Desmond and Brigit Mulqueen, the last Mulqueens to live in Kilree. She scanned the rest of the page. They had no children of their own and willed the estate to the town when their nephews and only heirs died in a tragic accident. "How sad," she said softly, and flipped the brochure over. There was a map on the back with directions, telephone numbers, and an email address for reservations at the inn.

She worked into the wee hours of the morning and when she finally allowed sleep to wipe her mind clean of names and historical dates, she dreamed about potatoes crossing the Atlantic Ocean in rowboats. ☺

chapter three

A single shaft of light from the afternoon sun braved the clinging shadows and warmed her where she sat upon her rock.

The smell of the ocean filled her senses, and the wind sprayed her with icy salt water. The glow of Mrs. Cox's surprised smile when Jackie had presented her with not only the signed note, but also the history project and delinquent homework still gave her an odd feeling of pleasure and more than made up for the lavender smudges under her eyes. Kyle had been right. She turned to a fresh page in her journal and began writing. The minutes drifted by....

Jackie gazed out over the water and chewed thoughtfully on her pen. A flicker of movement in the trees across from her caught her eye. She watched in surprise as a figure emerged from the forest. A boy, she decided, but who? He stepped out of the shadows and the light glinted off his silvery-blond hair. Montgomery Dawson.

He paused for a moment, and she knew he had seen her. He seemed to hesitate, then began skirting the edge of the cove. Jackie watched curiously. Surely he wasn't going to come over and talk to her! The other boys had certainly told him all about her by now.

Montgomery Dawson began clambering out over the rocks toward her. Even on the treacherous boulders he moved with agility and confidence. At last he reached her rock and sat down beside her.

"Hi."

"Hello."

Silence. Jackie closed her journal and waited.

Montgomery's dark eyes roved over the walls of the cove. "What is this place?"

"It's called Winds Cove."

He nodded.

Jackie absently twirled a long strand of hair around her finger.

"It's peaceful here," he said.

"Ayuh."

"Do you come here a lot?"

Jackie nodded. "It's kind of like my second home. I come almost every morning to watch the sunrise." She waited for an expression of incredulity or a sarcastic remark. None came.

"That's really nice."

"Where do you come from?" she asked, unable to contain her curiosity any longer.

"We moved from Boston," he said, and for the first time she detected the faintest trace of an accent.

"The city! Is it nice? It must be glorious to live in the city! So much excitement! Do you go to the ballet and the opera?"

Montgomery smiled. It was the first time she had seen him smile. It was nice—a kind of lopsided grin.

"The city's okay. I never went to any ballets, but I've been to a couple of operas."

"It must have been absolutely magical!"

He smiled again. "Actually, I'm not really big on opera. I mean, the music's good and everything, but to be honest, sometimes they just feel like they go on forever. Especially when they're in another language. Symphonies are more to my taste. Rachmaninoff and Vivaldi. The Broadway musicals are good too."

"Musicals! How wonderful! Why did you move *here*?"

He was silent. "We needed a change," he said after a long pause.

Jackie hesitated for a moment. He seemed sad. Then she asked, "Do you miss the city?"

"Sometimes. I mean it's only been about a week. I miss my friends. But I like it here too. Life seems slower and kinder somehow."

Jackie didn't respond. Kinder? She wasn't sure life was all that kind anywhere.

"Have you always lived here?" he asked.

"Since I was eight."

"Where did you live before?"

"In the southern part of Maine. Still on the coast, though."

"Why'd you move?"

"My sister Shonda got married, and Kyle—that's her husband—got a job up here."

"So you live with your sister?"

Jackie nodded. She heard again in her mind Brent's harsh words, "she doesn't have any parents." She knew that was what Montgomery was thinking. She could almost feel his curiosity. But he didn't ask. He was different from the other boys. A lot different.

"My mother died," she said finally.

"I'm sorry." Sincere regret shone in his face. "How old were you?"

"Six."

Montgomery was silent. But it wasn't an awkward silence like she was accustomed to. He seemed to truly understand. She suddenly wanted him to know her mother—to know what she had been like, even if it was only the little bit that she knew herself. "My mother was wonderful."

"Was she like you?" He looked out at the water.

"Oh, no! She was a lot like my sister. She was funny and popular, and she had golden hair and blue eyes! *Everyone* loved her!"

"What was your father like?"

Her enthusiasm faded. "I don't remember."

"Did he die when you were really young?"

Jackie let her gaze slip out to where the ocean reached the sky. "My father isn't dead."

Montgomery looked surprised. "Oh. I'm sorry."

"It's okay. He left my mom when I was only one. My sister never talks about him." Jackie watched the water roll in, wave after wave after wave. She had tried to ask Shonda about him before, but Shonda always got angry. Then somewhere along the way, she had just stopped asking.

"Sometimes he sends us a Christmas card. I've seen them come in the mail, and I've read them, but Shonda never puts them out with the other cards."

They sat in silence for a long time.

She noticed a cord hanging around his neck and caught a glimpse of something shiny dangling from the end. "What's that?" she asked curiously.

He glanced down. "Oh. My grandpa gave it to me." He pulled the cord out from his shirt and she leaned closer to look at the pointed rock hanging off it.

"It's an arrowhead!" she exclaimed.

"Yeah. He got it when he was a kid."

"Cool. So how did you find the cove?"

"I was just walking in the woods, and I followed the sound of the ocean."

"Is your house close by?"

"Yeah. It's just beyond those trees. Maybe ten minutes. Hey, is that a cave?" He pointed to a black gash in the rock walls of the cove.

Jackie narrowed her eyes to see where he was pointing. "Ayuh," she answered. "The cove is full of them."

"Where do they lead to?"

She shrugged. "I don't know. I think most of them just run in circles."

"You've never been in any of them?"

She shook her head. "I've peeked into a couple, but I've never explored them."

He looked around, his dark eyes scanning the surface of every rock.

"There's an old Penobscot legend about a silver cave somewhere around here."

"Really?"

"Mmm-hmm." She twirled a long strand of hair around her finger, trying to recall the details of the legend.

"Was it a silver mine?"

"No. It was supposed to be a cave made all of silver."

"Do you believe it?"

"I don't know. The caves have been explored a thousand times, and no one has ever found anything like that. But there are rumors that the cove is haunted too," she said with a laugh, "but I've never seen any ghosts." She paused. "I'd like to believe it, though."

"That the cove is haunted?"

"No, that there's a cave of silver. There's just something spectacular about the thought of a silver cave. It's ever so much better than gold."

"Except that gold is worth a lot more."

"Only because it's more rare. I think silver is far more beautiful than gold. Gold is too gaudy. And you see it *everywhere*."

"'All that glisters is not gold,'" Montgomery quoted.

"Shakespeare," Jackie said with a surprised smile.

"*Merchant of Venice*," Montgomery said. His lopsided grin appeared once again. "Don't look much like a Shakespeare buff, do I?"

She shook her head.

"Well, that just goes to show you can't judge a book by its cover."

She felt her cheeks grow warm at the thought of her first assessment of him. "I'll bet you don't carry a volume of Shakespeare to soccer practice, though."

Montgomery grinned. "The guys at school don't know about my cultural side, if that's what you're hinting at."

"Why do you keep it secret?"

"I don't really. If any of them asked, I wouldn't deny it. But since I know that none of them are interested in it, I don't see any reason to shout it from the rooftops."

"I wish I could be so subtle."

"I can see how that would be hard for you."

"What do you mean?"

"Well, you look different from everybody else. I mean, with your hair and everything, you look kind of like a fairytale princess."

Jackie stared at him. His eyes were clear and honest. He wasn't mocking her. That, she thought, with a sudden rush of elation, was the nicest compliment she'd ever received.

"Thank you."

"You're welcome."

They sat silently for a long time. At last, Montgomery rose.

"I'd better get going. My mom hates it when I'm late for supper. See ya."

She said good-bye and watched him nimbly make his way back over the rocks. She continued to watch long after he had vanished into the trees. What kind of boy liked Shakespeare and Rachmaninoff? What kind of boy risked his popularity to talk to a social outcast? Jackie chewed on the end of her pen and returned to her journal.

"I need a bigger room."

Kyle and Shonda looked up from their dinner.

"I'd like a new truck," Kyle said.

"No, *really*. I *need* a bigger room. It's not a matter of desire or preference. It's a matter of *necessity*."

Kyle looked at Shonda. "Uh-oh. I think she's about to make a point."

"You can joke all you want, Kyle Lainson, but I'm very serious." Jackie took a bite of mashed potato. "I'm very thankful that I have a room, but there's no floor space and you practically have to jump onto the bed in order to close the door."

"Okay," Kyle said. "You need a larger room. Do you want me to build an addition onto the back of the house or should we just buy a new home?"

"Oh, no, that's not at all necessary."

Shonda rolled her eyes. "Well, that's a relief."

"I've done a lot of thinking about this, and I've come up with a couple of options."

"Okay, let's hear them," Kyle said and took another bite.

"Well, first we could turn this room into my bedroom."

"The dining room?" Shonda asked.

"Well, we don't really need it. We use the kitchen table for everything except supper."

Shonda was already shaking her head. "There's not enough room in the kitchen for my china cabinet."

"Well, if we got rid of the dining room table, we could move the living room into the dining room so the china cabinet could stay in here. And I could have the living room."

"Try again," Kyle said.

"Or we could move the dining room stuff into my bedroom and me into the dining room."

"Impractical," Shonda said.

Kyle shook his head. "The dining room is off the kitchen and your room is down the hall. It wouldn't make sense."

"Okay, that leads me to my final option."

Kyle set down his fork and leaned back in his chair, waiting.

Jackie took a deep breath. She had tested the waters. The alternative she favored most she had saved for last.

"Well, we could turn the attic into my bedroom."

Shonda shook her head. "What would we do with all the boxes and trunks up there?"

"Put them in my room. It's like a large closet anyway."

"I have a better idea," Kyle said.

Jackie's heartbeat quickened. He was considering it at least. Shonda could tell too by the skeptical look on her pretty face.

"That back corner of the basement is still empty. It's dry and cool down there. That would free up the attic for Jax."

Shonda frowned. "But the attic is so hot and stuffy."

"Only because there's no ventilation. When the windows on either end are open, a breeze comes through, and it's not that bad."

"The ceiling slants almost to the floor."

"It's high enough for me, and all of my things would fit," Jackie said.

"What would we do with her old bedroom?" Shonda asked, beginning to look defeated.

"I don't know. We could turn it into an office… or a hobby room."

"A hobby room?"

"Sure! For all of your crafty things. That way you wouldn't have to store it in our bedroom. And we could get you a worktable. That way there's no hassle. No post-inspiration clean-up."

Shonda threw up her hands in exasperation. "Oh, all right! I've exhausted all my arguments. It's fine with me."

Jackie beamed at her brother-in-law. He winked back.

"But this is your idea," Shonda said. She pointed a long finger at Jackie. "You're going to have to help. Homework first, then the room. No skipping out to leave us to do the work. Understood?"

Jackie jumped out of her chair and threw her arms around her sister. "Thank you!"

Shonda smiled. "Well, after all, we can't stifle your creative genius now can we?" ☺

chapter four

Kilree Bible Chapel was built of red brick with large white pillars across a broad front portico where the church members gave out food and clothes to the less fortunate. It was a pretty church, Jackie thought as she and her sister and brother-in-law walked down the sidewalk Sunday morning. Though it looked simple compared to the ornate Catholic church that sat across the street.

Once inside, she headed for her Sunday School room. Though she liked her teacher, Mr. Armacost, who was also Kyle's partner in their small accounting firm, she didn't particularly enjoy Sunday School because the class was comprised almost entirely of her school classmates. As if five days of torture weren't enough, she thought to herself as she took her seat.

When the class was over, she joined Kyle and Shonda in the sanctuary. She glanced around to see if the Dawsons were there, but didn't see them.

Pastor Hallowell approached the pulpit and beamed at his congregation.

Jackie smiled. Pastor Hallowell was a great man. He was also a very old man. Though plagued by arthritis, he was nevertheless fit and physically active. In spite of his advanced years and infirmities, there was nothing slow or infirmed about him. His movements were quick and purposeful, as was his speech. Jackie loved listening to him.

He had been preaching a series from the book of Esther—her favorite book of the Bible. She loved all the dramatic irony.

Pastor Hallowell greeted his congregation and then opened the morning service with prayer.

Monday morning dawned beautifully on Winds Cove. The chill wind blew through Jackie's long hair. She imagined she was a princess in an island fortress.

At school the morning passed quickly, and after lunch Jackie went outside and sat under the trees with her journal, shutting out the incessant chatter of the other students. She wrote for a few minutes, then closed the book and set it on the grass beside her. She leaned back against the tree trunk and gazed dreamily at the clouds drifting through the sky. Like stretched out cotton balls, she thought.

The whisper of sneakers on grass warned her that someone was behind her, but before she could look around, someone dashed by and snatched her journal. Kris.

Jackie jumped to her feet. "Hey!" she cried. "Kris, please..." She ran after him.

A group of students gathered around Kris as he held up her journal like a trophy.

"Let's see what the loser writes about all day long!" He opened the notebook and randomly selected a page. "Listen, listen!" he shouted above his classmates' voices. He read dramatically, "'The sunrise was so glorious this morning it made me want to weep!'" Several of the boys made gagging noises. "'Shonda said Mama always got up to see the sunrise. I wish I could remember her better. It's getting harder and harder to see her face.'" A hush fell over the group. "'Sometimes when I see kids out with their moms and dads it hurts so much. If only Mama was still alive...'"

Kris' voice trailed off.

Jackie stared at the ground. She could feel tears springing to her eyes.

A movement among the students caused her to look up.

Montgomery pushed through the crowd.

Kris straightened. He was the tallest boy in the class, but somehow he looked much smaller just then. The boys stood for a moment, eyes locked on each other.

Montgomery reached out and took the book out of Kris' hands.

"I think you've read enough," he said.

Kris stared defiantly at Montgomery for a moment longer, then averted his eyes from the other boy's dark gaze.

Montgomery stepped away, and the other students made a path for him. He handed Jackie the journal. "I'm sorry," he said.

Jackie took it without a word, but she met his gaze gratefully. She turned and walked back to the trees. Murmurs started again behind her, but she refused to listen.

The rest of the day passed like a dream. No one spoke to her. Not even Montgomery.

Never had she felt so alone.

Jackie didn't go home that afternoon. Right after school, she headed for the cove.

The ocean breeze felt good on her hot cheeks, and the endless cadence of the waves beating on the rocks calmed her. She took a deep breath and exhaled slowly. It was no big deal, she reasoned with herself. So that nasty Kris had stolen her journal. And read it. Out loud. In front of *everyone*. She caressed the worn cover and the familiar words.

Out of the corner of her eye she saw someone approaching. She knew before she even turned that it was Montgomery.

"Not gonna jump, are you?" he asked.

She smiled faintly. "Not today."

He grinned and handed her a tissue.

She took it in surprise. She hadn't even realized she was crying.

Montgomery sat down. "I thought I'd find you here."

"Were you looking for me?" She sat down next to him.

"I just wanted to save you from doing something drastic," he said with a wry grin.

She sighed. "Why do the boys have to be so dumb? I know they don't like me, and I don't care about that. I'm used to it. But why do they have to go out of their way to humiliate and hurt me?"

"They don't understand you," Montgomery answered simply. "You're different from the others in our class. You're *deeper.*"

"Oh." She guessed that was a compliment.

"I understand you."

"Really?"

He gazed out at the water. "Yeah. You, uh—you kind of remind me of someone."

"Who?"

He was silent for a moment. "His name was Perry." He didn't offer anything further, and Jackie decided not to ask.

"So where is your family going to church?" she asked instead. "I mean, I didn't see you at Kilree Bible, and I just wondered if you were going somewhere else."

"Well, actually, we've been going back to Boston on the weekends. We're still sort of in transition, I guess you could say. The house hasn't sold yet, and my dad has some business there that he's still wrapping up. We'll probably go to your church when we're settled."

After a while he stood up. "I want to check out that cave."

Jackie followed his gaze to the crevice splitting the face of the rock.

"Are you coming?" he asked.

"I don't know. Do you think it's safe?"

"Why wouldn't it be? You said people have explored them before, right?"

"Yes, but..."

"Then why not?"

"I don't know... they're so mysterious and forbidding. I'm not sure if I want to know their secrets."

"It'll be fun!" He grinned down at her, and in spite of herself she smiled back. He reached out a hand and pulled her to her feet.

"I used to pretend that faeries lived in those caves. I guess I just don't want to go in and be disappointed by ordinary rock."

"Nothing about the world is ordinary unless you make it ordinary," he told her.

"I guess."

She followed him back over the rocks and up to the crevice in the cove wall. She peered over his shoulder, trying vainly to penetrate the gloom. It was useless. She could only see in a few feet. The rest was swallowed in blackness.

Montgomery stepped in without hesitation.

Jackie held back.

"C'mon," he called back to her.

She took a deep breath and stepped inside. Two paces into the cave the ceiling sloped downward, and she had to duck her head. She paused for a moment to let her eyes adjust to the dim light. Where was Montgomery? She squinted through the dark. The air was dank and musty and the rock slick with moisture. She could almost feel the walls closing in around her.

At last she made out Montgomery's dim figure several feet away.

"There's a tunnel," he said, his voice bouncing off the rock somewhere ahead of them.

"How can you see anything?"

"I can't see much." His footsteps faded.

Jackie waited. Her back was beginning to ache. She could see better now, the light from the entrance casting the dusty air with a faint glow. Finally, Montgomery returned.

"We'll have to come back with flashlights," he said.

"How far did you go?"

"Not very. A few steps into the tunnel, and I couldn't see anything at all."

Jackie sighed with relief when they re-emerged into the fresh air.

The cove was engulfed in shadows. It was only about five o'clock, but the sky was already beginning to darken.

Jackie paused outside the cave opening and frowned. Something didn't feel right. Like when Shonda rearranged the pictures on the walls without telling anyone. She couldn't put her finger on it, but she could tell something was different.

What? What was it?

Montgomery's dark eyes were already scanning the surrounding forest. "There."

She followed his gaze. Above the rock of the cove, a tree branch moved slightly. A shadow detached itself from the tree and vanished into the woods.

Someone had been watching them. ◡

chapter five

Jackie and Montgomery were quiet as they walked home.

Montgomery finally broke the silence. "Maybe it was just someone out for a walk. People go for walks all the time, right?"

Jackie nodded. "Yeah." But she knew that neither one of them believed it. The cove was on the far end of town, and no one ever came there. The older people said it was too dangerous, and the younger ones were always at the beach in the summer, snowmobiling in winter and hanging out at the town common in between times. "Maybe it was one of your soccer rivals trying to learn your secrets."

Montgomery's tense face relaxed into a grin.

They had reached the end of the trees, and the road lay like a boundary separating them from the real world.

They stood for a moment quietly.

"Maybe we shouldn't say anything about…"

Jackie nodded. "Shonda and Kyle wouldn't let me come back if they thought it was dangerous."

"My folks are kind of overprotective."

"Well…"

"See you tomorrow," Montgomery said.

Jackie nodded. "Yeah. Tomorrow."

They turned and headed in opposite directions. Jackie knew

it was probably nothing. Nothing ever happened in Kilree. It was probably just someone out for a walk like Montgomery had said. But she couldn't shake the creepy feeling it had given her. Even so, it was with reluctance that she crossed the asphalt boundary into the world of responsibility and school and homework assignments. She walked home slowly.

"Where have you been?" Shonda asked as soon as Jackie walked through the door.

"At the cove—"

"That attic won't empty itself out, you know."

"Shonda, I'm sorry. I know I should have come straight home, but I had a perfectly insufferable day at school, and I didn't even think. Don't be angry, please?"

Shonda sighed. "I'm not angry. I just wish you would learn to be more responsible. You didn't do your homework there by any chance, did you?"

Jackie shook her head.

"All right. Supper at six."

Jackie shut herself in her room and forced herself to concentrate, blocking out all thoughts of the mysterious watcher at the cove. She was surprised how quickly she finished. The assignments really weren't that hard. She just didn't often discipline herself to do them. After supper, she returned to her room and, struck with a sudden inspiration, worked as far ahead in all of her subjects as she could, teaching herself the new concepts in math and reading ahead in science and history. Learning came easily to her. It was the forcing her mind to study instead of daydream that was difficult. It was late when she finally went to bed, exhausted, but she felt a deep satisfaction she'd never before experienced. Shonda surely wouldn't mind if she went to the cove tomorrow, just for a little while.

"Jackie," Mrs. Cox called again.

"Oh, I'm sorry, Mrs. Cox. What was the question?"

Mrs. Cox repeated the question and Jackie answered it correctly. Again.

At first it had been fun, knowing everything the teachers were going to teach before they taught it. But after a while, Jackie's mind began to wander. This was the third time Mrs. Cox had called on her. Each time she had answered correctly, but she could tell her teacher was getting annoyed. She would try harder.

Noon found Jackie in the cafeteria lunch line. She grimaced at the murky vegetable soup and selected a cheese sandwich and some salad. She sat at an empty end of one of the long tables and began eating.

A tray materialized across from her.

Jackie looked up in surprise.

Montgomery grinned. "This seat taken?"

Jackie glanced around. The tables near her had suddenly fallen silent as dozens of eyes watched.

"Uh—no."

Montgomery grinned and sat down.

Jackie stared at him. "You're destroying your social life."

"I have no social life. What kind of sandwich do you have?"

"Cheese. Don't you care what they're saying?"

"Do you?"

"Well, no, but—"

"Then stop worrying, because I don't care either."

"But you're popular."

Montgomery laughed. "Not really. The guys hang with me because I play soccer. That's the only reason. And they respect me because I'm better than they are."

"I knew you were cocky."

Montgomery laughed again. "I had a private coach in Boston, and I played varsity last year."

"In eighth grade?"

"Yeah. Just second string, but all the guys in my class hated me so I'm kind of used to being on my own too."

"Oh. Are you on the varsity team here?"

"Nah. The coach told me I was lucky just to make JV since I came late. He had just bumped someone off the team so there was a vacant spot. There's a home game next week. Are you coming?"

"I don't know. I've never gone to one."

"You should. It would give you something different to do."

"What do you mean by that?"

"Just that variety is the spice of life." His mouth twitched into his lop sided smile, and he took a huge bite of his sandwich.

Jackie hesitated. Going to a soccer game meant willingly putting herself in close proximity to the people she was always trying so desperately to avoid. "I'll think about it."

By the end of the school day Jackie had managed to drown out all the whispers buzzing through the halls about Montgomery and her. It was appalling how immature teenagers could be. A boy talks to a girl, and everyone thinks they're "going out." Jackie shook her head. Utterly appalling.

"What?" Montgomery fell into step beside her as she followed the stream of students pouring down the hallway to the front entrance where the buses waited.

"Nothing. I was just reflecting on the maturity level of the average fourteen-year-old."

Montgomery grinned. "You're not letting them get to you?"

Jackie sighed. "No. I've just never really been in this position before."

"What position?"

"You know."

He gave her a blank look.

Jackie took a deep breath. "They're saying that you like me."

"Of course I like you."

Jackie rolled her eyes. How could someone so smart be so dense? "No. That you *like* me."

Realization dawned on his face, and he suddenly laughed so loudly that students nearby turned to stare. Jackie wondered if she ought to feel offended.

Montgomery regained his composure and then grinned at her. "Let them think we're engaged if they want. I don't care. Do you?"

"I guess not." Jackie sniffed. "You didn't have to guffaw so loudly at the notion though."

Montgomery chuckled. "Sorry. I'll try to keep my 'guffawing' to myself from now on. Did you go to the cove this morning?"

Jackie nodded. "No sign of our spy. It must have just been someone out walking."

"I guess. Still planning on exploring those caves with me?"

"Yes. Oh, but I forgot a flashlight! I'll run home first, then meet you there, okay?"

"Sure. See you there!" he called back as he boarded the school bus.

Jackie hurried across the road and headed for home. "Winds Cove," she whispered to herself as she walked. "I wonder what secrets you'll share with me today."

She burst into the house and ran to her room, stripping off her long blue skirt and pulling on an old pair of faded jeans and a scruffy sweatshirt. She quickly retrieved the powerful flashlight from the hall closet and then ran back to the door, just avoiding a collision with Kyle.

"Whoa! Where's the fire, Jax?"

"I'm going to the cove!"

"What about your homework?" he asked.

Shonda suddenly appeared in the doorway.

"I finished it last night." She looked from one skeptical face to the other. "Really, I did! I worked ahead so I could go to the cove this week."

"How far ahead did you work?" Kyle asked.

"I don't know. I think I finished everything for the week."

Kyle and Shonda exchanged glances.

"Mrs. Cox did give us a hand-out to do, but I finished it in class."

"Well... good," Shonda said. "But I think you should check with us first before you go running off."

"I'm just going to the cove. I go there every day."

"Yes, but I think you need to realize that you have responsibilities here as well. If you really want the attic for a bedroom, you're going to have to be willing to invest some time in it."

"I know. But today—"

"Will be an excellent time to start. Kyle came home early this afternoon so he could help."

"That's great! Really! But I'm supposed to meet Montgomery—"

"Well, you should check with us before you make plans like that. I'm sure after a few minutes he'll realize you aren't coming. You can explain at school tomorrow."

Jackie sighed. This was obviously one argument she wasn't going to win. She thought fleetingly of Montgomery. Would he explore the caves without her? She shrugged the thoughts away.

"Now before we can do anything to the attic, we have to clean out all the junk," Shonda said. "So why don't we start on that now?"

Jackie nodded and headed back to the closet to return the flashlight.

"What were you doing with the flashlight, Jax?" Kyle asked.

"We were going to poke around in a couple of the caves." She put the flashlight back on the shelf and then followed her brother-in-law down the hall to the attic stairs.

"Going exploring, huh?"

"Yeah. We wouldn't go in really deep or anything."

"Hmm. Just be careful, okay?"

"Of course."

"And mark your way so you don't get lost."

"Okay."

"And don't go alone—Wait a minute," he paused and turned to look at her. "Who's 'we'?"

"I was going with Montgomery Dawson."

Kyle frowned. "On second thought, I think I want to meet him before you go wandering off into a catacomb of caves with him."

"Oh, Kyle, you won't do anything weird, will you? I mean he's not... we're not... you know."

He looked at her blankly.

"Just don't do anything weird."

"Weird? No. I just want to make sure he's not the type to save himself before my favorite sister-in-law."

Jackie thought of the journal. "I think he's exactly what you would want."

Kyle raised his eyebrows. "Exactly?"

"Are you two coming?" Shonda's voice called down from the attic.

"We're coming!" Kyle jogged up the steep flight of stairs to the attic. He could just barely stand up straight. The top of his head brushed the ceiling.

"Are you sure you want this for your room?" he asked.

Jackie laughed. "Absolutely."

"Seems to me like you'll be more cramped up here than you were downstairs."

"It's a different kind of cramped," she said. "Up here it's a vertical cramp. Down there it's a horizontal cramp. Vertical's better because I'm short."

"It's a Shonda and Jackie-sized room. It isn't a Kyle-sized room," Shonda explained at her husband's dubious expression.

"That's for sure."

Shonda cranked open a window at one end of the attic, and the musty air began to stir with the faintest whisper of a breeze. "Much better." She looked around, hands on hips, and surveyed the room. Piles of boxes were stacked from slanted wall to slanted wall. "Okay.

Kyle's already cleaned up the area down cellar, so all we have to do is take the boxes down. Now everything is already organized, so we'll just go pile to pile and stack it the same way in the cellar."

The three of them grabbed a couple of boxes and trooped single file down to the basement.

"This isn't working," Kyle said as they filed back up the steps, nearly tripping over each other. "We're just getting in each other's way. We should set up a relay. Shon, you get the boxes and hand them to Jackie; Jax, you meet her on the stairs and bring them to me, and I'll organize the stuff in the cellar."

They were making good progress when a knock sounded on the front door.

Jackie was struggling down the attic steps with an armload of stuff, so Kyle answered the door. Montgomery stood on the front doorstep.

"Hi. I'm Montgomery Dawson. You must be Jackie's brother-in-law."

"Kyle Lainson. How're you doing?" They shook hands.

Jackie set her load down by the cellar door and joined them at the front of the hallway. "I'm sorry," she began, but Kyle interrupted.

"We put her to work," he said. "If it had been up to her she would have been at the cove all afternoon."

"It's no problem at all. I figured something probably came up, but I just wanted to make sure everything was all right."

"We're working on a new room for Jax."

"My present room is the tiniest bedroom in existence. So I'm going to move into the attic."

"Cool," Montgomery said. "Need any help?"

"Oh, no, that's okay—"

"Never turn down an extra pair of hands," Kyle said. "We'd love some help."

What remained of the afternoon sped by, and before long the attic was nearly empty. Both Kyle and Shonda seemed to genuinely like Montgomery. Shonda even invited him to stay for dinner, but he graciously declined and went home.

After the dinner dishes had been loaded into the dishwasher, Jackie went back up to the attic and looked around. A few odds and ends were all that remained. She took a broom and began sweeping. An old table sat in one corner next to a dusty trunk. She swept around them as best she could, thinking of how she could use them both in her new room. If the trunk were cleaned up a bit, it would look really neat at the foot of the bed, like a hope chest or something. What was in it anyway? Old blankets? Sweaters? She propped the broom against the rickety table and knelt before the trunk. She tried to open it. It was locked.

Jackie frowned at the trunk for a moment and was about to get up and finish sweeping when she saw it—a tiny grayish corner of something sticking out from beneath the lid. She bent closer to examine it. It was paper of some sort. A picture maybe? She gently pulled, afraid she might tear it. It didn't move. She pulled harder. Finally, it slid free. Jackie stared at the object she held in her hand. It was an old photograph of a man and a woman. The woman she recognized instantly as her mother. But who was the man? Even as she asked the question, she knew the answer.

She had never seen a picture of her father. All these years she had only imagined what he must look like. But she knew it was him. It had to be. The man in the photograph looked just like her. ✎

chapter six

The flashlight's yellow beam sliced through the darkness and washed the gloom from the cave walls. Jackie followed Montgomery's lean form as he started into the tunnel. The ceiling was even lower in the tunnel, and they were forced to hunch over to keep from hitting their heads. The flashlight beam was swallowed up in the darkness ahead.

"Ow!" Montgomery stopped suddenly, and Jackie bumped into him. "What is it?"

"A stalagmite. I didn't even see it." He moved aside so she could see the jagged pillar of stone rising up from the ground.

Montgomery rubbed his knee and then moved on.

Soon the tunnel came to an end and opened into another cavern.

Jackie shined her own light around. The ceiling was a bit higher here, and she could stand up straight again, much to her relief. Montgomery could too, though the top of his backwards baseball cap brushed the stone. Stalagmites dotted the floor, and stalactites jutted down in stony icicles.

"Awesome," Montgomery said, trying to shine his light everywhere at once.

"I haven't seen any faeries," Jackie said.

"Of course not," Montgomery said over his shoulder. "They're all in hiding. We're intruders in their fortress, and they want to see if we're friend or foe before they appear to us."

Jackie smiled. It felt so nice to have someone play along.

They began edging their way through the treacherous maze of stone. Montgomery spotted an opening in the rock wall on the other side of the cavern and angled toward it.

They paused at the jagged crevice, and Montgomery fished something out of his pocket. A piece of white chalk. He made an x on the rock and then started forward again. The ceiling was even lower here than the first tunnel, and they both stooped as they walked, alert for any rocky projections. The dank air clung clammily to Jackie's skin. She wrinkled her nose. It smelled like wet, dirty laundry. Damp rock brushed the top of her head. She stooped lower and noticed Montgomery was now moving in a crouch.

"Montgomery!"

"What?"

"The ceiling keeps getting lower and lower!"

"I kind of noticed that." He paused for a moment to rest.

"Well, maybe we're going the wrong way. Maybe this doesn't lead anywhere."

Montgomery shook his head. "It's got to lead somewhere." He wiped the dampness from his forehead and started forward again, nearly crawling now.

Jackie scowled after him. Boys! They thought they could do anything!

Montgomery glanced back. "Are you coming? Or are you going to sit there all day?"

Jackie briefly considered doing exactly that. But one look at the lurking shadows that leapt and flickered every time the flashlight moved convinced her it was best to stay together.

"Come on!" he urged. "This has got to lead somewhere!"

"How does a city boy know so much about caves?" she muttered.

"Don't worry. We'll reach the end soon."

Sure we will, Jackie thought. We'll both be slithering on our stomachs like snakes, but we'll get there.

It seemed like they crawled forever. Jackie's back ached. She didn't think she'd ever be able to stand up straight again.

Then the faintest whisper of air brushed her cheek, and the confining walls to either side of her fell away to nothing.

The beam from Montgomery's flashlight flooded a huge chamber, fading away before it reached the far side of the cavern.

Jackie slowly eased into a standing position and added her beam to Montgomery's.

The cave was enormous, stretching away to either side, its walls and ceiling lost in the darkness.

"Wow." Montgomery looked around, his dark eyes wide with awe. "This is incredible." He carefully marked the tunnel they had just emerged from with the chalk and then slowly led the way around the perimeter of the cave.

Crevices and tunnels opened into the stone every few feet, some of them burrowing away into the rock, others merely shallow alcoves.

"Do you hear that?" Montgomery asked. His voice echoed throughout the cave.

"Hear what?"

"Shh. Listen."

Jackie listened. A strange rushing sound reached her ears.

"What is that?" Montgomery asked. "The wind?"

"It's the ocean," Jackie said. She passed Montgomery and shined her flashlight around the cavern, trying to pinpoint which tunnel it came from. "One of these tunnels must lead outside."

They walked around the edge of the cave, listening intently.

Jackie paused halfway between two openings in the rock. "It's louder here," she said.

Montgomery listened and nodded.

Jackie glanced from one yawning tunnel mouth to the other. "Which one?"

Montgomery shined his flashlight down each, then marked the entrance of one and boldly entered. Jackie followed. The tunnel twisted and turned through jagged projections, and the walls sloped away among boulders and stalagmites.

The pitted floor angled upward. They hadn't gone far when the passage abruptly ended.

"What in the world..." Montgomery shined his light around.

Jackie sighed and pushed a strand of hair out of her eyes. "It's a dead-end. We took the wrong way."

Montgomery scowled at the rock.

"Come on," Jackie said. She turned around and headed back the way they had come. She brushed the wall with her fingers. It was damp and sticky. She wiped her hands on her jeans. The shadows seemed much darker now that she was in the lead. They clung to corners until her light swept them away like cobwebs. They gathered along the craggy floor and pooled in dark crevices.

Jackie's foot caught on a protruding rock, and she pitched forward. She reached out, trying to catch herself, and tumbled into a pile of loose stone at the edge of the tunnel with a jarring impact. *Ouch!*

Montgomery called to her, but his voice was drowned out by a gravelly crumbling sound.

Suddenly the ground beneath her gave way. Her flashlight clanged to the ground, and the beam winked out. She began sliding downward amidst a shower of loose rock. She reached out, grasping, trying futilely to stop herself. Montgomery was shouting something to her. She broke free from the rock around her, and then she was falling. ☺

chapter seven

"Jackie? Jackie!" Montgomery's voice sounded far away.

Jackie opened her eyes. Light from his flashlight filtered down to where she lay.

"Jackie, can you hear me? Jackie?"

"I'm here," she said. Her voice sounded distant in her own ears.

"Are you okay?"

Stupid question. She tried to survey her body and make sure everything still worked properly. She looked around. The world spun dizzily about her. She tenderly touched her forehead. Her fingers came away wet and sticky. Her stomach constricted. Blood.

Loose rock slid down from the hole she had fallen through and plunked to the ground beside her. She watched it dully. Her head ached. She was dimly aware of Montgomery dropping lightly to the rocky floor. So he was coming to rescue her. Too late, she thought wearily. She had felt the blood. She knew the truth. The walls around her spun in circles.

"Jackie?" The beam from the flashlight momentarily blinded her.

"Tell Shonda and Kyle—that I love them."

"Where does it hurt?"

"My head… the blood…"

Montgomery touched her forehead gingerly. He wiped his fingers on his jeans.

She could feel everything slipping away.

"Jax," he said softly.

She tried to focus on him.

"You're not bleeding."

Jackie blinked. Some of the fuzziness faded.

He touched her head again and showed her his fingers. They glistened wetly, but they weren't red.

"I think the moisture from the rocks dripped on you after you landed." He looked up at the stalactites hanging overhead. As if in answer, a drop splashed onto her forehead, splattering her face.

Jackie's head stopped spinning. Her mind cleared. She started to sit up.

"Whoa, whoa, whoa!" Montgomery grabbed her shoulders and firmly stopped her. "Not so fast. Take it slow and easy until you're sure you're all right."

She shrugged his hands away, grumbling, "I'm all right. I'm fine." She felt cheated.

"'The lady doth protest too much methinks,'" Montgomery quoted with a grin.

Jackie smiled in spite of herself. "Thanks, Hamlet. Now be a gentleman and help me up."

He helped her to her feet.

"How did you get down here?" she asked.

"Climbed."

Jackie looked up. The opening was about half way up the sloping wall.

"It looks like the rock was already weak and when you tripped and fell there, the impact was just enough to break it loose," Montgomery said. "Lucky for you the fall wasn't far."

She shuddered. It had been bad enough *thinking* she was dying.

"Feeling okay?" Montgomery asked.

She nodded. The ground felt steadier beneath her feet. "I think I'll have a couple of bruises, but that's all. My head doesn't hurt anymore. How are we gonna get out of here?"

Montgomery glanced around.

Several dark crevices led out from the narrow chamber they were in.

"I think we should try to get out the way we got in," he said. "We should be able to climb out okay. I'd kind of like to check out where these tunnels lead, but I think we should find our way out. We can come back later."

Jackie nodded, not at all sure she wanted to come back down here. The smell was worse, and the caverns looked positively inky.

"Okay, I'll go first," Montgomery said. He handed her the flashlight and started to climb. Rock crumbled down around him, but he kept going. He reached the jagged opening and hauled himself through. "Okay. Toss the flashlight up."

Jackie looked dubiously at the flashlight and then at Montgomery. "What if I miss, and it falls and breaks?"

"Don't worry, I'll catch it."

She was more worried about her aim. She took a deep breath and gently lobbed the light upward. Montgomery caught it easily and then shone it on the rock wall so she could see to climb.

She tentatively began easing her way up, thankful the distance wasn't far. Rock slid beneath her feet, and the wall was damp and slippery. At last she reached Montgomery's outstretched hand and climbed through.

"That wasn't so bad," Montgomery said as they brushed themselves off.

Jackie grimaced and retrieved her flashlight from where she had dropped it earlier.

They stayed away from the sides of the cave after that and after what seemed like an eternity they re-emerged into the huge echoing chamber.

"Should we head back the way we came?" Montgomery asked.

Jackie glanced toward the other tunnel, listening to the distant crash of the sea. "If this one leads out, it will be a lot faster than worming our way back through those wretched tunnels."

He nodded. "Let's give it a shot."

They started down the second tunnel. The sounds of the ocean intensified as they walked. After a while the air seemed to grow moister and colder.

"It's getting lighter!" Jackie said.

The faint light brightened, and before long Montgomery shut off his flashlight.

The tunnel widened and opened onto a shelf overlooking the ocean. Waves pounded the rock beneath and sent up geysers of salty spray.

Montgomery squinted against the light as Jackie breathed in the fresh sea air and sighed in relief. She had never thought of herself as claustrophobic, but she certainly didn't fancy the thought of going down into those caves again.

A narrow path led off the shelf and wound through boulders and scattered rock. Jackie looked closer. The twisting trail looked well worn. Someone must travel it often. But who? She came to the cove every day, and she had never seen anybody except Montgomery.

"Maybe the cove *is* haunted," she murmured.

"Huh?"

She pointed to the trail.

Montgomery frowned. "Ghosts don't make trails." He glanced up at her. "Do they?"

She shrugged. "There must just be someone else who comes here. I mean, it's not like I'm here all day. I like to think of it as mine, but it's public property. Anyone can come out here. And obviously, someone does. They just don't come at sunrise or right after school."

"Kind of weird that you've never seen them though, don't you think?"

She nodded.

They followed the path up the bank to the forest and then stopped. Scrub brush overwhelmed the trail and choked it from sight.

"What's on the other side of these trees?" Montgomery asked.

"I don't know. Nothing really. The woods go on for miles—all the way up to the next town."

Montgomery eyed the woods for a moment, then looked at Jackie. "Well, I think we'd better head home. You should come to my house and just have my mom make sure you're okay."

"I'm fine, really."

"Well, not to sound like a big brother or anything, but you did hit the ground kind of hard, and it would be better to have someone look at it now than find out tomorrow you've got a concussion. C'mon. You've never met my folks, anyway."

Jackie nodded and trudged along through the woods after him. A few minutes later the trees thinned and opened out onto a freshly mowed lawn at the back of a brown two-story house. They stomped their feet on the back step to wipe off the dirt and then went inside.

The smell of supper cooking greeted them when they walked into the kitchen.

"Mmm," Jackie closed her eyes and inhaled. "Spaghetti?"

Montgomery opened the oven a crack and peered in. "Lasagna."

Mrs. Dawson peeked around the corner. "Hey, Monty!" She smiled at Jackie. "Hello!"

"Mom, this is Jackie."

"Hello, Mrs. Dawson. It's a pleasure to meet you."

"We've heard a lot about you, Jackie. I'm glad to finally meet you. I'd come shake your hand, but I'm up to my elbows in dirty laundry."

Even so, Mrs. Dawson looked just as elegant in jeans as she had in her business suit. Jackie was suddenly very aware of her unruly curls springing out in every direction and her dirt-streaked skin and clothes.

"Supper's almost ready. Will you stay and eat with us?"

"Oh, I couldn't—I'm such a mess!"

"Nothing that won't wash off. Do you like lasagna?"

"I love anything Italian. Could I call my sister and check with her first, though?"

"Go right ahead. The phone's on the wall by the door."

"First, Mom, Jackie fell and hit her head. Can you just make sure she doesn't have a concussion or anything?"

"Oh, goodness!" Mrs. Dawson dropped the armload of clothes and hurried over.

"I'm fine. I really don't think—"

"Where did you hit your head? Does it still hurt? Are you dizzy at all?"

Jackie answered the barrage of questions and stood quietly while Montgomery's mother carefully felt her head and had her follow her finger with her eyes. At first Jackie felt uncomfortable, but after a minute or two, she began to enjoy the motherly attention. Shonda fussed, of course, when she hurt herself, but it wasn't the same.

"Well, you seem in pretty good shape," Mrs. Dawson said at last. "No bumps, good clarity and coordination." She stepped back. "What were you doing?"

"We were at the shore—at that cove I told you about," Montgomery said.

"I tripped over a rock," Jackie added.

Mrs. Dawson frowned. "You need to be careful out there."

"We will," Montgomery assured her. "I'm going upstairs to change. The bathroom's down the hall on the left," he told Jackie.

Jackie nodded and walked over to the phone.

Shonda picked up on the third ring. "Hello?"

"Hi, it's me. I'm at Montgomery's. May I stay for supper?"

Shonda hesitated. "Is it okay with his parents?"

"Mrs. Dawson invited me."

"Well, all right. Don't be too late though. If you need a ride, just call, okay?"

"Okay. Thank you!"

"Everything okay, then?" Mrs. Dawson asked after Jackie had hung up the receiver.

"Yes. I think I'll try to clean up now."

"There are towels and washcloths in the bathroom closet. Just use whatever you need."

Jackie thanked her and stepped out into the hall. An arched

doorway across from the kitchen revealed a spacious, beautiful living room. Another door led to a den, and Jackie was strangely delighted to see that the room was rather messy. Unable to contain her curiosity, she slipped into the room and looked around.

The living room was elegant, but this cozy room seemed more like where the family would lounge during holidays and weekends and snuggle down on cold winter nights. Large windows dominated two walls and captured the afternoon sunlight, basking the room in a warm glow. French doors opened onto a small patio where Jackie could just glimpse a grill. Another wall was floor to ceiling bookshelves and the fourth boasted a fireplace. A fat leather couch and chair faced an entertainment center, and a coffee table was cheerfully cluttered with dirty dishes and a board game, still in progress. Jackie ran her fingers along the back of the sofa. Leather had such a wonderful feel. The picture over the fireplace captivated her interest. It was a painting of a boy's face, eyes closed in tranquil sleep. Words scrawled across the upper left-hand corner. Jackie strained her eyes and breathed the words aloud:

"Good night, sweet prince. And flights of angels sing thee to thy rest."

Suddenly a hand grabbed her fingers, and Jackie jumped nearly six inches off the floor. A head as unruly as her own appeared over the back of the couch as Mr. Dawson slowly sat up. He blinked the sleep from his eyes and stared at her owlishly.

"I—I—I—" Jackie stammered. She could feel herself blushing to the roots of her wild hair.

Mr. Dawson watched her a moment longer, then a slow, lopsided grin spread across his features. "You must be Jackie."

"I—I—I'm *so* sorry, sir."

He extended his hand and shook hers warmly. "Quite all right. Nothing like a good fright to get the old adrenaline flowing. But by the looks of you, I'd say I scared you just as bad."

Jackie managed a smile, but she felt like crawling under the couch and hiding. "I was looking for the bathroom," she began, the words tripping over each other in their haste to escape her mouth. "I just needed to wash up because Montgomery and I were dirty from exploring the caves, and I was just admiring your house and especially this room because it looked lived in..." Jackie snapped her mouth shut before anything else came out.

Mr. Dawson glanced around the room and chuckled. "I guess it does look 'lived in' at that." He ran his big hands through his hair, but Jackie was too embarrassed to be jealous when it obediently fell into place. "Well, I'll tell you what. You go ahead and get cleaned up, and I'll try to reduce the amount of 'life' in here by a few dishes."

Jackie nodded and fled from the room. She closed the bathroom door behind her and took a deep breath. She almost cried when she looked in the mirror and saw the smudges of dirt on her red cheeks and her disheveled curls sticking out from her ponytail. She found a washcloth and hand-towel in the closet and scrubbed her face and hands clean. She wiped off the loose dust and grime from her clothing. There were a few stains on her jeans and one that she could see on her sweatshirt, but they blended with the dark colors. She finger-combed her hair, gradually taming the ringlets into some semblance of order, and then left it hanging long and loose down her back. She couldn't wash the embarrassment from her cheeks though. At last she gathered enough courage to return to the kitchen. She met Mr. Dawson on the way.

He grinned. "It's a good thing you woke me up, or I'd have slept through dinner!"

She couldn't think of anything to say, so she just smiled and tried not to think about how red her face was.

Montgomery looked up from setting the table when they walked into the kitchen.

"Well, I see you found Jackie," Mrs. Dawson said, smiling at her husband.

Jackie glanced sideways at Mr. Dawson, but he just winked at her and then enveloped his wife in a bear hug, sneaking an olive from the veggie platter behind her.

Montgomery rolled his eyes.

Jackie's embarrassment faded away as she watched them, and her throat constricted with sudden tears. Kyle and Shonda were wonderful. But they weren't her parents. What must it be like to grow up with two parents who adore you? She would never know. One had died so long ago she barely remembered her. The other had left because he wanted nothing to do with the family he'd created. She wondered fleetingly where he was and if he ever thought about them. She made a mental note to tell Montgomery how lucky he was.

She sat across from Montgomery at the oak table. Mr. Dawson blessed the food and then dished out the lasagna, serving Jackie first, then his wife, followed by his son and himself.

"So, Jackie, tell us about your sister and brother-in-law," Mr. Dawson said as he spooned out a large helping of lasagna for himself.

Montgomery must have told them about her parents. "Kyle works with a partner at a small accounting firm in downtown Kilree—they handle pretty much all the accounting for the local businesses—and he coaches peewee hockey in the winter. And Shonda manages the Kilree Country Store."

"Do they have any children?"

"Not yet. I guess they figure they have enough to deal with just with me," Jackie said with a grin.

"Nah," Montgomery said. "They've just been waiting for you to get older. They'll start anytime now that they've got a free babysitter."

Jackie chuckled ruefully. "You may be more right than you know. But more likely it's because they've never had room for a baby. Our house is pretty small," she explained to Montgomery's parents.

"Well, pretty soon they'll have an extra room," Montgomery said.

"They're turning the attic into a bedroom for Jackie," he explained to his parents.

"You know, I hadn't thought of that," Jackie said. "My room would make a perfect nursery! I hope they do have children soon. I think everyone should have lots of children."

The Dawsons didn't say anything. Jackie glanced up. Mr. and Mrs. Dawson shared a long look, and Montgomery stared at his plate. Jackie toyed with her food uncomfortably.

"Monty tells us you're interested in the more cultural aspects of life," Mr. Dawson said, quickly covering up the awkward pause.

"Yes, sir. I'm an avid reader of plays and poetry."

"Do you like Shakespeare?"

"He's one of my favorites!" Jackie exclaimed, beaming.

"He's a favorite in our house as well," Mrs. Dawson said.

"Well, maybe next time we go to a play, you'll have to come with us," Mr. Dawson said.

Jackie stared at him. She knew she must look like a fish with her mouth hanging open and her eyes popping out of her head, but she couldn't help it. No one had ever offered to take her to a play.

Montgomery was grinning at her, and she finally snapped her mouth shut. The Dawsons smiled, and she smiled back.

They discussed drama and literature and the Dawson's adjustment to rural life, and dinner passed in a whirl of happy conversation.

"That was delicious, Mrs. Dawson," Jackie said as she finished the last of her lasagna.

Mrs. Dawson smiled. "Would you like some more?"

"Oh, no, I couldn't. I'm stuffed!"

"Well, I hope you saved a little room for dessert," Mr. Dawson said, "because I saw fresh peaches on the kitchen counter."

"Oooh…" Jackie quickly evaluated how much more she could eat before she would be sick.

"I thought we'd have peach cobbler," Mrs. Dawson said.

"I'll make room," Jackie said quickly.

Mrs. Dawson laughed. "Good. I'll need about twenty minutes so if you kids want to go play a game or something, I'll let you know when it's ready."

"Can I help you with dishes?" Jackie asked.

"Thank you, but I think my husband is on dish detail tonight."

Mr. Dawson grinned. "A pleasure after such a culinary masterpiece."

Jackie followed Montgomery out of the kitchen and into the living room while his parents began clearing the table.

Montgomery threw himself into a plush, sage-green chair. "So have you decided if you're coming to the soccer game yet?"

Jackie hesitated, then shrugged. "Why not?"

"Good. And who knows? You may find you like it. And maybe," he continued slyly, "you'll even decide to become a cheerleader."

Some of the horror she was feeling must have shown on her face, because he burst out laughing.

She sniffed. "I'll have to make sure it's okay with Shonda and Kyle first. They've been pursuing this room thing voraciously. You'd think it was their idea."

"Are you having second thoughts?"

"About my new room? No! Not at all. I guess I'm just a little slower-moving. Shonda likes to start and finish projects in the same day. I like to take my time." She grinned ruefully. "So if I was doing it by myself, it would probably never get done."

"I'll bet Kyle would like to come to the game. Invite him. Invite both of them. Then they'll let you come."

She nodded. "Okay. They would probably like it actually—me *wanting* to attend a social function."

They fell silent, and she glanced about the room. Her gaze fell on the piano.

"Who plays?" she asked, walking over to the instrument and sitting on the bench.

"My mom."

She traced her fingers over the keys. "My mom played too." She looked at the pictures artistically arranged on the piano top. "There wasn't room in the house for the piano, so we had to sell it before we moved up here." Faces smiled up from each photograph. She recognized Mr. and Mrs. Dawson and Montgomery. And an elderly man that looked so much like Montgomery, she knew it had to be his grandfather. But there was another face as well. A boy's face. She looked more closely. He was the boy from the painting in the den.

"Who is he?" Jackie asked finally.

Montgomery cleared his throat. "That's Perry."

"Oh. The one you said I remind you of?"

He nodded.

Jackie looked down at the smiling face in the photograph. He had the same white-blond hair as Montgomery, but his eyes were much lighter. "Do I look like him or something?"

"No. It's just your personality. He was kind of dreamy like you. Dramatic. He loved Shakespeare."

Jackie hesitated a moment. "Perry's your brother," she said, but she already knew the answer.

Montgomery nodded.

Jackie waited, giving him the same courtesy he had shown her when he first found out about her mother. But he didn't say anything further. She glanced at him out of the corner of her eye. His dark expressionless gaze didn't move from the picture. At last he looked away and flashed her a bright, artificial smile.

"I think the peach cobbler's almost done. Let's go get some."

Jackie nodded. She was so curious she wanted to shake the information out of him, but she ignored the impulse and followed him into the kitchen.

Later that night, when she was lying in bed, she stayed awake for a long time thinking. So Montgomery had the younger sibling she had always longed for. And had lost him. She wondered suddenly if it was better to have never had a brother or sister at all than to have one and lose him. She thought of Mr. and Mrs. Dawson. It was horrible enough to lose a parent. How much worse it must be to lose a child! To not only bring a person into the world but see him leave it as well. She sighed and rolled over. It didn't seem fair that such a perfect and beautiful family should have to endure that kind of tragedy. She reached beneath her pillow and pulled out the worn photograph of her parents. At least Perry had a loving and wonderful family while he had lived. She fell asleep thinking what it must have been like to be Perry Dawson. ☙

chapter eight

The warm autumn sun beamed down on the soccer field as the players went through their drills. Jackie sat on the bleachers as far away from the cluster of girls on the other end as she could manage.

By the time soccer practice was halfway through, she had finished her homework and was desperately wishing she'd brought a book to read.

The other girls started giggling.

Jackie glanced over, and four smirking faces quickly turned the other way.

She wished she'd told Montgomery that she would just meet him at the library to work on their science papers instead of agreeing to wait at school for him. She was tempted to leave anyway.

One of the girls looked over again and then hid a giggle behind her hand.

Giggle. That was all they seemed to do. She had been in their class for years now and though she knew their names were Amy, Heather, Sarah and Jennifer, she was never completely sure which was which. They all seemed to look alike in a Gap fashion plate sort of way.

After what seemed like forever, the coach blew his whistle, and practice was over. As soon as Montgomery had showered and changed, they headed for the library.

"That's the church you go to, right?" Montgomery asked as they approached downtown.

Jackie glanced across the street at the red brick building. "Ayuh."

"Where's the parsonage?" he asked, looking around.

"It's just outside of town. Near us, actually. It's that little white house about halfway between school and home."

"Who's that?" Montgomery asked.

Jackie followed his gaze to an elderly man rooting through the Salvation Army bags beside the church. "Oh. That's Sam. Silent Sam."

"Silent Sam?"

"Yeah. Every town needs someone a little weird, you know? Our town character is Sam. He's a little odd, but he seems harmless enough."

"Why 'Silent' Sam?"

"He can't talk."

"Is he deaf?"

"No, I don't think so. He seems to be able to hear us fine; but he never speaks. He uses hand signals when he needs to communicate something but most of the time he just ignores you. Pastor Hallowell tried to take him to a doctor once, but Sam wouldn't go."

"Where does he live?"

"No one knows. He's not around much. He only shows up in town once in a while. For the soup kitchen or to raid the good will bags. Most people just leave him alone."

Montgomery watched him curiously for a moment longer, then they walked up the front steps to the town library.

"Shonda, what are we going to do with this old trunk?" Jackie asked later that afternoon.

Shonda glanced up from sanding the attic floor boards. "It's in pretty rough shape. Maybe I'll just throw it out."

"Oh, no, don't do that!"

"Why not?"

"I could use it up here!"

"Whatever for?"

"For *effect*. It would look wonderful! Especially with that old table, too! I'm going to strip and repaint it. If you'll unlock the trunk, I can clean that up, too!"

Shonda studied the trunk for a moment then returned to her sanding. "Why don't you let me take care of it."

Jackie watched her sister carefully. She thought of the picture of her parents now tucked securely between the pages of her Shakespeare anthology. "What's in it?" She tried to sound casual.

Shonda didn't look up. "Oh, just stuff."

"Whose stuff?"

"My stuff."

"Oh. Then why do you keep it in this old trunk?"

Shonda sighed. "Because the trunk was Mama's."

Jackie waited. Shonda didn't say anything more. "Would it bother you if I kept the trunk up here? I'll just clean it up a bit, I won't paint it or anything."

Shonda was silent.

"I've never had anything of Mama's," Jackie added quietly.

Shonda stopped sanding. She looked at Jackie. She looked at the trunk. "All right," she said at last. "If it means that much to you. I'll clean out the stuff inside sometime this week."

"Oh, thank you, Shon! If you want, I'll empty it out. I can just stick everything in a box and put it down cellar."

"No. I'll do it."

"Okay." Jackie decided to let the matter drop. She helped Shonda sand the floor, and by the time Kyle got home, they were almost done. He had brought a pizza with him, and they took a break and ate dinner. Afterwards, Kyle moved the trunk and the table to the downstairs hallway and helped them finish sanding.

"Looks good," Kyle said when they were done. He stepped back and surveyed the floor.

"Feels good," Jackie said. She rubbed her bare foot along the dark silky boards. "What's next?"

"Polyurethane. I'll get some tomorrow. So what do you say we call it a night?"

"Excellent notion," Shonda said, climbing to her feet with a groan. "My knees are *killing* me." She looked around the room. "But at least the first phase is done."

Jackie nodded and sighed. It was a lot more work than she had counted on, but when it was finished, it would be so worth it.

"Definitely a cause for celebration," Kyle said, putting his arm around his wife's shoulders and squeezing. "And I was thinking along the lines of... oh... great big fat hot fudge sundaes?"

Shonda smiled wearily. "Sure."

Kyle could eat any kind of ice cream with any kind of topping at absolutely any time of the day, but Shonda was more of a brownie a la mode girl. Her sister was working the afternoon shift tomorrow, so Jackie decided she would make some brownies for Shonda as soon as she got home from school. But for now, sundaes would have to do. Not that Jackie would be suffering at all. She liked anything with chocolate.

"That sounds great!" Jackie exclaimed and ran downstairs to get the ice cream.

When they arrived at church on Sunday morning, Jackie glanced about, but there was still no sign of the Dawsons. They must be in Boston again, she thought. She went into her usual Sunday school classroom and sat in the back corner.

They were about to begin when the door opened, and Montgomery walked in. He sat in a chair by the door and pulled out his Bible. Mr. Armacost smiled cheerfully and welcomed Montgomery to the class, then opened their time with prayer. When he said "amen," Montgomery glanced around the room and smiled when he saw Jackie.

Mr. Armacost led them in a recitation of the verse he wanted them to memorize and then launched into the lesson.

When class was over, Montgomery waited for her outside the door. "Hey," he greeted her.

"Hi. I thought you'd be in Boston."

He shook his head as they walked out to the church auditorium. "I think we're done with our weekend visits. My parents are getting anxious to settle in and become a part of the community, you know?"

She nodded and glanced around the sanctuary. She spotted Mr. and Mrs. Dawson talking to Pastor Hallowell and weaved through the people toward them, Montgomery trailing behind.

"Hello, Jackie!" Mrs. Dawson smiled.

Jackie beamed. "Hello, Mrs. Dawson. You look lovely!" she said, admiring her long skirt and silk jacket.

"Why, thank you!"

"Hey, what am I? Chopped liver?"

"Hello, Mr. Dawson," Jackie felt her smile stretch even wider and fought to keep it under control. If she wasn't careful, her whole face could turn into one giant mouth. "You look nice too. Very impressive and distinguished."

Montgomery's father grinned and then winked at his wife. "I like her!" Mrs. Dawson laughed.

"Kyle!" Montgomery suddenly called out.

Jackie turned as her sister and brother-in-law joined them. "Mr. and Mrs. Dawson, this is my sister Shonda Lainson and her husband Kyle."

The two couples shook hands warmly. "Call me Tony," Mr. Dawson was saying.

"And Lara, please," Mrs. Dawson added. "It's a pleasure to meet you."

They talked for a few minutes and then sat together when the service began. Jackie sat between Shonda and Mrs. Dawson and for some reason, enjoyed church even more than usual.

Pastor Hallowell continued his series in the book of Esther and preached that morning on the governing providence of God. He said that God was not specifically mentioned anywhere in Esther, yet throughout the book you could clearly see the presence of the Divine.

"The Book of Esther is rife with coincidence. Vashti's timely deposition and Esther's consequential ascension to the throne, Mordecai uncovering an assassination plot against the king and the oversight of his reward, Esther's delay in petitioning the king, Ahasuerus' sleepless night and the random selection of Mordecai's service and lack of reward read from the book of records of the chronicles—it goes on and on. The king rewards Mordecai, and then Haman, the man who was plotting the genocide of the Jewish People, is hanged on the very gallows he erected for Mordecai. Coincidence? No. Providence. In each development of the plot, you find a new chance discovery, accident, or 'twist of fate.' But to the eyes of the believer, it is the unmistakable hand of God.

"That is how it is in our lives as well. We may not hear His voice in our ear, we may not see His face with our eyes, we may not feel His guiding hands with our own. But He is there.

"Some of you are going through some tough times. Those of you who aren't, you will soon enough. And I want you all to remember something. That job that didn't work out, that promotion that passed you by, that loved one who died, that illness that struck—they are not mistakes. It's sometimes hard to find comfort in times that try and test us—but there *is* comfort to be found, and it is this: life has a plan. We are all threads in a beautiful tapestry that God is weaving. This life is a work of art more exquisite than anything Michelangelo painted on a Roman ceiling, richer than any of the treasures in the Louvre. There is a plan. And it is God's plan." He seemed to make eye contact with every single person in the church. "There are no accidents. There are no mistakes. There are no coincidences. There is only Providence."

When the service was over, Jackie turned to Montgomery's mother to ask her how she had liked the sermon, but quickly bit back the question. The Dawsons sat quietly, sharing a long look. Mr. Dawson held his wife's hand tightly and gave her a gentle smile. Mrs. Dawson nodded and smiled back. Jackie wondered if they were thinking about Perry. Then several families came over and introduced themselves, and the moment had past.

Jackie hesitated, then asked Montgomery, "Did you like the sermon?"

He nodded. "Yeah, it was… perfect."

She decided to not ask any questions.

"I like Pastor Hallowell," Montgomery said.

Jackie nodded. "Everyone loves him to death. He was a missionary in France for almost sixty years. He came back to New England to retire but then agreed to take the church on a temporary basis. That was seven years ago," she added with a laugh.

"How old is he?" Montgomery asked.

Jackie shrugged. "He must be in his eighties, but you'd never know it. He's an avid skier."

"Really?"

"Yeah. And he only gave up basketball a couple of years ago. I guess his arthritis was getting really bad. He said nothing could keep him off the slopes, though." She laughed. "He said even if he was confined to a wheelchair, he'd glue skis on his wheels."

Montgomery grinned. "He sounds fun. Do you ski?"

"Not really. Kyle took me once, and I broke my wrist." She smiled grimly. "I haven't skied since."

They walked outside into the sunlight and paused.

Sam stood on the walkway that led from the church steps to the sidewalk, staring up at the brick building, a conflicted look on his weathered face, almost as if a battle was waging inside of him. When he saw them, he turned away and shuffled across the lawn to the Kilree cemetery.

"What do you suppose he wanted?" Montgomery wondered.

Jackie shook her head and watched as the old homeless man opened the iron gate and wandered off into the graveyard. ☙

chapter nine

An Indian summer had descended, encouraging energy levels to rise and minds to wander. Bright sunshine filtered through the classroom windows, and a light breeze rustled the papers on the desks.

Mr. Hudson, KCA's highschool math teacher, was out sick, and since Mrs. Cox refused to teach math beyond long division, their class received an unexpected study hall. Five minutes into class, Mrs. Cox suggested they all take their work outside.

Jackie leaned up against her favorite tree on the school grounds and used the time to finish up her assignments for the next day.

"Hey," Montgomery said, plopping down in front of her with his history book. "I heard the youth group's going to have a party on Halloween. Are you going?"

"No way."

"Come on! It'll be fun!"

"No!" Jackie hissed. "They'll call me Jackie-lantern!"

"What?"

"They always call me that around Halloween. Once Kris even carved a pumpkin so it looked like me. It even had freckles."

Montgomery turned away, but not quick enough to hide his smirk.

"It's not funny!" Jackie shouted furiously. "It's *persecution*!!"

Several of the students turned and stared. Mrs. Cox glanced their way but didn't say anything.

Montgomery winced and rubbed his ear. "Okay! I'm sorry!"

Jackie glared at him. She wasn't convinced. "You're mocking my pain."

"Well, if it's any consolation, I think you blew my eardrum out."

She felt a faint glimmer of satisfaction and nodded. "It is." She returned to her homework. She could feel Montgomery's disapproving frown. "I won't change my mind," she said without looking up.

"Oh, fine," he grumbled. "We'll have fun without you."

"They always do," she said softly.

It rained all night. When morning came, the rain fled with the dawn, and the rising sun chased the clouds away.

"It's a great day!" Montgomery said, breathing in the fresh rainswept air as they stepped outside after their last class ended.

Jackie nodded. It was exactly the sort of day that made you wonder how anyone could want anything over their head other than the great blue sky.

"Are you going to the cove?" he asked.

She shook her head. "I can't. I have to get some milk from the store and bring it home for Shonda. She's making tapioca pudding for dessert."

"I'll walk with you," he said.

"Okay."

They walked down the sidewalk to the tiny market at the far end of Main Street. The road curved into a roundabout, circling the town common. The green was ringed in maples and scattered with trees and stone benches. Little brick paths wandered through the grass and around shrubs, and a gazebo stood at the center.

"Hey, can we go out to the common?" Montgomery asked, his eyes fixed on the little tree-lined park. "I've seen it driving by, but I want to take a closer look."

Jackie hesitated. She didn't go out to the common very often. That was where the teens liked to hang out after school. Already a few of them were gathered there. She swallowed. "Okay. I'll go ahead and get the milk, and I'll meet you out there."

"Okay!"

Jackie ducked inside and purchased a gallon of low fat milk, then crossed the street to the green. She passed the gazebo, avoiding the gazes of the teenagers sitting there. She found Montgomery examining a marble fountain enclosed in a small grove of red maples. In the center of a round pool stood a tall Celtic cross with a beautifully carved angel hovering on either side. One of the angels held a harp and the other a pitcher that poured water down into the pool. Old pennies glimmered at the bottom, and the dark green of moss and climbing roses that bloomed white in the summer crept over the base and trailed leaves in the water.

"This is great!" Montgomery exclaimed. "What's the story behind it?"

"I don't know," Jackie said. "I think it's been here for a long time. It's really beautiful." She looked up at the angels' faces. They were youthful and boyish and looked almost real. "I never come here except for the town picnic on the fourth of July. I haven't really looked at it in years. I'd forgotten... it's exquisite."

He nodded. Then he glanced at her and grinned. "Wanna make a wish?"

She smiled. "Why not?"

He dug around in his pocket and found six cents. "You can have the nickel," he said chivalrously. "More expensive wishes are bound to come true."

She laughed and took the coin. She closed her eyes and then tossed it into the fountain.

Montgomery made his own wish, then began examining the fountain more closely. Something caught his attention, and he knelt down at the fountain's base.

"What is it?" she asked and peered over his shoulder.

"There's something written on it." He pulled the vines away and brushed at the moss.

"What does it say?" she asked, leaning closer.

Montgomery squinted. "There's moss and junk all over it. Looks like something *Queen*. No, wait, I see an 'M.' McQueen, maybe?"

"Mulqueen," Jackie said. "It must be for the Mulqueens."

He glanced back at her. "Who are the Mulqueens?"

"The Mulqueens founded Kilree. The inn on the other side of town was once their estate."

"Oh. Cool. Do any of the family still live around here?"

She shook her head. "There's no one left. The family died out."

"Oh. That's too bad."

"Yeah. Well, I'd better get going. I've got to get the milk to Shonda."

He nodded. "Okay."

They walked back through town and out toward their homes. Jackie turned off when she reached the little lane that ran past her house and said goodbye.

Shonda was cooking when she reached the house. Jackie did her homework, then helped her sister in the kitchen. They played music while they worked and talked about their day.

"Do you know anything at all about the Mulqueens?" she asked her sister and brother-in-law at dinner.

They shook their heads.

"Just that they were the founders of the town," Shonda offered.

"That was Josef and Fiona. What about Desmond and Brigit? They were the last Mulqueens to live here."

"Sounds like you know more about them than we do," Kyle said. "Why the sudden interest?"

"I don't know. I wrote a paper on them, but there wasn't much information to draw from and now I'm just kind of curious about them."

"How long ago did they live here?"

"Well, they died in the Sixties, so really, not that long ago."

Kyle nodded. "You should ask around at church. Some of the older people are bound to know them."

She nodded. "Maybe I'll try that."

The rest of the week flew by and before she knew it, the weekend had come.

Shonda and Kyle were eating breakfast when Jackie returned from the cove Saturday morning.

"Good morning," Kyle greeted her sleepily. Shonda put some pancakes on a plate for Jackie and set it on the table.

Jackie sat down with them, said a silent prayer, then began eating hungrily. She glanced up after a few bites.

"There's a soccer game at school today, and I thought I might go."

They both stopped eating and stared at her.

"Are you feeling all right?" Kyle finally asked, only half joking.

"Oh, for goodness' sake, I'm not *that* much of a recluse!"

Shonda arched an eyebrow.

Jackie sighed in exasperation. "Okay, maybe I am. But just because I want to go see one little soccer game doesn't mean I've undergone some weird social conversion."

"You've never wanted to go to one before," Shonda said, exchanging an uncertain glance with her husband.

"I've never had a friend on the team before," Jackie replied simply.

They both nodded slowly.

"So you really want to go to the game?"

"Yes!"

A light appeared in Kyle's eyes. "Let's all go!"

When afternoon arrived, the three of them walked to the school soccer field. A cool autumn breeze ruffled the leaves on the trees, but the sun shone warmly on their faces and made the stroll a pleasant one.

Kyle's enthusiasm seemed to grow with each step. "This will be great!"

"Why are you so excited?" Jackie finally asked, panting slightly as she and Shonda tried to keep pace with Kyle's long strides.

"I tried for years to get you to do stuff like this, and you always refused. I haven't been to a soccer game in ages!"

When they reached the field, Jackie's stomach did a little flip-flop. Most of her classmates were there, walking or standing around or sitting on the bleachers. She bit her lip but smiled quickly when she saw Kyle glance at her. It was no big deal, she told herself. It was just a soccer game. Invitations weren't required. She took a deep breath and followed Kyle to the bleachers, coolly ignoring the surprised glances from her peers. A wave caught her eye, and she saw Mr. and Mrs. Dawson sitting on the top bench and gesturing for Jackie and her family to join them.

She clambered up the metal bleachers, Kyle and Shonda right behind her, and greeted the Dawsons with a mixture of joy and relief.

"Jackie!" Mrs. Dawson said with a smile. "We're so glad you came!"

Mr. Dawson grinned his lopsided grin. "This crowd could use a little refinement."

They greeted her sister and brother-in-law next, and Kyle and Mr. Dawson shook hands. Jackie squeezed herself in between the two couples and was suddenly and unexpectedly very glad she'd come.

When they had all settled in, she looked around for Montgomery and saw him at last, huddled with the rest of the soccer team in a tight circle around their coach. Kris and Brent were both on the team, too, as well as most of the boys from her class. She glanced over at the other team. They looked bigger. Maybe it was just the orange uniforms.

The referee called both teams to the center of the field and then the school principal prayed for the safety and good testimonies of each player. When he was finished, amen's echoed all over the field and a moment later, the players had taken their positions. Montgomery and Kris stood at the center of the field.

The referee blew his whistle. Kris kicked the ball forward a few inches; Montgomery darted forward and started dribbling the ball toward the left side of the field; the opposing team charged forward and the game began.

Jackie had never really watched a soccer game before. She'd never even been interested. But with the whole school humming with energy around her, Mrs. Dawson cheering wildly on one side of her and Kyle clapping and yelling on the other side, it was hard not to get caught up in the excitement. Mr. Dawson's voice boomed out praises and instructions to his son every few seconds.

Mrs. Dawson leaned closer to Jackie and grinned. "By the next game, he'll know every player's name and will yell to them as much as he does to Monty."

Jackie chuckled. "Montgomery's really good," she commented as he drove the ball down the field again. When he had the ball, he seemed almost untouchable.

Mrs. Dawson nodded proudly. "He is very good. I'm just glad the other boys are really letting him play now."

Jackie glanced at her in confusion. "What do you mean?"

"His first game, none of them would pass to him. And I guess they were all pretty rough on him during the practices. Especially that boy Kris and his friend Brent."

Jackie turned her gaze back out to the soccer field. "He never mentioned it," she said quietly.

"He never complains. He likes to keep his troubles to himself. He's always been that way."

Jackie watched in silence for a moment, in wonder if not shame that her only friend had a whole set of problems she knew nothing about. "Well, at least they seem to value him now," Jackie said. Kris passed him the ball a lot.

"Yes. He had to work very hard to gain their respect. Over halfway through his second game, one of the players was in trouble, passed to him out of desperation, and Monty scored the game-winning goal. He hasn't had any trouble since then."

Jackie watched her friend with newfound admiration and respect.

The teams surged back and forth over the field, each struggling for possession of the ball. An opposing team member drove the ball down the center of the field until a Kilree defender intercepted him and with a mighty kick, sent the ball flying to the other end of the field. Montgomery leapt up and headed the ball to Kris who slammed it passed the goalie into the goal.

A huge cheer went up from the Kilree fans, but Jackie cried, "Oh! Is he okay?"

"What?" Kyle asked. "Who?"

"Montgomery! It hit him right in the head!"

Kyle smirked.

"What?"

He put his arm around her shoulders and whispered, "That's a soccer move, Jax. It's part of the game."

Jackie stared incredulously out at the boys on the field. "Well, now I know why guys act the way they do."

"What do you mean?"

"I wouldn't think you could let hard, rapidly approaching objects bounce off your head too many times without it having some kind of permanent affect."

Kyle laughed. "If you do it right, it doesn't hurt."

Jackie watched the players dubiously. "If you say so."

Kris scored again right before half time, and Montgomery scored three goals of his own before the game's end, while the Kilree goaltender let only one slip by him. Then, with three blasts of the referee's whistle, the game was over.

Jackie felt a strange burst of pride as she looked at the small flip scoreboard on the scorekeeper's table. *We won!* she thought, the word *we* sounding odd to her mind's ear. The opposing teams shook hands and then the visiting school climbed wearily aboard their bus and headed for home.

The Kilree team gathered around their bench and drank thirstily, then sprayed each other from their water bottles when they'd gulped down enough.

The Dawsons stood up, and Jackie and her family followed. After a few minutes, Montgomery jogged over to them.

"The game was supposed to be a lot tougher than that," he said, mopping his face with a towel while his father clapped him proudly on the back. "I heard their lead scorer was out with chicken pox."

"You would have beat them anyway," Kyle said.

Montgomery grinned. "I hope we play them again when he's better. It's more fun when the game's close." He took a long drink from his water bottle. "I'm glad you guys came," he added to Kyle, Shonda and Jackie.

"What's next?" Mr. Dawson asked. "Ice cream or showers?"

"The guys were just talking, and I guess the whole team always goes out for ice cream after a win. If you don't mind waiting a few minutes, I'll go grab a shower in the gym, and then we can all go." He glanced at Jackie and her family. "Are you guys coming?"

Jackie looked questioningly at her sister and brother-in-law.

"Sure! Why not?" Kyle said with a grin.

Jackie smiled. Kyle would use any excuse to get ice cream.

"Great! Be right back." Montgomery jogged off toward the school after his teammates.

He returned a few minutes later, and Jackie, Kyle and Shonda all crammed themselves into the backseat of the Dawson's SUV while Montgomery caught a ride with some of the other soccer players.

The DoubleDip Ice Cream Shoppe was the local ice cream parlor which doubled as a coffee shop. The brightly colored booths were reminiscent of the fast food restaurant that formerly occupied the building, but a whole section had been cleared out in the front to make room for sagging second-hand couches and a couple of over-stuffed chairs, all covered with Hawaiian-print slipcovers from the clearance table of the nearest department store. The owners had opted not to go with all new furniture since they would inevitably get ice cream dribbled over the upholstery anyway.

Mr. Dawson let everyone out at the door before he parked so they could get a table before the soccer team arrived.

Mrs. Dawson's eyes were glowing. "This is the first time they've really included Monty in anything," she told Jackie as they claimed a couch and chair situated around a low table.

"I haven't seen him this happy since…" she paused and glanced at Jackie uncertainly. "Has he talked to you at all about…"

"Perry?" Jackie felt a pang in her chest at the sadness that filled Mrs. Dawson's eyes at the sound of his name.

She nodded.

"Only a little," Jackie answered. She hesitated, then asked softly, "Was it an accident?"

Mrs. Dawson shook her head. "Cancer."

Jackie's stomach twisted at the thought of watching a loved one die like that and was suddenly thankful her mother's passing had been mercifully quick. "I'm so sorry," she said, knowing the words were inadequate but unable to think of anything else to say.

Mrs. Dawson nodded slowly, then took a deep breath as if to collect herself and looked over at Shonda who was fumbling for something in her purse, obviously trying not to listen. "Well, at least Monty's talking about it now." She smiled at Jackie. "I think you've helped him more than a dozen soccer teams. Now let's be happy, okay? This is a good day for him. For all of us."

When Mr. Dawson came in, Mrs. Dawson and Shonda stayed where they were to save their spot, and Mr. Dawson, Kyle and Jackie went up to the front to order. They only just beat the rush as soccer players and their friends and families swarmed into the DoubleDip. Jackie spotted Montgomery with Kris as they quickly got in line. Mr. Dawson called to his son and ordered for him when he reached the counter. Montgomery's ice cream was shoved into Jackie's hands as the men juggled their own dishes and returned to their wives. Jackie fought her way back through the line toward Montgomery.

"How come you're not on varsity?" Montgomery was asking.

Kris rolled his eyes. "I should be. But Mr. Kroy—he's the varsity coach—has six kids and every *stinking* one of them is on the team."

"Are they any good?"

He shrugged. "They're okay. If their dad wasn't the coach, you can bet they wouldn't all be on the team, though. But some of the other upperclassmen guys are really good, so the team does okay." He grinned. "We played them once last year and almost beat them."

"Yeah?"

He nodded. "I'll bet we could take them this year." He glanced over and noticed Jackie standing there with two sundaes. "Hey, it's your girlfriend," he said, his brown eyes mocking.

"Oh, grow up!" Jackie snapped, handing Montgomery his ice cream. "I'm not anyone's girlfriend, and I don't intend to be."

"To the everlasting gratitude of all mankind."

Jackie opened her mouth to retort, but Montgomery smoothly stepped in and steered her away.

"Just ignore him," he said. "You should know by now that he's just got a big mouth."

"He's such a jerk!" Jackie spluttered.

Montgomery shrugged. "He's not so bad."

Jackie stopped and stared at him like she'd never seen him before. How could he say that? Kris and Brent were practically her lifelong tormentors!

"He's a good soccer player," Montgomery offered hopefully.

"I don't care if he can kick a ball into a big net! So what?!"

He sighed. "Fine. Let's just go eat our ice cream, okay?"

Her indignation faded, and she felt a stab of guilt. She hadn't meant to dampen his good mood. "Congratulations, by the way. You played a great game."

"Thanks."

She grimaced painfully, took a deep breath and said, "And Kris did too. I guess he is a good soccer player."

Montgomery's lopsided grin flashed across his features. "Yeah. He is. I'm glad you noticed."

Jackie bit back the retort that rose unbidden to her lips and forced a smile.

Montgomery laughed.

They joined their families. Jackie squeezed in next to Mrs. Dawson, and Montgomery sprawled in the big chair. "Thanks, Dad," he said as he took a huge bite of his ice cream.

"You only get a sundae because you won. If you'd lost, you'd get a kiddie cone."

Montgomery grinned and took another bite. ☺

chapter ten

"Good morning," Mrs. Cox said at the beginning of English class. The students fell silent and turned their attention to their teacher. "Before we begin," she said, sitting at the edge of her desk, "I need to make an announcement. Normally at this time of year, we start discussing plans for the spring talent show. But this year, the other teachers and I have decided we're going to try something a little different."

Jackie pulled her gaze in from where it had lingered on the trees beyond the window. The people of Kilree were not known for trying different things, and the Academy was no exception. They had been having the annual talent show as a fund raiser for as long as anyone could remember. So far, she had managed to escape doing anything totally embarrassing. Generally, enough students signed up to do things that the school didn't have to resort to mandatory participation. Besides, everyone was involved in one way or another, because every class would sing a song or recite a speech or poem together.

"We've decided that instead of having a show where everyone is doing something different, we would unify our efforts into a single production," Mrs. Cox continued. "So we've decided that this year, we are going to do a play."

A play! Jackie thought, impressed.

Mrs. Cox paused as the students started murmuring amongst

themselves excitedly. Montgomery glanced over and grinned at Jackie. She smiled back, though she wondered if this new idea of the teachers was a good one. In order for a stage to be worthy of the play, the actors had to be good enough to transport the audience to another place and time. At least with a talent show, you were bound to have something good even it was just in comparison to the rest. With a play, it was hit or miss.

"We thought we'd try something a little more traditional this year and see how it goes. We're thinking of Shakespeare's *Tempest*."

A few of the students groaned at the mention of Shakespeare, but most of them seemed open enough to the idea. Jackie ran through the play in her mind, trying to picture who among her classmates or the upperclassmen could fit the roles.

"What about the little kids?" one of the students asked.

"The younger grades will be putting on their own program which we'll incorporate into the annual spaghetti dinner. Play tryouts will be one week from today right after school in the cafeteria. Montgomery?"

"Do we need to memorize something or bring something to read?"

"No. Just bring yourselves. We'll have everyone read from the same selection. There will be plenty of other ways to be involved in the production for those of you who won't be acting in the play. We'll discuss those areas a little more at the tryouts. Any other questions?" She looked around the room. "Okay then. Turn in your lit book to page 227."

The rest of the day flew by in a rush with the play the main topic of conversation.

"Pretty cool, huh?" Montgomery remarked as they walked home from school.

"What?"

"The play."

"Oh. Yeah, I guess so."

He looked at her, a puzzled expression on his face. "I thought you'd be excited."

Jackie shrugged. "Well, a play is only as good as its cast. I mean, the script and the direction is critical, naturally, but with a bad cast, it's sunk."

"That's why they're having tryouts. To find the best actors."

She said nothing.

"You're going to try out, aren't you?"

She hesitated.

"You have to," Montgomery said. "I mean, this is right up your alley. This is probably the most-Jackie-thing the school has ever done. And I know you'd do a great job. Besides, I thought you *wanted* to act."

"I do," she said with a sigh. "But, Montgomery, the final bell is what gets me through the school day. Staying longer than that would be like designing my own brand of torture." She shook her head. "Someday I will be in a play, but I don't want to act with these guys anymore than they want to act with me."

Montgomery stared at her incredulously.

"Don't you see?" Jackie asked. "They would suck all the magic right out of it and make it miserable. It would be a better experience for me if none of them were a part of it. And a better play for them— and therefore for the school—if I was not a part of it."

Montgomery shook his head. "You can't really believe that. I mean, it'll be the whole school, not just our class."

"I know. But if I'm going to be part of a real play, I want it to be memorable—in a good way."

"It's not like the teachers are going to let them dismember you onstage," Montgomery said. "Bad for the whole fundraising thing, you know?" he added with a grin.

Jackie smiled. "I know. But you don't understand—"

"What don't I understand? I'm not exactly Mr. Popular, myself."

"But you have an *in* with them, a link. Soccer. I have nothing."

"Let the play be your link."

Jackie was silent. She hadn't honestly thought about it that way. "I'll think about it, okay?"

She could tell it wasn't okay with him and that he thought she was being stupid and paranoid about the whole thing. And maybe she was. She just wanted her first play to be perfect. Was that such a bad thing?

"So what's the talent show usually like?" Montgomery asked.

"It's okay. People sing and play instruments and recite poems and speeches and stuff. Everyone's favorite is the duet acting. Kris and Brent did one last year that had everyone in hysterics."

"Were they good?"

Jackie shrugged. "I don't know. I mean, I guess maybe I would have found it funnier if…"

"If what?"

"If Brent hadn't been writing fake love letters to Kris and signing my name to them."

Montgomery laughed and then quickly clapped a hand over his mouth.

Jackie glared at him. "It wasn't funny."

He shook his head. "No. No, I can see that it wasn't."

She gave him a withering look. Boys! There were nice ones and mean ones, but they were all still part of the same club.

Jackie stuffed her school books into her backpack when she had finished her homework and turned her gaze out to the soccer field where the team was scrimmaging. When practice was over, Montgomery and Jackie walked home, enjoying the warmth of the afternoon sun.

"How's the room coming?"

"Good. Tomorrow we'll give the floor its last coat."

"Cool. What are you working on today?"

"That little table that was in the attic. Kyle's got some stuff that will strip the old paint off, and then I'm gong to sand it down and repaint it."

"What color?"

"I haven't decided. I'm leaving the floor boards brown. The walls are tricky because the ceiling slants down to just a few feet above the floor. I have tons of glow in the dark stars all over the ceiling in my room now. I could just put those all over the slants." She kicked at a pebble and sent it bouncing away. "I have a book on constellations. I could chart the stars out more accurately."

"Or you could paint a mural."

"A mural?" Jackie paused. She had never thought of that.

Montgomery stopped after a couple of steps and glanced back.

"I've sketched before, but I've never done any painting." She started walking again as she thought about it. "Do you draw?"

He shrugged.

"Will you help me?"

He shrugged again. "I don't know…"

She looked over at him. "Please? It'll be fun!"

"Well… maybe." His dark eyes turned away, and his face emptied of expression.

She watched him carefully and wondered if she had said something wrong, but decided not to press him.

When they reached the house, she paused at the end of the driveway and checked the mailbox. Shonda usually got the mail, but she was working an extra shift today at the store and would be home later.

Jackie thumbed through the stack of envelopes.

"Oh! I got a letter!"

She pulled out a small white envelope.

"I never get mail! Look!"

She waved it in Montgomery's face.

"I see it! I see it! Just open it!"

She shoved the rest of the mail into his hands and tore open the envelope. She pulled out a card, and her eyes flew over the outside eagerly. Her enthusiasm drained away. She opened it and read the inside. "It's from my father." She put it back in the envelope and started down the driveway.

Montgomery followed. "Well, that's good, isn't it?"

"It's a birthday card."

"It's your birthday?"

"No. My birthday was six months ago."

"Oh."

Jackie didn't mention the card to Shonda when she got home a few minutes later.

Montgomery helped strip and sand the table and by suppertime it was silky smooth.

"Would you like to stay for supper?" Shonda asked him.

"No, thank you. My parents are really into the eating-together-as-a-family thing. Thanks anyway, though. See you tomorrow," he said to Jackie as he headed for the door. "Don't forget about the science test."

"We have a science test?"

Kyle laughed. "He knows you too well already."

Montgomery grinned. "Chapters five and six."

Jackie racked her brain. "I don't remember her saying anything about a science test."

"She did. See ya." He closed the door behind him.

Jackie studied for the science test after supper, but her mind kept wandering back to the birthday card. What kind of father didn't know his own children's birthdays? The question seemed to answer itself. The same kind that would abandon his family. She pulled the photograph out from her Shakespeare. They looked so happy. What had gone wrong? ☺

chapter eleven

"I aced the science test!"

Shonda looked up from the laundry she was folding. "Excellent. I knew you could be a good student if you really tried. Now isn't that more rewarding than coming home soaked from spending hours sitting on a rock reading old plays?"

It wasn't exactly the sort of praise she was looking for, but it would do. She smiled.

"Since there's paint drying in the attic, and I don't have any homework, can I go to the cove this afternoon?"

Shonda hesitated, and Jackie knew she was searching for an excuse, but she finally nodded. "I suppose so. But be careful."

"I'm always careful."

"I know. It's just… I was talking to a lady at work today, and she was horrified that I let you go there alone."

"Shonda, it's not like I'm still in diapers. I'm fourteen."

"I know. And that's what I told her. Well—not the diaper part, but—you know. But I guess the place has a history."

"A history?"

"Yeah. She said some kids drowned there a long time ago."

"Really?"

She nodded. "So just promise me you'll be extra careful, and I won't nag you about it again."

Jackie smiled. "I promise."

She met Montgomery there a few minutes later and told him what Shonda had heard. "Maybe that's where the ghost rumors came from," she mused.

"Maybe. There was this old house on my street in Boston that's supposed to be haunted. Some Civil War general lived there. It's an inn now, and the owners swear they can still hear him walking around at night with his sword clanking on the floor."

"Cool!" Jackie said, fascinated. "I would so love to live in a place like that!"

"What, a haunted house?"

"No! A city with culture and history! What made your family pick Kilree anyway?"

Montgomery shrugged. "My grandfather was born here, then his family moved to Boston when he was a teenager. It's as good a place as any, I guess."

Jackie pushed a lock of hair back from her face. "That's kind of neat, you know?"

"What?"

"Well, a couple generations ago, it might have been your grandfather and one of his friends sitting out on this rock."

Montgomery glanced around, a look of vague surprise on his face. "I never really thought about it."

"Does he ever talk about when he lived here?"

He shook his head. "No. At least not to me. I didn't even know he'd ever lived anywhere else until Dad suggested we come out here for a while. I think he asked Gramp to come too, but he said no. He likes his life in Boston too much, I guess. He has a lot of friends."

"Do you miss him?"

"Yeah. Especially after Perry died, he really started spending a lot of time with me; wanted to be sure I didn't think it was my fault."

"Perry died of cancer. Why would you feel responsible?"

Montgomery shrugged. "It's hard to explain, really. There's just something about a younger brother—you feel like it's your job to protect him. I know there was nothing I could have done. But for a while, I really did feel like I'd failed him." He was silent for a moment, then glanced over at Jackie and smiled. "Gramp was the only one who saw that. He really helped me through it."

"It's strange, isn't it? Why God allows the things He allows? Me losing my parents, you losing your brother. Do you suppose we'll ever know why?"

Montgomery looked out over the water. "I've thought a lot about that. I think if we focus on the why too much, we'll just make ourselves crazy." He was quiet for a moment. "But I do have a theory."

She waited expectantly.

"Maybe… maybe it's to help shape us into the people we're going to become."

She nodded slowly. "Maybe it is." She thought about her parents and wondered what sort of person she would have been if they'd been around to raise her. She thought about Shonda, too. If their parents had raised them, Shonda would have a thriving career right now and maybe even a couple of kids. Both she and Kyle would have their own cars, and they wouldn't have to sit in the kitchen once a month, madly punching numbers into calculators, trying to figure out how to make the mortgage. And where would she be? She thought for a moment and then decided it didn't matter where she was because she would be with her mother and father. What kind of people were these circumstances shaping Shonda and her into? She shook her head. Nothing better than what they would have been if they'd been raised like normal kids. She didn't like thinking about it. It left her with the wretched feeling that she was some kind of horrible mistake. That her very existence was a cosmological blunder.

She shrugged the feelings away and tried to think of something else. Anything else. "Well, I can't imagine choosing this place over Boston."

"I don't understand why you want to leave it so badly," Montgomery said. "This is a really cool town."

"It is nice, I guess," Jackie conceded reluctantly. She shrugged. "Maybe if I liked the people better…"

Sudden irritation flashed across his face. "You know, you're always complaining about the people. Wherever you go, there are going to be people you don't like. Maybe it's time you just dealt with it and learned to be content where you are."

Anger flooded through her, and she glared at him, stung at the reprimand. He flinched a little but didn't look away from her gaze.

"You've seen how they treat me, and I don't do anything—"

"No, you don't do anything. That's just it. Maybe it's time you did."

"What are you talking about? You said yourself they don't understand me."

"You're using that as a crutch. I'm not excusing them, but, you know something? You're every bit as critical and judgmental of them as they are of you."

Jackie said nothing.

"Give them a reason to see past what they don't understand."

"How?" she asked quietly.

"I don't know. Stop hiding from them. Stop avoiding them. If you spent time with them, you'd see they're not all bad. And they'd see you're not so weird and stuck up."

She stared at him, hurt and anger warring inside of her. He returned her gaze, then abruptly looked away and shrugged. "Just stop complaining about it and *do* something. I've gotta go."

He climbed off the rocks and walked away without a backward glance.

She walked home slowly, his words repeating themselves over and over in her mind. She felt awful, but wasn't convinced he was right.

After dinner she tried reading, but couldn't seem to concentrate. She'd never had a close friend, so she'd also never argued with one. It was a horrible, unsettling feeling. Finally, she fell into a troubled sleep.

When she went to the cove the next morning, she half expected him to show up. But he didn't.

At school she remained cool and aloof, and though he was civil, he didn't go out of his way to talk to her. He sat with Kris and Brent during lunch.

At the end of the day, Mrs. Cox reminded everyone about the play tryouts that were going to be held that afternoon and then dismissed them all with prayer.

Jackie held back to avoid the crush of students surging out the door and found herself standing next to Montgomery.

"Hey," he greeted her.

"Hey. Are you trying out?"

He nodded. "Yeah."

"Good luck."

"Thanks." There was an awkward pause. "I'll catch up with you later."

Jackie watched him go, then left the school and started for home. The wind sent leaves skittering across the road and blew harshly in her face, pushing against her, and slowing her progress. Why did everyone want her to be in the dumb play anyway? Just because she was passionate about drama didn't mean she intended to lower her standards and act with a bunch of.... The thought trailed off unfinished, and Montgomery's voice suddenly shouted in her mind. *"Just stop complaining about it and do something."*

"Do something," she echoed.

The wind shoved at her.

She stood there on the side of the road, frozen in indecision for several long minutes. Finally, she took a deep breath and turned back toward Kilree Christian Academy, the wind blowing her cheerily along.

The cafeteria was bustling with activity. She was surprised to see so many of her classmates. Especially the boys. Both Kris and Brent were trying out! She frowned. A school play didn't seem the sort of thing they'd be interested in. Faces turned her way in amazement.

Clearly they had not expected to see her either. She steeled herself against their gazes.

Mrs. Cox stood up at the front of the auditorium and called for everyone's attention. "Thank you all for coming. We'll begin having readings for the speaking parts of the play in just a few moments. For those of you who don't want to act in the play, there are still plenty of ways you could help out with the production. And the same goes for those who do not get the parts they're hoping for. Those of you who are trying out, please form a line off to the right of the stage and come up one by one and read from this paper on the podium. Boys, read Prospero's part; Girls, read Miranda's."

Jackie went to join the line that was quickly forming and stood behind Alicia Lewis, a pretty girl from the senior class. Montgomery was several people in front of her.

Once the readings began, the line moved swiftly. Most of the students simply read the part as they would read a selected reading in English class. A few went over the top, saturating each beautiful line with melodrama that made Jackie cringe. But some of them treated it like an audition for Broadway and put everything they had into it.

When Montgomery's turn came, he strode to the podium, and his eyes scanned the paper in front of him. Then he looked out at the people in the auditorium and began speaking. He changed the pitch of his voice slightly so that it sounded older and more powerful. "'Our revels now are ended. These our actors, as I foretold you, were all spirits, and are melted into air, into thin air, and like the baseless fabric of this vision, the cloud-capp'd tow'rs, the gorgeous palaces, the solemn temples, the great globe itself, yea, all which it inherit, shall dissolve, and like this insubstantial pageant faded leave not a rack behind. We are such stuff as dreams are made on; and our little life is rounded with a sleep.'"

"He's really good!" Alicia whispered back to her.

Jackie smiled and nodded, feeling a surge of pride similar to when she had seen him help win the soccer game.

Alicia read soon after, and then it was Jackie's turn.

When she stepped onto the stage and saw all the faces turned her way, she nearly walked right by the podium and out the nearest door. But she stopped at center stage and breathed a quick prayer that God would steady her nerves. She felt like she'd eaten a whole butterfly farm for lunch instead of a salad. She skimmed the passage she was to read and cleared her throat. Alicia had read the part in a feathery light voice that Jackie thought emphasized Miranda's lack of strength as a character. So she spoke in her own voice in an attempt to strip away the Shakespeare's-weaker-sex stereotype and make her real. Fixing her eyes on the back wall to imagine the horrific storm conjured by Prospero to wreck the ship—and to avoid the gazes of everyone watching—she took a deep breath and began. "'If by your art, my dearest father, you have put the wild waters in this roar, allay them. The sky it seems would pour down stinking pitch, but that the sea, mounting to th' welkin's check, dashes the fire out. O! I have suffered with those that I saw suffer. Poor souls, they perish'd. Had I been any God of power, I would have sunk the sea within the earth or ere it should the good ship so have swallow'd, and the fraughting souls within her.'"

When she finished, she quickly left the stage, keeping her gaze on whatever wall was ahead as she walked until Montgomery's grinning face appeared directly in front of her.

"That was great!" he exclaimed.

She thanked him and tried to smile nonchalantly while her heartbeat gradually returned to normal.

A sheepish look came over him. "By the way," he said, "I'm sorry. Yesterday was a bad day. I shouldn't have snapped at you like that."

"No." Jackie shook her head. "You were right. And I needed to hear it."

He smiled gratefully.

"And good job yourself," she added. "You'll get a part for sure. No one else has even come close. I was sure Prospero was in the building." To her surprise, he actually blushed.

The next student was auditioning, so they fell silent and watched. When everyone had finished, Mrs. Cox thanked them again and said she would let everyone know the outcome as soon as possible.

"Also," she added, as everyone started leaving, "there will be a signup sheet posted here in the cafeteria for those who want to help out in other ways. We will be constructing our own sets for the most part, painting our own backgrounds, and, though the home-ec class will be working on costumes, anyone who can sew is desperately needed. Family members and friends are welcome to help out."

The students surged out of the cafeteria. Soccer practice had been cancelled due to the play tryouts, so Montgomery offered to come help out with Jackie's room.

"So what part do you want?" Jackie asked as they walked.

"Prospero," Montgomery said. "I know he's old, but he's really cool, and Ferdinand is a sap. How 'bout you?"

"Well, as usual, there aren't too many female roles to salivate over. But I'd like to play Ariel."

"The spirit?"

"Yeah. I think his—or her—character is one of the most interesting of the cast. Why was he trapped in the first place? Where did he come from? What will he do once Prospero frees him? He's fascinating. And because he's a spirit and not technically a 'he,' a boy or girl could play him. In fact, a girl—especially a short girl—could probably be more convincing."

He nodded. "You're not interested in Miranda?"

She grimaced. "She's okay. But since most of the time she's drooling all over Ferdinand, she's not terribly interesting to me."

When they reached Jackie's house, they grabbed a quick snack from the kitchen and went upstairs. Shonda was up there already, a handkerchief holding back her golden hair. The paint cans were all set out with the colors Jackie had requested.

"Are you sure about this?" Shonda asked, looking dubiously at a can of dark greenish-brown paint.

"Absolutely. It won't look like a real forest if you can see white paint behind the trees."

"But why a forest?" Shonda asked. "That'll make it so *dark*."

Jackie glanced around. She was right of course. "I know. I've thought about that a lot. But I think it'll be worth it to live in a wooded glen."

Shonda closed her eyes and shook her head. "Whatever you want."

"Just the walls; not the ceiling slants. And it doesn't have to be perfect," Jackie said, as she pulled her hair back into a ponytail and the other two grabbed paint brushes. Most of it's going to be painted over anyway. This is just background."

Shonda winced as she brushed the murky paint across the clean white walls. She seemed almost glad when the phone rang, and she dropped her brush onto to the paint can and rushed downstairs.

"This could be therapeutic," Jackie said, vigorously splashing paint onto the short walls.

"Painting is good for the body and soul," Montgomery said, sweeping the walls with broad strokes.

"Who told you that?"

"My art teacher."

"Did you have private lessons?"

He nodded.

Jackie made a series of splotches and then swirled them all together. Her back was beginning to ache, so she knelt on the drop cloth that was protecting her floor. "Ahh. Much better. So why was it a bad day yesterday?"

Montgomery was quiet for a moment, and at first she thought he wasn't going to answer her. Then he said softly, "Yesterday would have been Perry's thirteenth birthday."

She winced. "I'm sorry," she whispered.

He nodded.

She tried to think of something appropriate to say, but couldn't, and decided it might be best to say nothing at all.

They painted in silence for the next few minutes, lost in the feel of the paint-laden brushes whisking along the walls and their own thoughts and memories. Shonda's voice drifted faintly up the stairs.

"Did you cry?" Jackie asked suddenly, the words slipping out of her mouth before she had even thought through the question.

Montgomery glanced at her in surprise.

"When Perry... did you cry?"

"'To weep is to make less the depth of grief,'" he quoted, turning back to his painting.

She wasn't satisfied. "Did you?"

"Yeah. I cried."

Jackie smeared more paint along the wall. "I can't remember ever crying when Mama died. I can't remember Shonda crying. I'm sure we both must have."

"Do you miss her?" he asked softly.

She nodded. "But, you know, it's funny. I don't know if I really miss her or if I just miss the fact of her. I can barely remember her at all. There's just... fragments. A look, a phrase, a color. Every year, her memory gets a little fuzzier. I keep a picture of her in my room. Shonda thinks it's because I loved her so much. And I did. But really, I like to keep it close by just so I can keep the image of her face fresh in my mind. So I won't forget, you know?"

He nodded slowly. "Yeah. I know."

A few long strands of hair had drifted down around her face, and Jackie pushed them back. "So are you good?"

He glanced at her questioningly.

"At drawing and painting."

He shrugged.

"Can I see something you've done sometime?"

He hesitated. "There's a picture in the den. Over the fireplace."

Jackie stopped painting. The boy sleeping—she remembered it well. "You did that?"

He nodded and kept his eyes fixed on the wall in front of him.

"Montgomery, it's beautiful! I saw it when I was there for dinner. It's perfect!"

"Thanks."

He was quiet for a long time.

Jackie heard Shonda clanking dishes in the kitchen. It must be almost supper time.

"I drew it while he was in the hospital. He was sleeping, and I felt like if I could just capture that moment, capture him, then maybe he would just sleep forever, you know? And not die." He took a deep breath and then swallowed. "But he was gone before I had finished it. I haven't drawn anything since."

"Why not?" she asked softly.

He shrugged. "I don't know. I just haven't wanted to."

"But to have a gift like that…" She looked over at him, but his face might have been carved from stone.

He left soon after. "I've got to get home for supper. See you tomorrow."

"Bye," she called after him as he descended the stairs. She shook her head and kept on painting. It was amazing. He could listen and comfort and encourage and advise, but when the tables were turned and he was on the other end, he could turn people off as effectively as if he carried a little remote control in his pocket.

She had finished painting by the time Shonda called her down for supper.

Over macaroni and cheese, she told her sister and brother-in-law about the play tryouts.

"Jackie, that's wonderful!" Shonda exclaimed.

Kyle grinned his agreement. "Way to go, Jax."

"Do you know what part you'll get?"

"Well, I don't know if I got any part yet. But I'm hoping for Ariel. Ariel's a spirit who had been imprisoned and was freed by Prospero."

"Did Montgomery try out?"

She nodded. "He was amazing. He got a part for sure."

"When will you know?" Kyle asked.

"Pretty soon. I don't think they'll deliberate all that long. It's only a high school play after all."

"Well, even if it is 'only' a high school play," Kyle said, "we're very proud of you."

Shonda smiled and nodded.

"And just think," Kyle added. "This could be the beginning of a long and illustrious career on the stage."

"Just don't forget us when you're rich and famous," Shonda said, her eyes twinkling.

"I won't," Jackie said with a grin.

At school the next day, an announcement was made in Homeroom that the roles for the play had been cast and the list had been posted in the cafeteria. Before the next class, students raced to the lunch room and struggled to see the audition results. Jackie peered over the shoulders of a boy standing in front of her and squinted to make out the fine print on the sheet of paper. The roles were listed in alphabetical order. "Ariel, Ariel, Ariel," she murmured. Adrian, Alonso, Antonio, *Ariel!* Her eyes flew to the student's name next to it. *Alicia Lewis.* Her heart plummeted in disappointment.

"Hey!" Montgomery jostled his way through the crowd and squeezed in next to her. "Congratulations!" He was grinning ear to ear.

"What do you mean?" Jackie said. "I didn't get it. Alicia did."

"You didn't get Ariel, dummy, but that doesn't mean you're not in the play. You got the part of Miranda!"

"I did?" Jackie's mind whirled, and she stood up on her tiptoes to stare at the paper again. And sure enough, there was her name right next to Miranda. Her heartbeat quickened, and she read the name again. She did! She got the part, and she would be playing Miranda in Shakespeare's *Tempest*! The keen disappointment of not getting the part of Ariel faded before the onslaught of excitement. What about Montgomery? Her eyes flew over the rest of the names, ashamed she hadn't looked for him right away. Ferdinand was being played by Josh Fielding, a junior. Juno… Sarah Lane, Miranda… Jacqueline Randall—she thrilled to see her name there again, Nymphs… There! A few spaces below her name, 'Montgomery Dawson' leapt out at her from its place next to the name Prospero. "Prospero!" she shouted joyously. "You got Prospero!"

"I know!"

"Montgomery, this is fantastic!"

He nodded, his dark eyes glowing with excitement. "This is going to be great! We both got great roles!"

Her smile took on a rueful edge. "Well, at least one of us got the part we wanted. I'll be spending most of my time acting lovestruck over Josh Fielding."

"But she's the lead female role, you big dope! Instead of an invisible spirit, you'll be princess of the island. That's not so bad."

"I know." Her enthusiasm returned, and she could feel her grin stretching way out of control as a new thought struck her. "And you know what else?"

"What?"

"This means I'm playing your *daughter*."

Montgomery laughed. "I hadn't thought of that."

"Just be nice to me, okay? Sometimes Prospero treats his daughter like she's dumb and calls her names—and maybe they weren't offensive in Shakespeare's day, but they sure don't sound very nice now. So don't do that to me. I'm your only daughter so be nice."

Montgomery grinned wickedly.

"Hey, congratulations, you guys."

Jackie and Montgomery glanced over and saw Alicia Lewis had forced her way back to where they stood.

"Thanks," Montgomery said.

Jackie nodded. "You too."

Alicia smiled. "Thanks. I had a feeling you both would be in it. Well, see you around."

Most of the students chosen were upperclassmen. Jackie and Montgomery were the only two from their class to get lead roles, though there were several understudies, including Kris Cappencella and his sidekick, Brent, Jackie noted unhappily.

"Brent is the understudy for Caliban," she read. "Well, that's appropriate. And Kris…" She groaned. "Look at this, Montgomery! Kris is the understudy for Ferdinand!"

Montgomery started laughing.

"It's not funny!" Jackie exclaimed. "They'll probably pull some stupid prank and ruin the whole play!"

"They're just understudies," Montgomery said. "They probably won't even be in it."

"Can you imagine if they are, though?" Jackie said. "Brent as my tormentor wouldn't be anything unusual but *Kris*?! Kris as my—my—"

"Your one true love?" Montgomery asked with a huge grin.

Jackie glared at him.

"It might not be that bad. And they might be really good. You said they had a good duet acting routine last year."

Jackie shrugged. So everyone had said. "Let's just hope that none of the cast members get sick. If I have to, I'll follow Josh around and disinfect everything before he touches it."

Montgomery laughed and then glanced around the nearly deserted cafeteria. "Come on, we're late for class."

"Why do you suppose they decided to cast understudies?" Montgomery asked as they hurried down the hall to their science class.

Jackie shrugged. "This is the biggest fund raiser of the year. They like to be prepared. They always have backups for the talent show, because someone is inevitably sick or doesn't show. I guess they don't want to be any less prepared for the play."

Montgomery nodded. "It would be a lot worse to have a cast member not show than a talent show participant."

"Yeah."

Later that morning, a high school assembly was held to discuss the fund raiser. After a few opening announcements, Mrs. Cox called the cast members and understudies aside to a corner of the cafeteria while the principal, Mr. Norris, continued to talk to the rest of the high school about all the other areas of the production.

Mrs. Cox opened a cardboard box and started pulling out slim paperbacks and handing them out. "This is the version of the play we'll be using," she said.

Jackie glanced through hers. The play had been abridged of course. No doubt if they had tried to do the whole thing, they would put the audience to sleep.

"Now, the first thing to do is have everyone memorize their lines. That's why we're starting early. The sooner everyone has his or her lines down, the sooner we can concentrate on the play itself. There's a synopsis in the front of the book. I would advise everyone to read that first and then read the play. We'll have another meeting next week after school to discuss it and answer any questions you might have. After that, we'll start having line checks every other week to see how it's all coming. Understudies, it's just as important for you to have your lines down as it is for the main cast, so no slacking. Now, does everyone have a copy of the play?"

The cast nodded.

"Okay, so we'll meet back here one week from today after school. Any questions?" She looked around the group. "Good. You may return to your classes."

The larger group was finishing up too, and the students all filed back to their classrooms. Jackie read the play synopsis as she walked, but suddenly voices behind her caught her attention.

"...can't believe they gave the role to *her*."

"I know. Makes me glad I'm just an understudy."

"You'd better hope Josh doesn't get sick or anything…"

Jackie shut their voices out. She didn't need to look to know who they were. Her stomach twisted into a knot and seemed to stay that way. She wished she hadn't tried out for the play, much less received a part.

"What are you talking about?" Montgomery demanded that afternoon when she voiced the sentiment as they were leaving.

"Don't you see? It's just like I said it would be. They're glad, Montgomery, *glad* they didn't get main parts, just because I'm in it!"

"They're just jealous and you know it. Don't worry about them."

Jackie wasn't so sure.

So when's the next soccer game?" she asked.

"There's an away game coming up. We're going all the way to Bangor."

"Cool. Did Perry play soccer?" she asked

Montgomery was quiet for a moment. "Yeah," he said at last.

"Did he have a private coach, too?"

"No," he answered quietly. "He didn't play that much. We just liked to kick the ball around."

"What about art? Was he an artist, too?" she asked.

He shook his head. "He was more into drama." He kept his eyes fixed on the road ahead of them, but she could hear the sadness in his voice.

"So what kind of art do you like best?" She asked, steering the subject away from his brother.

Montgomery shrugged.

"You paint obviously. Do you sculpt or do any three dimensional stuff?"

"I've done a bit," he said. His face looked tense and his words were clipped.

"Uh oh," she said.

"What?"

"You're retreating to that place."

He glanced over at her. "What place?"

"That mental place you go to when people ask too many questions."

His eyebrows lowered. "I don't know what you're talking about."

"Your face gets that leave-me-alone look and you get all dark and broody."

"I do not."

"Yes, you do. You should look in a mirror."

Montgomery shrugged and didn't answer.

Jackie watched him carefully, but let the matter drop. He would open up when he was ready. ◡

chapter twelve

The water swirled around the cove in a circular pattern, an impenetrable gray like the sky. With one storm passed and another on its way, there was barely time for the sea to calm. The wind blew her hair across her face and ruffled the pages of her copy of *The Tempest*. She tucked her curls behind her ears and closed the book with a snap. "'Be of comfort. My father's of a better nature, sir, than he appears by speech. This is unwonted which now came from him.'" She spoke her lines into the wind. She had almost the first act down pat, but wanted to learn her entire part as quickly as possible so she wouldn't have to worry about her lines when rehearsals began.

A stick went swirling by and caught in a crevice in her rock. She reached down and plucked it out of the water absent-mindedly.

A strong gust of wind roared through the cove and shook the last stubbornly clinging leaves from a skinny ash tree growing precariously between the rocks at the water's edge. The leaves danced on the air for a few moments before fluttering down to the churning sea water below. Jackie watched as they were sucked in and then caught up in the whirling motion of the water. That's how I feel, she thought. "Like I'm just along for life's ride." She reached out with the stick to poke at one of the leaves as it swirled by. She missed. She knew God was in control of course. Pastor Hallowell preached on it all the time. But sometimes it was so hard to actually feel God there. The leaf floated by again. She snatched and missed. She thought about Shonda and what she could have done with her life if things had been different. "If she hadn't been stuck with me." Not that her life was a waste. She had a husband and a house and a good job. But Jackie couldn't help but feel that her sister could have done so much more. She followed the leaf with her eyes as it circled the cove again. She reached out over the water as it came back toward her, stretching as far as she dared. She almost had it—

A hand suddenly gripped her shoulder and yanked her back from the edge. She yelped in surprise.

"Oh! Honestly, Montgomery, I wasn't going to fa—" She turned around.

It wasn't Montgomery.

An old man perched on the rock behind her, his white hair shaggy and unkempt.

"Sam!" she exclaimed.

He released her and leaned back, watching her carefully, his brilliant blue eyes intense.

"Thank you," Jackie said uncertainly. "I come here all the time," she added, "and I've never fallen."

He continued to sit there, his face empty of expression.

She didn't know what else to say, so she sat quietly and waited, though she wasn't sure what she was waiting for. Sam's flannel shirt was stained and torn in a dozen places, and under it she caught a glimpse of an old tee shirt with "Hawaii" written across it in hot pink letters. The soles of his shoes were worn thin.

He moved at last, but instead of leaving as she expected, he began tracing circles in the air with his finger.

She watched, completely clueless.

He made a sweeping gesture that encompassed the waters of the cove and then again used his finger to make a circular motion in the air. She imitated him, feeling rather foolish, but hoping that copying his movement would help her understand what he was trying to communicate. It didn't.

She stopped and looked at him questioningly.

He drew his air circles faster.

She was beginning to wonder about the state of his mental health when he reached for the stick she was holding. She gave it to him. He leaned down and stirred the water with the stick, moving it in a circle slowly at first, then faster and faster. Then he made a peculiar sucking sound and shoved the stick under the water and let it go. He looked up at her pointedly. The stick bobbed up and floated away, but she didn't suppose that was the point.

"The water sucks things down... a whirlpool?" she asked tentatively. "A whirlpool. The water makes a whirlpool."

He nodded vigorously.

"But it's not like it's that dangerous. I've been coming here for years. I've even gone swimming in it during the summer."

He fixed her with a penetrating stare.

She looked out over the cove as if she'd never seen it before. Shonda and Kyle had always told her to be careful, and of course there was the rumor about the kids who had drowned. But she'd never really thought it was any more dangerous than any other place on the coast of Maine.

She looked at Sam, intrigued. "You come here a lot too, don't you?"

He nodded.

It must have been Sam watching Montgomery and her that afternoon.

His gaze shifted to the book in her hand, and his eyes lit with interest.

She glanced down at her copy of *Tempest*. "Shakespeare," she said. She held the book out.

He looked up at her, eyes wide.

She smiled and put the book in his hands.

He rubbed the cover gently and slowly opened the book.

Jackie felt a pang in her chest. His fingers were trembling.

He turned each page carefully, and his gaze never wavered from the printed words. Jackie waited quietly. The minutes passed slowly. Wind rustled the pages and ruffled her hair. The water churned and crashed on the rocks as the waves increased in size and force. Jackie shivered and brushed the spray from her face. It was getting cold and the storm was almost here. But Sam never even looked up.

He didn't stir until the first cold drops of rain splashed down onto the pages. He glanced up and then looked at Jackie as though he had forgotten she was there. Reluctantly, he closed the book and handed it back to her.

"Why don't you keep it?" Jackie said. The words were out of her mouth before she could think better of it.

He blinked, and his brows lowered slightly.

"No, really. I have another at home. In fact, I probably have a couple. Shakespeare is one of my favorites."

He hesitated.

She could see in his eyes that he desperately wanted to, but something seemed to be holding him back—as if he was too proud. But what could a homeless man be proud of? She tried another tactic. "Have you read *The Tempest* before?"

He didn't answer.

"You can take it hom—er—you can hang onto it and if you like it, you can keep it, and if you don't, you can give it back. But I have a couple copies of the play, so I really don't need this one."

He looked longingly at the book.

She put it back in his hand.

He looked up at her, and slowly a smile spread across his weathered features. He tucked the book inside his shirt to protect it from the rain, then pointed up at the darkening sky and stood up. She followed him off the rocks, slipping and skidding as the rain fell faster and the waves splashed higher. He seemed to have no trouble on the wet stone.

When they had reached the edge of the forest, he paused and glanced at her. He touched the bulge in his shirt where the book lay snugly hidden and smiled again. Then with a nod, he turned and walked off into the woods.

She watched him go and then slowly began making her way back home. She didn't regret giving him her copy of the play, though it would be harder to learn her lines toting her heavy collected works. What a strange man he was. She couldn't tell if it was the play that moved him so or just the book in general. Maybe he didn't have any books of his own. The rain was starting to soak through her clothes. She rubbed her arms briskly and began to run. ○

chapter thirteen

"You gave him your copy of the play?" Montgomery asked for the third time.

"*Yes.*"

"Why?"

"I told you. He just looked like he really wanted it. Montgomery, you should have seen him!"

"So you think he was the one watching us that day?"

"I think so."

"And when you left, he just walked off into the woods?"

"Yes."

"Do you think he lives out there?"

"In the woods?"

"Yeah."

"Maybe," Jackie said, furrowing her brow.

"You said no one knows where he lives."

"Yeah. There's a shelter in the next town down, but I don't know. Maybe he does live in the woods." Jackie frowned. "That's sad."

"I'd rather live in the woods than in a homeless shelter."

Jackie shook her head. "I'd rather have a roof. And plumbing."

He shrugged. "Maybe it's a pride thing."

After school, they hurried to the cove in hopes that Sam would come again. But he didn't. They waited until the early darkness of approaching winter had settled, but still there was no sign of the old man.

"I've got to go," Jackie finally said, reluctantly rising. "Shonda gets mad when I'm out after dark without a flashlight."

He nodded. "Okay."

They started up the path, then Montgomery reached into the front pocket of his backpack. "Wait, here." He pulled out a tiny flashlight. "It's not much, but it's light. You have farther to go than I do," he added before she could protest.

"All right. Thanks."

"See you tomorrow."

During the next few days, Montgomery staked out the cove during his free hours, which, between school and soccer practice and play practice, did not amount to very many.

"It's not fair," he grumbled irritably, pulling his coat closer around him.

Jackie smiled to herself. It had been a week, and Sam had not shown himself. "He's shy," she said.

"He came to see *you*."

"I *told* you," she said, trying to be patient. "He pulled me back from the edge of the rock. I think he just thought I was going to fall in."

Montgomery didn't look convinced.

"Oh, don't be such a grump!" Jackie snapped. "If you want to meet him so badly, fall in." She gestured to the cold waters swirling below. "Then maybe he'll show up and jump in after you."

He actually looked like he might be considering it, and Jackie rolled her eyes and stood up. "It's freezing out here. I'm going home."

Montgomery muttered to himself but followed her off the rocks.

They said goodbye, and Montgomery headed off through the woods toward his house. Jackie followed the trail back to the road and walked home.

"Good morning, Mr. and Mrs. Dawson!" Jackie beamed at Montgomery's parents when she saw them before church Sunday morning.

"Good morning, Jackie." Mrs. Dawson smiled warmly.

"And how does fair Miranda?" Mr. Dawson asked with a grin.

Jackie smiled and blushed.

"Rosy red," Montgomery said, looking thoroughly bored.

"How is the play coming?" his mother asked her.

"Fine. I have almost all my lines down."

"That's wonderful. I know Monty still has a way to go." She glanced at her son with a slightly reproving smile.

"I have a lot more of them than fair Miranda," he said shortly.

"Don't get defensive, sweetheart." The organist began playing hymns, and Mrs. Dawson said, "It looks like they're about to start. You can sit with us if you like."

Jackie quickly agreed and glanced around for her sister and brother-in-law. She spotted Kyle across the aisle and waved to him.

"I'm going to sit with the Dawsons. Is that all right?" she called.

Kyle shrugged and nodded.

Throughout the service, Jackie found herself glancing around at the different members of the congregation, trying to see who looked the most approachable to ask about the Mulqueen boys. She had chickened out last Sunday, but today she was determined to ask someone. When the service was over, Montgomery went over to talk to Kris and some of the other guys from school.

Jackie took a deep breath and headed for the front of the church. She had settled on Mrs. Harrison. She was the oldest person she knew, and as long as you caught her on a good day, she was quite a nice old lady.

"Good morning, Mrs. Harrison," she said timidly.

Mrs. Harrison peered over her glasses at Jackie. "Good morning."

"How are you feeling today?"

"Pardon?"

She groaned inwardly. On good days, Mrs. Harrison was hard

of hearing. On bad days the woman was practically deaf. She was very sweet about it, but Jackie didn't want to have to announce her question to the entire church.

"How are you feeling today?" she said, louder this time.

Mrs. Harrison beamed. "Oh, thank you, dear; I always liked this dress."

Jackie opened her mouth to correct her, but then thought better of it and just went with it. She nodded and smiled.

"How is your sister?"

"She's fine. Um…" She took a deep breath and bent closer so the woman would be sure to hear her. Here goes nothing. "Mrs. Harrison, I wanted to ask you a question."

Mrs. Harrison nodded and smiled pleasantly.

"Do you remember the Mulqueen boys? Desmond and Brigit's nephews?"

The older woman's smile faded. "Yes," she said softly.

Jackie leaned even closer and said loudly and clearly. "Could you tell me what happened to them?"

The woman sagged wearily back against the pew and slowly shook her head. "It doesn't do anybody any good to talk about such things. This town has enough ghosts." She looked up. "You're too young to be concerning yourself with sad stories like that, dear. Now run along."

Jackie masked her disappointment and thanked her, then walked away. Shonda and Kyle were talking to some friends, so she wandered outside.

The sky hung low and gray. She walked down the steps and then on impulse turned toward the cemetery. The iron gate creaked as she swung it open.

She roamed through the graves, old and new, reading names and epitaphs. An impressive monument stood at the center of the cemetery, remembering the founders of Kilree, but Jackie was drawn to a plot nearby with two stones enclosed in a wrought iron fence. She lifted the latch on the narrow gate, expecting it to protest, but it swung silently inward on well-oiled hinges. A lilac stood guard over the graves, and climbing roses twined about the fence in thorny spirals. She wondered what color they were. She peered at the stones. Desmond Mulqueen, the first one read. The second belonged to his wife, Brigit. Jackie read them sadly, thinking of the picture of the solemn couple on the brochure.

A cool breeze blew through the graveyard and chilled her. She shivered and drew her coat tighter about her, and as she slipped out of the little enclosure, she couldn't help noticing how lonely the two gravestones looked, walled away from the rest of the sleeping community.

Monday afternoon Montgomery had soccer practice but promised to come work on her mural as soon as he was done. She stopped at Winds Cove on the way home to enjoy a few minutes of peace and quiet. She hauled her heavy collected works of William Shakespeare out of her bag and looked out over the water as she studied her lines. Memorization came easily to her and for that she was very thankful.

She shivered. The pale sunlight had barely warmed her at all, and now the earth's closest star was hiding behind the trees.

She pulled her jacket closer about her. She was about ready to pick up and leave when she saw him.

He was standing beneath the willow tree at the water's edge, watching her.

Her heart skipped a beat. It was almost creepy.

She waved. "Hi, Sam."

He hesitated a moment, then nimbly picked his way among the rocks and joined her. She recognized his coat as one Kyle had donated to good will years ago.

Sam sat down, and there was a funny look on his face. He almost looked nervous. Probably because he's not used to being around people, she thought. But then he slowly pulled a book out from inside his jacket and shyly handed it to her. She took it, more than a little bewildered. It was an old hardback Sherlock Holmes mystery, protected by an ugly dust jacket. The Dewey Decimal label on the binding announced it was or had been a library book. The inside cover was stamped "Discarded" in red ink. The pages were worn, and the binding was loose. He must have read it a hundred times.

"I love Sherlock Holmes," she said, glancing at the summary on the back. "I've never read this one, though. It looks really good." She tried to hand it back, but he shook his head. He seemed to want her to keep it. "It's for me?"

He nodded.

And then she understood. A gift for a gift. She had given him her copy of *Tempest*. He was giving her a book of his own in return.

She smiled. "Thank you."

He beamed and his face crinkled into a myriad of wrinkles.

He leaned over and looked curiously at the heavy tome of Shakespearean plays and poetry. He pointed to the title at the top of the page she was on and glanced at her questioningly.

"Yes, I'm still reading *The Tempest*," she said with a laugh. "My school is putting the play on as a fund raiser, and I'm in it."

His bushy eyebrows rose, and he pointed to the character names on the page.

"I'll be playing Miranda," she told him. "And my friend Montgomery is playing Prospero. We're both pretty excited."

He nodded appreciatively, but his eyes were fixed on the heavy volume in her lap.

"It's a collection. All of Shakespeare's known works. You can look at it if you want."

She handed him the book, and he took it almost reverently.

It was an odd sight, really—a homeless man sitting on a rock and pouring over a Shakespeare anthology.

He flipped through the pages, his eyes flying over the words. He was skimming through the sonnets when he stumbled across the picture of her parents. He gingerly picked it up and examined it, then glanced at her, eyebrows slightly raised.

"Those are my parents," she said. He nodded and studied it anew. He fingered her mother's face and gave her a little smile.

"Yes, she was beautiful."

He looked up, his blue eyes penetrating.

"She died. When I was young. I don't really remember her much."

He pointed to her father questioningly.

"No, he's still alive. But I don't live with him. I've never even met him actually. He left when I was a baby."

Sam's blue eyes glinted with sadness, and he gently touched her shoulder. He could not have expressed his sympathy more clearly if he had spoken the words aloud.

Jackie smiled. "I'm okay, though. I live with my sister. She and her husband have pretty much raised me. So I'm really okay."

She didn't sound all that convincing, even to herself.

Sam looked at her like he knew better, but nodded and replaced the photograph. He handed the book back to her and then climbed to his feet. She held up the Sherlock Holmes novel and thanked him again. He smiled sheepishly. Then, with a brief wave goodbye, he was gone.

By the time she got home, Montgomery was already there. Kyle was home early, and the two of them were playing catch in the front yard.

They greeted her cheerfully and after a few more throws came inside.

While Montgomery and she worked on the mural, she told him what had happened at the cove.

"What?!" he exclaimed. "The one day I don't go..."

At first she was afraid that his dismay would cause a relapse into another obsessive after-school vigil at the cove. But then he shrugged. "There must just be something about you," he said as he painted a broad tree trunk.

"Well, I've been going there alone for years. Maybe he identifies with me on some lonely subconscious level." She reflected for a moment on that possibility. "Or maybe he was just thanking me for the book."

"I'll bet that Sherlock Holmes was his favorite," Montgomery said.

"Oh." Jackie stopped painting. The thought of him giving up his one treasured possession seemed so horribly sad.

"Where does he keep things like that?" Montgomery asked. "Books and stuff. I wonder if he has a hole somewhere or something. There was this alley in Boston a few blocks from our house where a bunch of homeless people lived in boxes. Just like you see in the movies. Cardboard boxes stuffed with newspaper."

"That's so sad." Jackie thought of Sam sleeping in a box and felt tears spring to her eyes. She quickly blinked them back before Montgomery noticed. "And to think I complained about the size of my bedroom."

"Human nature," Montgomery replied. "Nothing is ever good enough or big enough."

"I don't know," Jackie said, looking around at her new room as it slowly began to take shape. "I think I'll be incredibly happy when I'm all moved in up here." She smiled as she thought about it. The mural was coming along nicely, and after Montgomery's initial reluctance to work on it with her, he seemed to throw himself into the project. In fact, she noted, he seemed happiest when he was painting. They rehearsed some of their lines together, then Montgomery left in time to get home for dinner.

There was a *Tempest* meeting after school the next day, and when it was finished, she stopped by the library on her way home.

The librarian smiled as Jackie dropped her books through the return slot of the book bin.

"Hello, Mrs. Neilson," Jackie greeted her cheerfully.

"Hello."

She walked quickly to the microfiche machine but stopped halfway there when she glimpsed the out of order sign taped to the screen. Her heart sank. She returned to the librarian's desk. "Any idea when it will be fixed?" she asked.

Mrs. Neilson shook her head. "Unfortunately, it's nothing that can be repaired locally. It's got to be sent out." She started pulling books out from the return bin and piling them onto her desk to catalog. "They were suppose to pick it up yesterday, but no one came. I'm afraid small towns are often low priority for this sort of thing. In fact, many don't have them at all."

Jackie nodded glumly.

"Anything in particular you were looking for?"

"Just more information on the Mulqueens."

Mrs. Neilson arched an eyebrow. "Didn't you finish that history project already? Why the sudden interest?"

She shrugged. She wasn't sure she knew herself. "Just curious."

"Well, the microfiche won't be much help anyway if that's what you're looking for. Nearly everything before 1960 was destroyed in the fire." She shook her head. "Whatever we have is from what families have donated—old records and newspapers and things. There's not much."

Jackie sighed. "But what about the last Mulqueens? They were still alive in the Sixties weren't they?"

She nodded. "Yes. They passed on in the late Sixties, I believe. So you'll be able to get their obituaries, I'm sure. And I think there might have been an article on them too."

"Did you know them at all?" Jackie asked.

"I remember them vaguely when I was a little girl. Very sad people."

The picture from the brochure flashed in her mind. "Because of their nephews?" she asked.

Mrs. Neilson shrugged. "I suppose. That was all before my time."

"Do you know what happened to them?"

She shook her head. "Just that they died in an accident."

"Oh." Jackie thanked her and turned to leave. She was nearly to the door when Mrs. Neilson called after her.

"Do you know Mrs. Jamison?"

Jackie paused and shook her head.

"She knew Mrs. Mulqueen fairly well, I believe. She's been a bit reclusive since her husband died, but she usually stops by in the afternoons. She might be able to tell you more."

"Thank you!" Jackie thanked her enthusiastically and hurried home.

The next afternoon, Jackie rushed to the library after school. Mrs. Neilson pointed to the back, and Jackie smiled and waved her thanks.

At the back of the library, an elderly lady sat at a large card table covered with puzzle pieces. Her thin frame was wrapped in a blue and green kimono, and her snowy hair was up in a bun with white feathery wisps curling around her face.

Jackie liked her instantly.

"Mrs. Jamison?" she asked shyly.

Mrs. Jamison looked up, and her bright eyes crinkled as she smiled.

"I'm Jacqueline Randall," Jackie said. "Mrs. Neilson thought you might be able to help me. I'm doing a little research on some local history stuff."

"Lovely. Do you like puzzles?"

Jackie nodded, and Mrs. Jamison gestured gracefully toward a chair.

Jackie joined her at the table.

Now that she was closer, she could see the woman's eyes were a deep violet. She must have been devastatingly beautiful in her youth, Jackie thought. "Have you always lived here?" she asked, finding it hard to believe she could have missed such a colorful dresser.

"This is wonderful. I could use another pair of eyes. No, no not always. I moved here with my parents when I was fifteen. How old are you?"

"Fourteen."

"Ah. A good age. I liked it very much anyway. Here's the cover of the puzzle box so you can see what we're trying to put together." She waved a cardboard cover at her that showed a collage of birds, bees and butterflies.

"Did you know the Mulqueen family at all?" Jackie asked.

Mrs. Jamison looked vaguely surprised but nodded. "Yes. Yes, a bit. Mrs. Mulqueen hired me to do a bit of cooking for them, and the wages were sorely needed as my mother was a cleaning woman and my father was particularly good at doing nothing."

"Well, I wondered... what could you tell me about them? What were they like?"

"Does that look like a humming bird's beak to you?"

Jackie peered at the small puzzle piece. "Ummm..."

"They were nice folks. Fairly quiet really. No, that's not a humming bird's beak at all, is it?" She scrutinized the puzzle piece from every angle and then dropped it and snatched up another. "I remember they were particularly fond of my maple walnut pie."

"So your relationship was more professional."

"I wasn't one of the family if that's what you mean. But we got on well enough. No, dear, don't force the pieces. It never works in the long run, and it upsets Mrs. Neilson."

Jackie smiled and pulled apart the pieces she'd jammed together. She had never had the patience for puzzles. "Were you there long?"

"A few years. Long enough, really."

"Did you know their nephews at all?"

Mrs. Jamison looked up in surprise "Yes. Yes, I knew them. They were good boys, both of them." She shook her head slowly, and her gaze left the cardboard conundrum before her and turned to the trees outside the window.

Jackie fumbled with the puzzle, trying to decide the best way to pursue the topic. "Were you there when... when the accident happened?"

She did not answer for a moment, her large eyes shining with remembered sadness. "Yes..." she finally said, her voice soft and full of memory. "Those were sad days. Heartbreaking. The whole town just seemed to stop breathing. And after... the house was too sad. I couldn't bear to be there anymore."

Jackie wanted to ask for every morbid detail on what had happened to the Mulqueen nephews, but Mrs. Jamison's cheerful face had fallen, and she looked close to tears, so Jackie asked quietly instead, "How long did you work for them?"

"Until I was nineteen. Then I met Jamison, and he whisked me away to see the world." She smiled faintly. "He took me to Italy for our honeymoon and everywhere else in the world after that."

"You must have been very happy," Jackie said.

Her violet eyes pierced Jackie's. "If wealth and travel and adventure equated happiness, I would have been the happiest woman alive."

Jackie looked down at her puzzle pieces, at a loss for the appropriate thing to say. "I'm sorry," she said softly.

"No need to be. I wouldn't advise marrying for money any more than I would promote arranged marriages. Fortunately, in spite of my vain selfishness and my parents' antiquated ideas, I did grow to love him." She fingered a blue puzzle piece. "And he adored me." She looked up and smiled at Jackie. "I may not have always been happy. But I learned to be content. Now where do you suppose this one goes?"

Jackie turned her attention to the puzzle, but her mind was bursting with questions, both about the Mulqueens and Mrs. Jamison herself. She bit down on her lip to keep her mouth shut and painstakingly assembled a butterfly.

"Does that look like a butterfly antenna to you?"

Jackie studied the fine black line at the edge of the piece Mrs. Jamison held out to her. "Ummm… maybe?"

"See if it goes with the butterfly you're working on."

Jackie frowned at it. The edges didn't look quite right. "I don't think it will…" she began doubtfully.

"Try it and see," Mrs. Jamison urged her.

Jackie pressed the piece into the space above her butterfly's little insect head. To her surprise, the interlocking grooves fit smoothly together. "It does fit!"

"You can't always tell at first glance how the pieces will fit together."

Jackie looked up at her.

Mrs. Jamison just smiled.

"Well," she said, "I've met my puzzle quota for the day and then some, so I'll be off. Lovely to have met you, dear."

Jackie followed her to the door and watched as the older woman pulled a mountain bike out of the rack in front of the library and cycled away, her kimono robes billowing behind her. Then she turned and slowly headed for home. She met Montgomery on the road, walking home from soccer practice and told him about Mrs. Jamison.

He laughed. "She sounds like a trip."

Jackie nodded thoughtfully. "But to have so much and still not be happy."

"It's people, not possessions that make you happy."

"I know."

"Well, it sounds like she's managing just fine."

"Yeah. I guess. But to be only content… it just seems like there should be more."

Montgomery shrugged.

They said goodbye at the turn off to Jackie's house. She walked slowly down the little lane and into her driveway, her thoughts consumed with images of a grief-stricken town and a young Mrs. Jamison with sad violet eyes, cooking maple walnut pies for a heartbroken couple.

chapter fourteen

To help reinforce her lines, she had written them out on a sheet of notebook paper. She took the paper out now and read through them once, then started saying them into the wind.

Movement caught her eye, and she glanced up as Sam sat down beside her.

"Hello," she said.

He greeted her with a smile and looked questioningly at the sheet of paper in her hand.

"They're my lines. Writing them out helps me learn them faster. Isn't this marvelous weather?" she said, holding out her arms to the wind and reveling in the feeling of it whipping through her hair. "The wind is a grand audience. Unfortunately, it doesn't tell me when I've made a mistake."

He reached for her paper, and pointed first to her, then to the lines and himself, looking at her with raised eyebrows.

"I can say my lines to you?" She was getting pretty good at interpreting his strange sign language.

He nodded.

"Wonderful! Okay..." she closed her eyes and envisioned them on the paper. She spoke them slowly and clearly the first time through and Sam waved his hand when she made a mistake. By the fourth time through, she could deliver them flawlessly.

Suddenly Sam lowered the paper, and his blue eyes narrowed. Jackie followed his gaze.

Montgomery stood at the shore, watching them hesitantly.

"Oh, that's my friend Montgomery," she said. "He's great. You'll love him." And she waved to Montgomery to join them before Sam could decide to leave.

Montgomery walked out to the large boulder at the end and sat down.

"Montgomery, this is Sam. Sam, meet Montgomery Dawson."

Sam stared at Montgomery oddly. The color drained from his face, and his blue eyes went cold.

Montgomery glanced at Jackie uncertainly, then smiled at the older man. "Hi." He held out his hand tentatively.

For a moment, Sam didn't move. Finally, he stretched out his own hand and shook Montgomery's.

"Sam was helping me with my lines," Jackie said, trying to fill the awkward silence. She turned to Sam. "Montgomery is in the play, too. He's playing Prospero."

Sam nodded, and his eyes lit with interest.

Going with the Shakespearean appeal, Jackie asked suddenly, "Would you do us a huge favor and listen to both our lines? We were going to practice a scene together, but that's hard to do with no one to check if we're getting our lines right."

He nodded, and Montgomery handed him his copy of the play.

They rehearsed their lines for Sam for nearly an hour until the warmth of the sun faded with its setting, and the cold penetrated their winter clothes.

"My fingers are going numb," Jackie said, standing up.

Sam and Montgomery rose with her.

"This has been great," she said to Sam. "Thank you so much!"

Montgomery thanked him too and suggested they do it again. Sam nodded.

They said goodbye when they reached the trees, and each headed off in separate directions. Jackie pulled her hat down lower over her ears. She enjoyed the cold, but the knowledge that a fire would be burning merrily in the wood stove in the living room spurred her on to walk faster. She smiled to herself, relieved that Montgomery had at last met Sam. But there was something vaguely troubling about the older man's reaction to meeting her friend. Nothing she could really put her finger on, but still there, nagging at the back of the subconscious. She replayed the scene again in her mind. Once they had made it through the introductions, Sam had been fine—even cordial, and Montgomery seemed to be at ease. But there was something Montgomery hadn't noticed. All the time he had been speaking, instead of following Prospero's lines in the book, Sam had been staring at the arrowhead around Montgomery's neck.

Line checks were held the Wednesday before Thanksgiving. Jackie made it through hers and only stumbled when Brent and Kris looked at her cross-eyed in unison. Honestly! She thought. You'd think we were still in grade school!

The Dawsons left for Boston that afternoon so they could spend Thanksgiving with Mr. Dawson's family.

Thanksgiving at the Lainson house passed as it always did, with lots of food and a special prayer time of praise for everything they'd been blessed with.

Friday was spent moving all of Jackie's furniture upstairs into her new room. The mural was only a few details away from being done. She and Montgomery had worked on it nearly every day, and the few things left she could take her time with. By mid afternoon, she had her new room all arranged. She stood at the door and surveyed her work. The room looked fabulous. The wall ended a few feet to the left where a bean bag and a squashy chair faced each other next to a window with a small table and a bookcase nearby. The walls and slants were painted with rolling green meadows and periwinkle skies, with a beautiful fairy-tale castle rising up from the hills. The fields became a dense forest which grew down toward the opposite end of the long room where her bed, dresser, nightstand, desk and second bookcase were. Her mother's trunk lay at the foot of her bed. It was a little dark. But she didn't care. Walking from one side of the room to the other made her feel like she really was walking through the woods. She knew her trees weren't entirely accurate—her branches curled and swirled too much. But it created just the right sort of atmosphere. Like she was in an enchanted wood.

She sighed with satisfaction. She wanted to sit for a moment, but she was absolutely parched, so ran downstairs to get something to drink. She opened the refrigerator for some apple cider and stared at the shelves packed solid with Thanksgiving leftovers. Throughout the time of traditional over-eating, Sam had never been far from her thoughts. She wondered where he was. What he was eating? If he was eating. She had felt a mixture of guilt and gratitude with every bite she had taken. Kyle had gone into town to put in a couple of hours at the office. She chewed her lower lip thoughtfully and glanced out the window.

Shonda was sitting on the swing in the back yard.

She made up her mind and quickly began packing turkey, stuffing and cranberry sauce into containers and then piling them into a grocery bag. She filled a freezer bag with rolls and squeezed three pieces of pie—apple, chocolate and lemon—onto a plate and covered it with tin foil and put them in the bag as well. She looked around the kitchen and snatched some apples out of the fruit bowl. Then she found some harvest-patterned napkins and dropped them in along with a plastic fork, knife and spoon. She grabbed her backpack and carefully put the grocery bag inside and headed for the door. As a last thought, she went back to the kitchen and filled up an old thermos with cider and stuffed that into her bag as well. Then she slipped out the front door and hurried down the road to the cove.

When she arrived, she scanned the area for any sign of Sam, but found none. She sat down and waited for several minutes. She hoped he wouldn't be offended or think she felt sorry for him and was being some kind of do-gooder. Although she did feel sorry him…

and she supposed it was charity—but the biblical kind of charity. Not insincere sympathy. What ever had happened to him, she wondered. He couldn't have always been this way. She tried to imagine what he might have looked like when he was younger but failed. The cold was starting to penetrate her jacket, and she wished she'd brought gloves. She forced herself to sit there a little longer, but when he didn't come, she pulled the grocery bag out of her backpack and left it beneath the willow. She rummaged around in the bottom of her bag until her fingers located a scrap of paper, and she hastily scribbled a note. *Sam, We cooked too much food yesterday, and I wondered if you wouldn't mind helping us take care of it before it spoils. Happy Thanksgiving! Jackie.*

She left the note lying at the top of the bag. As an afterthought, she removed her red scarf and tied it around the bag. She only hoped he would find it. She glanced around one last time and then headed home.

She breathed deeply of the wintry air as she walked. Kyle and Shonda's house came into sight, the bare branches of the maple trees embracing it with skeletal arms. She was checking the mailbox when the car appeared. It pulled into her driveway and stopped abruptly before it was even all the way off the road. A sticker on the windshield announced that the car was a rental. A man got out and approached her.

Jackie stared. He was probably in his late-forties, but his handsome face was still youthful. Fine lines creased the sun and wind-weathered skin around his oddly familiar pale green eyes, but not a lock of his kinky dark hair was gray.

He smiled.

It was her smile.

"Jacqueline?"

She dropped the mail. It scattered over the driveway, fluttering in the cool breeze.

It was the man in the photograph.

She felt her heart leap into her throat and then drop down to her toes.

It was her father. ◎

chapter fifteen

She stood there staring at him for what seemed like hours. She knew she should say something, but she couldn't think of any words that matched what she was feeling.

He smiled again. "I guess we've never been officially introduced. I'm Mason Randall." He held out his hand.

She stared at it, then looked back up at his face and hesitantly held out her own hand. "Hi," she said finally, trying to keep her voice steady.

He shook her hand firmly, but seemed reluctant to let it go. "The last time I saw you..." His voice dropped to a whisper, and he slowly shook his head. "I had no idea..." He released her hand. "Happy Thanksgiving!" The grin was back on his face.

Jackie heard the front door opening but couldn't tear her gaze from the man before her.

He glanced toward the house, and the smile faltered for a brief moment, then broadened. "Hey, Shonnie. Surprise."

Jackie looked over at her sister. Shonda was standing rigid in the doorway.

"No smile for your old man?" Mason asked.

He walked slowly up the driveway, Jackie trailing after him. She'd forgotten all about the mail.

He paused a few feet from the front door. Shonda still hadn't said a word. Finally, she said softly, "Jackie, come inside."

"But—" Jackie looked up at her father, her thoughts whirling in a fuzzy incomprehensible mess.

"*Now*."

She slipped past Shonda into the house, but stopped a few steps down the hall and turned around.

"How dare you," Shonda was saying, her voice low and unsteady.

"Look, Shonnie, I know it's been a long time, but I just thought Thanksgiving, you know, family… that maybe it was time to—"

"*Family*?" Shonda echoed. "The only family I have live in this house with me." She slammed the door in his face, then leaned against the door, shaking.

Jackie stared at her, not sure if she should comfort her or be angry. She walked into the living room and dropped her backpack on the floor, then drew back the curtain and peered out the window.

Mason was picking up the mail and placing it back in the mailbox. He paused at the car door and looked back at the house. Their eyes met, and he raised his hand in a solemn wave.

She hesitated, then slowly gave a little wave back. He smiled and climbed back into the car. She watched as he drove away.

The weekend dragged by.

Jackie kept waiting for Mason Randall to come back, but he didn't. She began to wonder if she had imagined the whole thing, but Shonda was in too horrible a mood for it to have been a dream.

Where was he? What was he doing? She wondered if he would come again. Shonda hadn't encouraged a second visit, but he couldn't have driven all this way just to be dissuaded from a slammed door. Could he?

Her father's surprise entrance had driven all thoughts of Sam from her mind. Apparently, Shonda was equally distracted, because she hadn't noticed the missing food. It wasn't until Jackie tripped over the grocery bag full of clean, empty containers on her way out the door Monday morning that she remembered. Her scarf was in there too, as well as the note she'd left with a scribbled thank you on the back of it.

Shonda stared oddly at the bag when Jackie brought it in.

Jackie quickly explained what she'd done, and Shonda nodded in understanding and approval as she took the dishes out of the bag and began sanitizing them.

"There's something else I want to mention before you go off to school," Shonda said, when Jackie headed for the door a second time.

Jackie paused.

"Since… Mason Randall is in town, maybe—just for a few days—you should stay close to home."

"Oh. Okay."

"Just don't go to the cove alone and come straight home after school, okay?" She ran a hand through her bright hair. "I don't know what he's doing here, but it can't be anything good."

Jackie nodded mutely.

She felt like she was in a dream as she walked to school. A strange kind of dream where every movement seemed to be slow and significant. She wasn't sure yet if it was a good dream or a bad one. She was still deliberating when the car pulled up beside her and slowed to a crawl.

Her heartbeat quickened.

Mason Randall leaned across the seat and smiled out the open window.

"Good morning!" he called cheerfully. "Can I give you a ride to school?"

She shook her head. "No, thank you. I enjoy the walk."

"Well, that's good. Would you like a bagel?" He held up a bag with Brewster's Bagels emblazoned on the side of it.

"No, thank you," she said again. "I've already had breakfast."

"Oh. Okay. Well, I was wondering if you'd like to get together after school. We could get a snack and… ah… get to know each other a bit."

Jackie sighed. She was bursting with curiosity, but Shonda's words were still ringing in her ears. She stopped and turned to him. "Shonda doesn't want me to talk to you."

He nodded as if he had expected that and then looked at her with a challenge in his eyes. "You strike me as the kind of girl who has a mind of her own."

"Shonda is my guardian," Jackie returned evenly. "I have to obey her wishes."

He nodded again. "Well, perhaps another time. Have a good day."

She felt a pang in her chest as she watched him drive away and resisted a wild urge to run after him and tell him she'd changed her mind. But she kept walking and prayed that if God willed it, He would bring them together so she could meet him.

When she arrived at school, she sat quietly, waiting for the first bell to ring.

"Hey!" Montgomery said as he slid into the seat next to her.

"Hi."

She could feel him watching her.

"Is everything okay?" he finally asked.

"My father's here," she said tonelessly. She was still trying to believe it was all real and not some kind of warped dream.

"Your father?" he echoed. "The one who left you when you were a baby?"

Jackie glanced at him. "How many fathers do you think I have?"

"Sorry. I didn't mean... Why is he here?"

She shrugged. "I don't know. Just to see us, I guess."

"After all these years?"

She nodded.

He was quiet for a moment. Then he asked, "What's he like?"

"I don't know. I mean, I didn't really get a chance to find out because Shonda slammed the door in his face. But before that..." She turned to her friend. "He seemed nice. Really nice."

Then Mrs. Cox called for everyone's attention and the day began. Jackie couldn't seem to focus on anything. All day long Mason Randall's face seemed to float across her vision. By the time the last bell rang, Montgomery had nearly given up trying to talk to her. She tried to listen, and she appreciated his trying to draw her out, but she just couldn't seem to keep her concentration together long enough to figure out what he was saying.

He made a last effort as they filed out the door with the rest of the students. "Do you want to go to the cove?"

She shook her head. "Shonda wants me to go straight ho—" She stopped, her eyes fixed on the cars in the parking lot.

"What?"

"Shonda's here." Jackie stared in bewilderment. "What is she doing?"

"You think it has something to do with your dad?"

She didn't answer. "I'd better go. See you tomorrow."

"Bye."

She ran toward the car.

Shonda saw her coming and leaned over and pushed the door open for her. "Hi."

"Hi," Jackie said. "What's up?"

Shonda shrugged. "I just thought I'd pick you up. In case it rains or something."

Jackie stared at the cloudless stretch of blue overhead. "Oh. Thank you."

She half expected Shonda to launch into some kind of speech about their father or school or something. But she said nothing.

Jackie sat uncomfortably in the silence as they drove. She glanced over at Shonda. Her sister sat stiffly, knuckles white as she gripped the steering wheel. She cleared her throat a couple of times as if about to say something, and Jackie waited expectantly, but then she seemed to change her mind and remained silent.

Jackie decided not to tell her about seeing their father that morning.

"So what are you going to do this afternoon?" Jackie asked, her voice sounding unnaturally loud in the quiet car.

Shonda shrugged as she pulled in to their dooryard. "There's lots of housework to be done. Today seems like a good day for cleaning, don't you think?"

No, she didn't think so at all. It was a good day for being out under the sky. But she could see by the set of her sister's jaw, that no one would be doing anything outside.

When Kyle reached home, Shonda was on her knees scrubbing the kitchen floor, and Jackie was marching around with glass cleaner, with the mission of washing every window in the house.

"Hey, Jax," he greeted her quietly. He peeked around the corner at his wife, then turned back to Jackie. "What's going on?"

"Shonda's upset, I guess. She hasn't said anything, but…" she held up the glass cleaner and cloth.

He nodded, understanding all too clearly, she knew. Whenever Shonda was really upset about something, the entire house got cleaned from top to bottom.

"Has she talked to you at all?" Jackie asked. "About… you know… our father showing up?"

He shook his head. "Not really. She will when she's ready."

"Well, in the meantime, I suggest you find something industrious to do or you'll be put to work too."

He grinned and went into the kitchen. Jackie saw him bend over to kiss the top of his wife's head, then she turned away and attacked the living room windows with vigor. She had already dusted every part of the house she could reach and vacuumed all the carpets. When she came downstairs from washing her bedroom windows, Kyle was cleaning all the light fixtures. She bit back a smile and went looking for Shonda. She found her sister in the bathroom, feverishly scrubbing the tub, and offered to make something for supper. Shonda looked up distractedly and thanked her.

Jackie fixed hamburgers and salad and set the table. Shonda picked at her food and then told them she just wasn't hungry as she pushed her plate away. Kyle devoured his dinner in minutes and then ate Shonda's, too. After supper, Jackie escaped to her room to do some studying.

The next day passed quickly. Shonda again met her at school and gave her a ride home, then plunged into a cleaning frenzy. She started cleaning out the closets and sorting stuff into boxes and trash bags. Jackie endured silently and wished Kyle would come home.

"Here, Jackie, would you take this down to the basement? It's full of books, so be careful. It's a little heavy."

Jackie nodded and picked up the box.

"Careful," Shonda said again.

Jackie hauled the box down the stairs and was nearly to the cellar corner when she stumbled over another box, sending its cover flying. Through a series of ungraceful maneuvers, she managed to regain her balance and protect Shonda's books. She set them down with relief and then picked up the runaway box cover. She tried to fit the lid back on, but the box was stuffed full. It looked like some of Shonda's old college stuff—textbooks, folders, papers. She sighed and knelt down, then pulled out a couple of books to rearrange them. Something fell to the floor. She glanced down.

A bundle of letters.

She picked them up and began to stuff them back into the book they had fallen from, when something caught her eye. She looked at them more closely. They were addressed to *her*. Her forehead wrinkled in confusion. Why would Shonda have a bunch of letters meant for her…? Her gaze traveled to the return address in the top left corner. Her heart skipped a beat. *M. Randall.*

With trembling fingers, she opened the letter on top. *Dear Jackie,* it began. *I climbed the Eiffel Tower today—all 1,665 steps. I thought if you'd been with me, we would have had to take the elevator, but then you're probably big enough now to climb the stairs yourself.* She stopped reading and glanced at the other letters. There were six more. She heard a soft creak and looked up.

Shonda was standing on the bottom step.

"What are these?" Jackie asked, her voice low.

"Jackie—"

"What are these?"

"I was protecting you."

"From what?" Her voice was rising but she didn't care. "He wanted to *know* me!"

"Listen—"

"No, you listen! I stayed away from him because you wanted me to. Because I believed that he didn't care about us. Because I believed what you let me believe. I trusted everything you said, because I've never had a reason to doubt. But I do now."

"Jackie, please, we need to talk about this."

"What's there to talk about? You lied to me—"

"I didn't lie—"

"Oh, right, my mistake. You merely withheld the truth, and I ran with the implications." Jackie shook her head in disgust. "Well, I have new implications to run with now." She pushed past her sister and stormed out of the house, slamming the door behind her. She glanced down at the letters clenched in her fist and realized she was shaking. She didn't remember ever being so furious in all her life. She didn't even know where she was going, but her feet took her instinctively toward the cove.

She reached the end of the lane and turned down the main road until she came to the path and then followed the winding trail through the forest. She could hear the ocean before she could see it and breathed deeply of the salty air.

It was cool, and the wind was chill, so she sacrificed her usual seat on her boulder for a mossy stone beneath the willow that wept at the water's edge. Then she smoothed the letters in her hand and began to read them one by one.

They weren't poetic or beautiful or anything earth changing. They just sketched out what he'd been doing, places he'd been, things he'd seen. They asked lots of questions, too. Things like what her favorite color was, if she had a pet, if she liked to walk in the rain. She read them three times and then sat there in the shelter of the weeping willow, letting the wind dry her tears.

It was growing cold, but she didn't want to go home. She huddled under the tree until the stars glowed silver in the darkening sky and listened to the sounds of the night—the careless rush of the waves on the rocks, the willow boughs swishing softly in the breeze, crickets singing their evening lullabies. For a moment, she thought she heard something else—a voice maybe—but then realized it must only be the wind sighing through the trees. She hugged the letters to her chest. She knew she should go home soon. Just a few minutes longer, she told herself. Just a few minutes.

chapter sixteen

Jackie jerked upright with a start. She glanced about, shivering, and realized she must have fallen asleep. The moon shone coldly through the willow boughs, streaking shadows across the papers in her hands. She peered out through the cascade of leaves and caught her breath. She rarely came to the cove at night. As splendid as the ocean was by day, no sun could rival the moon's reign over the deep. Silver light lit the sea, and the wind stirred the water into a glittering whirl. She tried to guess how long she had been sleeping. She'd better get back. Her fingers and toes ached with cold. She rose stiffly and gently stretched her cramped limbs. She took one last look at the cove and turned back to the forest. The tall trees crowded out the pale evening light and left her in darkness. She stumbled along the path, relying more on memory than vision. The moon peeked down at her at intervals through the trees, and she walked slowly, so she wouldn't trip. Halfway through the forest, the trees grew more densely and screened out the weak night light. She stopped. Great. She was going to have to crawl.

Suddenly, she saw Sam's face, floating ghostlike a few feet in front of her. She jumped and stumbled back. "Oh!"

He smiled and took her arm and gently led her down the path. How he could find his way, she had no idea, but she was incredibly thankful for his presence.

When they reached the road, he waved goodbye and she thanked him, then hurried home.

She slipped quietly inside. There was a light on in the kitchen, and she supposed Shonda was waiting up for her.

She was wrong.

Kyle's silhouette appeared in the doorway.

"Hey, Jax," he said.

"Hey."

"You okay?"

"Yeah. I just needed some time."

He nodded. "Come sit with me for a minute."

Her heart sank a little in her chest. She was still shivering, but the kitchen was warm.

They sat at the table in silence for a moment.

"I'm sorry," Jackie began. "I just—"

He shook his head. "That's not what I want to talk about."

"Oh." She waited, slightly relieved she had averted the lecture, but leery of what was coming next.

"Did she ever tell you about the day he left?"

Jackie shook her head. "She never talked about him at all, really, and the few times she did, it was just… you know… how horrible and irresponsible he was. She never gave me specifics."

"He just left one day. He didn't take anything. He just went for a drive and didn't come back." He paused. "It was two days before her birthday."

Jackie looked down at the table, but all she could see was her sister's face. "That's horrible."

"They'd been planning a party, I guess, and he had promised her pony rides." He glanced up. "She never wanted you to know that. But maybe it will help you understand where she's coming from a little better." He paused. "Shonda loves you more than anything in this world, Jax. Maybe all her decisions weren't the right ones, but whatever she's done, she's done it with your best interest at heart.

I know that may not seem like enough, but she does her best." He smiled faintly. "That's all. I just wanted you to know that." There were shadows under his eyes.

"You didn't have to wait up for me."

He smiled sleepily. "Yes, I did."

"Goodnight, Kyle."

"Goodnight."

She wearily climbed the stairs to her room and sank into her bed, but as her gaze fell on the letters, her fatigue faded. She read them all one more time before she finally fell sleep.

The bell rang. The last bell of the day. Jackie slung her bag over her shoulder and sighed in relief, though her chest was tight with anxiety. She was the first one out of the classroom, and she slipped down the hall and out a side door to avoid the crowds. She didn't even say goodbye to Montgomery.

She ran down the sidewalk and didn't slow until downtown was behind her. She walked the rest of the way, but she couldn't seem to slow her heart rate. She didn't remember ever being so nervous in her life.

She was nearly on the other side of town when she saw it. An iron gate standing open between two stone walls. This was it. The old Mulqueen Estate. She breathed deeply a couple of times, in and out, and started down the driveway. It seemed to go on forever. The house was a rambling stone building two and a half stories high and sheltered by two towering oak trees. It must have been a lovely place to live, she thought, trying to take her mind off what she was about to do. But her imagination didn't want to consider anything else.

She walked through the front door, spoke quickly to the receptionist, then walked up the carpeted center staircase and down the paneled hall to the left until she came to the door with a large number seven on it.

Her heart was hammering in her chest.

She took a deep breath and knocked.

A minute passed. Then another. Maybe he wasn't there.

Suddenly the door swung inward, and Mason Randall stood there, looking down at her in surprise.

For a moment, both were speechless.

"I like to walk in the rain," Jackie said at last.

He stared at her wordlessly.

She pulled the bundle of letters out from her backpack. "I just received these." She smiled faintly. "They were a little late."

His gaze fell to the papers in her hand, and understanding dawned on his face. He nodded slightly. "Well, that's the postal system for you, isn't it?" he said quietly. Then his features relaxed into a broad smile, and he opened the door wider. "Come in."

"Where have you been?" Shonda demanded, as soon as she walked through the door. "I was there to pick you up at school today and you never came out."

Jackie set her bag down. "Well, maybe you should tell me when you're going to pick me up," she answered coolly, "so that I know to be there to meet you."

Shonda wasn't about to be put off. "Where were you?"

Jackie met her sister's gaze evenly. "At the Mulqueen Inn, visiting a guest."

"*Him?*"

"Our father."

Shonda's eyes flashed angrily. "How dare you go behind my back—"

"Behind your back?" Jackie felt her temper rising. "Who hid his letters from me all these years? I mean forget that it's a federal offense to steal mail. Forget that it's immoral and ungodly to lie. Yes, I went to see him myself. You obviously weren't going to give me a ride over and you've made it pretty clear that you don't want him in the house. I don't understand! He's not dangerous. He's not a criminal. He's our father, Shonda! And he just wants to see us. There's nothing wrong with that."

Shonda stared at her, the anger slowly draining from her face. She sank down onto the couch and put her face in her hands. "I can't do this, Jackie. Not with you. It's just... I know him. I know what's he's like. I know what he did to our family. And I don't want you to get hurt."

Jackie sighed and sat down next to her sister. "I know. And I appreciate your concern, I really do. But, I never got a chance to know Mom because God took her home. But our father is still alive. Please, just let me spend some time with him. Find out what he's like for myself. I really want to."

Shonda rubbed a hand across her eyes, and Jackie noticed with surprise the tear that trickled down one cheek.

She felt a stab of guilt. She shouldn't have gone without Shonda's permission.

"All right," Shonda said softly after a long moment. She looked up at Jackie. "But please, promise me you'll be careful. He's very charming. He could talk a vegetarian into cattle farming. Just be careful."

"I promise," Jackie said.

The following afternoon Mason picked her up after school. He smiled broadly as she slid into the car, and they drove into downtown Kilree.

"How 'bout some ice cream?" he asked.

"It's freezing out."

"I hear the DoubleDip is heated," he said with a grin. "Besides, it's never too cold for ice cream."

She laughed. "Okay then. Triple chocolate sundae, here I come!"

They settled themselves into a couple of fat chairs by the front window and talked as they ate their sundaes. Jackie was up at the counter getting a couple of extra napkins when a group of boys invaded the shop and ordered hot chocolate and brownies. Montgomery was with them.

"Hey," he said when he saw her. He glanced around. "Are you here with your dad?"

"Yeah. Come on, you've got to meet him!" He followed her back to the squashy chairs and politely shook Mason's hand when Jackie introduced them.

"I've heard a lot of good things about you, Montgomery," Mason said, gripping his hand firmly.

"Thank you. I've heard a lot of good things about you, sir."

"Well, that's a change. They must be true then," Mason said with a broad grin. "I hear you're a soccer player."

Montgomery nodded. "Yes, sir. It's my favorite sport."

"You any good?"

He shrugged modestly.

"Yes," Jackie said. "He's awesome."

"Are you thinking of trying to play professionally?"

Montgomery shrugged again. "I don't know." He glanced at Jackie. "I'm not *that* good."

"Well, if you ever want to pursue it, let me know. A buddy of mine was on the Olympic team, and he's got a lot of connections."

Montgomery's eyes lit up. "Wow. Thanks." He shook Mason's hand again. "Well, I'd better get back to the guys or they'll think I'm asking for your daughter's hand in marriage." He grinned at Jackie. "It was nice to meet you, Mr. Randall."

"Likewise. See you around." He watched him go and turned to Jackie. "Well, he seems like a great kid."

Jackie nodded emphatically. "He is. He's the first best friend I've had since... well... ever, actually."

"Ever?"

Jackie squirmed under the intensity of his gaze. "I don't really make friends very easily. I'm not exactly the popular type," she said.

She attempted a light laugh, but it came out more like a chicken squawk. She had never been so concerned about anyone's opinion of her as she was with him. People seemed to like him naturally. What would he say when he discovered his daughter was a total geek?

But all he said was, "Popularity is overrated. You can't determine how well people respond to you until you've been exposed to more of them. It's a scientific principle. Just wait," he concluded. "College will be a lot different."

So people kept telling her. But the question was, could she survive that long? She looked over at the boys slurping their drinks and playfully punching Montgomery. It wasn't fair. He could fit in anywhere.

"I could try harder to assimilate with the other kids," she said.

Her father glanced at her sharply. "No. Don't let the kids freak you out. Just be who God made you."

She nodded slowly. Easy for him to say. God had made him a naturally cool person. Her train of thought stumbled. Or had He? The reason they were sitting there in the ice cream parlor was that her father had abandoned her family. He lived exactly the sort of life he wanted. But in doing so, shirked all his responsibilities as a father, a husband, a spiritual leader. How cool was that?

The next morning Jackie decided to forego her usual ocean sunrise and met Kyle at the front door as he was about to go jogging.

"'Morning, Jax," he said sleepily.

"Good morning."

He blinked owlishly at her and then his eyes widened as he noticed her wind pants and running shoes.

"I thought I'd join you. Is that okay?"

"Sure." He gave her an odd look. "This must just be the year for new things, huh?"

She shrugged. "I just have something I wanted to talk to you about."

They stepped outside, and she breathed deeply of the morning air.

"So shoot."

"I love mornings," she said instead.

He watched her a little suspiciously but didn't push her. They stretched for a few minutes and then jogged down the driveway toward the road.

Jackie was puffing before they were out of sight of the house. "Wow," she panted. "I'm really out of shape."

"No exercise will do that," Kyle said dryly.

"I walk miles every day!"

"You use different muscles when you run."

She could tell.

"So what did you want to talk about?"

She hesitated. She had been up all night thinking about Mason and Shonda and their dysfunctional family. If she really wanted Mason to be involved in her life, she would have to get him back on speaking terms with Shonda.

"Well," she said, wheezing slightly. "I was thinking... and... well... uh... I was thinking maybe we should invite Mason over for supper. I know he's made mistakes, but I really think he wants to make amends, and you've never even really met him, and I know Shonda is really angry with him, but don't you think it's sort of our duty to try to... to... fix things?"

"You know you really should be talking to Shonda about this," Kyle said at last.

"I know... but you know Shonda. And I just thought she might be more open to the idea if it came from you."

He was quiet for a moment, then nodded. "All right. We'll see. If the opportunity presents itself, I'll mention it to her. But let's not rush her, okay?"

"Thank you!" Jackie exclaimed.

"I wouldn't hold my breath, though."

"I won't! But if you'll just try... Thank you!"

They jogged on, the early morning quiet disturbed only by Jackie gasping for air.

"Kyle?" she asked after a few minutes.

"Yeah?"

"How much farther are you going?"

"Another mile and a half."

"What?" She was already close to collapsing. "Would you mind— if—I didn't—"

"Hey, you're not quitting on me, are you?"

"Well—no—not exactly—but if—if I don't stop soon—the only place you'll be running—is to the hospital with—with me over your shoulder."

He chuckled. "Okay. Just slow down gradually. Make sure you cool down, all right? Walk it out."

She nodded and turned back toward home.

"See ya," he called after her.

She waved without turning around, concentrating on conserving what little energy she had left.

The day passed in a blur of quizzes and homework. She went to the bookstore after school and found an almost new hardcover volume of Roman mythology and a tattered copy of *A Tale of Two Cities*. Dickens was wonderful as long as you liked words. A lot of words.

She stopped by the country store to see if Shonda was still working.

"Hi, Jeff." She greeted the high school boy who worked the cash register after school.

He smiled. "Hey. Looking for Shonda?"

She nodded.

"She's in a meeting with the owner. I think they're going to be a while. Do you want to leave her a message or anything?"

"No. It's not important. I'll see her tonight."

She headed for home and decided to have dinner all ready for her sister and brother-in-law when they got there. She found some taco shells in the cabinet and hamburger in the refrigerator and quickly settled on a Mexican theme.

By the time Shonda and Kyle walked in the door, tired and hungry, the air smelled of spices, and the tacos were ready.

"Oh, Jackie, you're an angel!" Shonda gave her a quick hug.

They ate hungrily, and Shonda and Kyle talked about their day, but there was no mention of Mason coming for dinner. Kyle must not have talked to her yet.

It was okay, she told herself. She just had to be patient. Very patient. ☺

chapter seventeen

Jackie peeked out the living room window again. It was nearly six o'clock. He should be here any minute.

It had been a week since she had begged Kyle to persuade her sister to invite their father to dinner. Shonda had been a tough case, but Kyle had done his job well, and she finally relented. In the meantime, Jackie had seen her father almost every day. He continued to stay at the inn and showed no sign of leaving any time soon. She hoped he wouldn't be late. Shonda hated it when people were late. And tonight of all nights, Shonda didn't need to be in a bad mood. Not that she was in a particularly rosy disposition as it was. Jackie had been walking on eggshells all day, doing dishes and vacuuming and setting the table without being asked—doing anything she could think of to make things easier for her sister as she prepared dinner. Kyle seemed to have the same idea and tried so hard to be helpful that Shonda finally ordered him out of the kitchen.

The living room clock struck six.

The clock didn't make any particular bonging or cuckoo-cuckooing sort of sound. But the soft click as the long hand moved to the twelve seemed to resonate throughout the house.

Seven minutes after six, the rental car pulled into the dooryard.

"He's here!" Jackie exclaimed and ran for the door.

"What's the rush?" Shonda asked crossly. "He's obviously in no hurry."

Jackie ignored her and yanked the door open.

Mason grinned broadly. "Hiya, kiddo."

She ushered him into the living room where Kyle and Shonda stiffly waited. Jackie plunged into introductions to avoid the awkward silence she'd been dreading. "This is Kyle Lainson. Kyle, meet our father, Mason Randall."

She held her breath as the two men exchanged a measured look.

Then Mason offered his hand. "Good to meet you, Kyle. And about time too, I guess."

Kyle shook his hand and nodded civilly, but his brown eyes were missing the twinkle that Jackie loved so much.

"Well, Jacqueline sure raves about you," Mason said, putting his arm around her shoulders. "Sounds like there ought to be some kind of fan club."

Kyle smiled faintly.

Mason turned to his eldest daughter. "Hey, Shonnie. Sorry I'm a little late. All that traffic, you know." He winked at Jackie.

Shonda didn't look amused. "Dinner is waiting," she said coldly.

They filed quietly into the dining room. Mason looked about with interest. "This is a nice little house you've got. Cozy."

"Thank you," Jackie said quickly, afraid that no one else would answer.

Shonda had outdone herself on dinner, and everyone was quick to tell her so. The steak was thick and juicy, the homemade bread hot from the oven, the vegetables fresh. Even so, Jackie couldn't seem to find her appetite. The butterflies in her stomach kept interfering with the food. Under normal circumstances she could consume vast amounts of steak, fresh bread and sharp cheddar cheese, but tonight she gnawed nervously on the celery sticks and picked at the rest.

Mason had no problem putting it all away. "This is excellent, Shonnie! I'm surprised you remembered that steak is my favorite."

"I didn't," Shonda said. "It's what we had in the freezer."

"Oh."

Jackie felt a pang. If only Shonda would try.

"Jacqueline tells me she's going to be in a play," he said, changing tactics.

Shonda said nothing.

"Yes," Kyle said. "Shonda and I are very proud of her."

Mason nodded. "You should be. She's grown into a remarkable young lady, to your credit." He smiled at Jackie, then looked at Shonda. "You've done a commendable job raising her."

"Someone had to," Shonda said icily. She hadn't touched her dinner.

Without missing a beat, Mason turned to his son-in-law and inquired about his accounting business. Some of the tension drained out of Jackie as they talked, and she enjoyed a few bites of steak. Mason asked about Kyle's peewee hockey team and about his parents and his childhood, slowly drawing him out. Shonda shot her husband a couple of venomous looks and then settled back in her chair, a stony expression on her pretty face.

When there was nothing more for Kyle to tell about himself, he asked Mason what he did for work.

"Well, I float around mostly. Some construction here, mediation there; I've worked pretty much everywhere from chicken farms to national newspapers."

"Did you like any of your jobs enough to stick with them for more than three months?" Shonda asked.

"I like to move around," Mason replied evenly. "I don't like to stay in any one place for too long."

Shonda's eyes glittered angrily, and she opened her mouth to say something.

Jackie wanted to hide under the table. She was sure this wouldn't be pretty.

"So what did you study in college?" Kyle asked quickly, before Shonda could speak.

Jackie sighed in relief. Kyle was an angel.

Mason smiled. "Anything and everything I could. I've always loved learning. I double majored the first time around and got a Bachelors in history and theater; that was followed by a Masters in cultural studies, and now I'm a dissertation shy of a Ph.D. in English literature."

"Wow," Jackie said.

"Pretty impressive," Kyle agreed.

"It's amazing!" Jackie gazed at her father in admiration. Every time she talked to him, she found out something new. It was like looking at him in a constantly changing light.

"Well, there are plenty of people who think those studies are a tad boring." Mason chuckled. "But in fact, they were perfect for me because they gave me a broad base that has enabled me to pursue writing, acting, law, politics. Pretty much everything but medicine and math," he said with a grin. "And each area of emphasis has contributed to an even greater appreciation of my travels."

Kyle nodded toward Jackie. "We've been trying to talk Jax into college."

Mason glanced at her, eyebrows raised. "I'm surprised you'd have to talk her into it. But college isn't for everyone. Although it gives your intellect an added dimension, develops your gifts and polishes your demeanor. Well, a good college will anyway," he amended. "Go to a liberal arts school," he told Jackie. "Get a rounded education. There's really no substitute. I've heard a lot of people go on about life experience being better than a classroom. But really the ultimate is to have both. College is more than a classroom. It's a phase of life. And a good education will help prepare you for life experiences and will enable you to get more out of them—to enjoy more. It sure has for me anyway." His pale green eyes sparkled. "It's an expensive hobby, but worth every penny."

Kyle nodded emphatically.

"Well, the idea is certainly growing on me," Jackie said. "Right now I feel like I've had enough school to last me forever, but—"

"College is a lot different from high school," Mason said. "A lot more fun, too, because you're studying what you want. You'll love it. In fact, I think—"

He broke off as Shonda suddenly started laughing.

Everyone stared at her.

Jackie glanced at Kyle, but he was watching his wife, a perplexed look on his face.

"Does anyone else hear this?" she asked, when she could speak. She looked at her father and shook her head in disbelief. "You're giving Jackie advice? A nice fatherly chat about college?"

"Shonda," Kyle said gently, but she ignored him.

"You're a drifter," she told Mason. "There is nothing in your life to emulate. You just coast around from place to place; you can't hold down a job; you don't have a home because you're always moving!"

He returned her gaze steadily. "There's no law against my life style, and I have no family to take care of—you've seen to that."

"When are you going to take responsibility for your own choices?!"

Mason leaned back in his chair and replied with an easy grin, "Why should I? You're responsible enough for the both of us."

Jackie cringed. She was sure bloodshed would follow.

Kyle looked worried too.

Shonda was turning purple, and she looked as if she was about to throw herself across the table and resort to some kind of physical violence.

Jackie wanted to stuff everyone's mouths full of rolls so no one could speak.

"Okay, that's enough," Kyle said.

Shonda glared at her father. "Don't you dare—"

"*Enough!*" Kyle stood up. He silenced his wife with a look and then turned to Mason. "I think we should all call it a night."

Mason nodded and rose from the table. "Excellent meal, Shonnie." He pushed his chair in. "Thank you all for dinner."

Jackie followed him to the door. "That didn't turn out the way I wanted it to."

"It rarely does," he said with a sad smile. He gently touched her hair. "Good night, kiddo. I'll see you soon."

"Okay. Good night."

Shonda and Kyle came up behind her. She hesitated. She didn't want to leave her father alone with them. At least with her there, he had a bit of a cheering section. But Kyle glanced at her and nodded slightly toward the dining room. "Right," she said. "I'll just go clear the table."

She returned to the dinner table and started clearing the half empty plates, but in their small house, she couldn't have drowned out the voices if she'd wanted to.

"I don't want you seeing Jackie anymore," Shonda was saying.

Jackie froze. *No!* She couldn't do that! She heard her father's voice.

"I'm just trying to get to know her. To be in her life like you haven't let me be in yours."

"You *chose* to leave our lives a long time ago."

"Yes, I did. And I've *chosen* to try to change that. I'm choosing now to be a part of her life."

"Being a parent is a full time job, Mason," Kyle said quietly.

There was no response. Jackie peeked around the doorway. Her father had put on his jacket and was walking out the door.

At the front step, he turned around and looked at Shonda. "Just because I don't have a nine to five job and a mortgage doesn't mean I live a worthless life, Shonnie. I'm happy. Are you? Is Jackie?"

Shonda didn't answer.

"Good night, Mason," Kyle said, and closed the door.

After that, no one seemed in the mood for apple crisp.

"How did you like Kyle?" Jackie asked the following day when she met her father after school at the DoubleDip.

Mason nodded. "Seems like a good guy. Guess he'd have to be to have Shonnie's stamp of approval."

"Yeah. He's the best." She hesitated, wondering if she should ask him the question that had kept her up half the night. "Something's been bothering me," she said finally.

"Okay, shoot."

"Last night you mentioned you didn't have a family to take care of—that Shonda had taken care of that. What did you mean?"

Mason frowned and seemed reluctant to answer. "I shouldn't have said that." He looked at her for a long time. "I don't think I should really talk to you about any of this," he said at last. "I don't want to cause any problems between the two of you."

Jackie hid her disappointment behind a smile and nodded as she took a bite of the giant snickerdoodle he'd bought for her.

She mentioned it to Montgomery the next day at school. "Should I push?" she asked. "I mean, my first thought is that it's none of my business. But it's my family. Of course it's my business."

He nodded. "Yeah. I don't know. I guess I would just forget it for now. If they don't want to talk about the past, don't force them. It won't make things any better."

"I suppose."

"You may not want to know anyway."

"What do you mean?"

He shrugged. "You just seem to, I don't know, worship your dad almost. And considering how little you know him…"

Jackie's defenses began to rise. "What?"

Montgomery shrugged. "Nothing. I just think you should be careful."

Mason took her out driving on Saturday. They drove up the coast, checking out light houses as they went, and enjoyed a hot take-out lunch on a deserted beach. Jackie was freezing, but she couldn't think of anyplace she'd rather be. She loved listening to him talk about all the places he'd been and things he'd done. From sky diving to African safaris, he'd done it all. His résumé must read like an adventure novel, she thought. He'd worked professions from photojournalism to tutoring to construction. An unorthodox way to make a living, he'd admitted freely, but it allowed him the flexibility to travel.

"Life's too short to spend it cooped up in an office from nine to five, you know?"

She did know. "That's how I feel about classrooms."

"That's different," he said. "Finish high school. Go to college. With a good education, you can go anywhere you want."

Later that night as they pulled into her driveway he asked, "So where do you want to go?"

Jackie sighed and leaned back in the seat. "Everywhere. I don't think there's a single place where I wouldn't want to go."

"Where do you want to go most?"

She smiled to herself. "To where the sea meets the sky." It was the sort of comment that often invited ridicule, but her father's smile held no hint of mockery.

"I know exactly what you mean."

And somehow, she knew that he did.

"I'd settle for anyplace right now, though," Jackie said with a laugh. "All my life, I've just wanted to travel. I've never even been outside of Maine."

"No? Kyle and Shonda don't go on vacations or anything?"

She shook her head. "Not really. Their last vacation was their honeymoon, and that was just some bed and breakfast place near Niagara Falls." She grimaced. "I had to stay with a neighbor. She was this old lady who smelled funny and must have had at least fifteen cats."

"But why don't they go anywhere?" her father pressed. "Why don't they take you anywhere? Theme parks, someplace."

"Well, we've done day trips to museums and things. And we spent a weekend at Bar Harbor last summer. But things are pretty tight for them. Mostly because of me," she said, looking down at her feet. "Shonda insisted I go to a Christian school, and the tuition has them really strapped."

Mason shook his head in confusion. "I don't understand why things are so tight when I send money on a regular basis."

Jackie looked at him blankly. "What?"

His eyebrows lowered. "I've been sending you and Shonda money for years. For your tuition, for clothes, for whatever either of you might need. That's why I work. I can live off my investments, but I take free lance jobs so I can help you girls out. You didn't know?"

She shook her head slowly.

He shot a dark look toward the house and shook his head, then reached across her and opened her door. "Well, thanks, kiddo. This was great. I'll see you later?"

"Sure."

Jackie watched him drive away and then went into the house, her mind whirling in anger and confusion.

Shonda was in the kitchen fixing dinner. Jackie set her bag down on the table. "Are you and Kyle going to be able to make the bills this month?"

Shonda looked up from the hamburger she was flattening into patties. "What?"

"Well, with things being so tight, I just wondered how you were going to make the payments."

Shonda's brow furrowed. "We'll manage, like we always do."

"No thanks to Mason, though. After all, he ditched us and never contacted us again, right? No letters." She felt a hint of satisfaction as Shonda winced. "No monthly checks. Nothing to help us out. He just left us to go it alone. Right?"

Understanding began to dawn in Shonda's eyes. "Jackie—"

"I'm sick of this! What else have you hidden from me? He said he's been sending money for years. Why don't you use it to pay off your mortgage or buy a second car or a bigger house? Are you so proud that you won't even allow your own father to help you? Or did you just hide it to make me hate him more? You're always acting like he owes us big-time, but then when he tries to pay up, you won't let him! What have you done with it anyway?"

Shonda straightened, her eyes flashing angrily. "It's in a bank account," she said coldly. "In your name."

"*My* name…?" Jackie stared at her, confusion replacing her fading anger.

Shonda sighed, and the ice melted from her gaze. "Kyle and I didn't want any handouts. And we didn't want any help raising you. I guess I thought that if I let him help, he would have some say in your life, and I didn't want that. And you're right. I didn't want anything that was from *him*. Money can't fix the damage he caused. I never wanted his money. I just wanted…" her voice trailed off. She cleared her throat and continued. "So I put it all in an account for you. We were going to tell you on your eighteenth birthday. There's enough to pay for college."

Jackie opened her mouth, but nothing came out. She wasn't sure what she had expected. But it wasn't this. He had provided a lot more than they'd ever given him credit for. And college paid for! She never even dreamed… She walked from the room, but turned back at the doorway. Shonda was still watching her. "Sorry," Jackie mumbled, and left the room.

She hoped her father would join her at church on Sunday, but he didn't. She had mentioned it while they were driving but he was reluctant about the idea and finally explained that he didn't want to upset Shonda.

The *Tempest* meeting ran a little long Monday afternoon, and Jackie found her father waiting outside the cafeteria door.

"Hi!" she said eagerly and turned to her teacher. "Mrs. Cox, this is my father, Mason Randall. He's visiting for a while."

"Mr. Randall?" Mrs. Cox blinked in surprise, then smiled quickly. "It's so nice to meet you."

"The pleasure's all mine," he said with a charming smile and shook her hand warmly. "I hope Jackie's doing well in school."

Mrs. Cox smiled. "She's outstanding in English class."

He grinned proudly and put his arm around her shoulders. "I'm not surprised. She knows almost as much about Shakespeare as I do—and I've been at it twenty years longer than she has!"

Jackie felt a warm glow spread through her entire being. There was nothing like the feeling of being praised by the person you admired most in the world.

Mason wished Mrs. Cox a good evening and they turned to leave.

Suddenly Mrs. Cox called after them hastily, "I'm sorry, Mr. Randall. But could I have a brief word with you?"

Jackie waited in the hall while they talked, the warmth she had felt at his praise quickly fading. Since she had started working harder at paying attention and completing her homework assignments, her grades had improved dramatically. But she wasn't quite a straight-A student yet. She felt butterflies whirl in her stomach and wondered what Mrs. Cox was telling him. It was only five minutes but it felt more like five hours before he returned. She glanced up at him questioningly, and he grinned broadly and winked.

She smiled back a little uncertainly. What did that mean? He must not be too disappointed in her if he was smiling like that. "Did she... did she say that I was..."

He put his arm around her. "She told me how much your grades have improved and how she thinks you have amazing potential."

"Really?"

"Yup." He winked again. "I told her you got it all from me."

Jackie felt her smile falter a little. That was kind of an odd thing for him to say considering their family history... but then of course he was just joking. She beamed at him. "What else?"

He grinned mischievously. "You'll find out."

"I'll find out?" she echoed.

He nodded. "Tomorrow."

Her forehead crinkled as she contemplated what he could be talking about but then decided to savor the anticipation. ☺

chapter eighteen

"Today, class, we have a special surprise," Mrs. Cox announced in history class the following day. Jackie glanced up from her history workbook. She'd started working ahead on all the worksheets during the spare minutes before class everyday. With her father in town and play practice taking up so much of her time, she realized she needed to utilize every minute possible during the day. "We have the honor of having a special guest with us today…"

Jackie didn't hear anymore. The door had opened, and her father had entered the classroom.

What was going on?

And then she remembered the conspiratorial grin from yesterday. Was this what he had been talking about? It couldn't be.

But it was.

Mason winked at her as Mrs. Cox introduced him to the class. For one horrible minute, Jackie was terrified the class would be awful to him because he was her father. But she didn't need to worry. Just as Shonda had said, their father was as smooth talking as they came. Within the first ten minutes of class, he had won over every single student. The guys laughed at his jokes and marveled at his adventures; the girls giggled and blushed at his charm. Jackie didn't even remember what he had talked about when class was over.

Everything he'd said had faded before the warm glow she felt when he smiled at her and the fierce pride that had welled up inside her when one of the girls whispered to her, "Your dad is *so* cool!"

He pulled her aside after class. "Bet you didn't expect to see your old man up here, did you?"

She shook her head.

"So, how'd I do? Your teacher wanted me to talk about Italy because I guess that's what you're studying, but I think to truly understand one culture, you need to get an overview of the surrounding cultures, you know?"

Jackie didn't have the faintest idea what he was talking about, but nodded. "You were amazing. Everyone thought so."

His grin broadened. "Well, there was only one person I wanted to impress."

She beamed.

"Hey, what are you doing after school? I've got a surprise for you."

"Really? Um… I have play rehearsal, but… I can meet you after."

"Great! I'll pick you up."

The rest of the day couldn't go fast enough. Several people told her how cool her father was, and she just smiled and agreed.

She normally enjoyed play practice, but even the rehearsal seemed to take forever, and when no one was looking, she slipped out early. They didn't really need Miranda that afternoon anyway, she told herself.

He was already in the parking lot, reading the latest Pulitzer prize winner, when she got outside.

"Hey!" he greeted her, sliding his book under the seat. "You're early."

She nodded. "Let's go."

He grinned. "You're going to love this."

She had no idea what he had in store, but she was beyond excited.

The clouds were low hanging, and heavy fog seemed to cling to the car as they drove. He turned onto the shore road and drove down to the narrow stretch of beach the Kilree residents sunned themselves on for two short months out of the year.

He parked right on the beach and got out of the car. She followed him, still clueless about what he was doing. He led her to a little rowboat that had been pulled up on shore. "C'mon," he said. "Get in."

"We're going out on the water?" she said incredulously. "But it's—"

"I know. It's freezing out. Button up your coat. There's a blanket in the stern."

She shook her head and laughed as she climbed into the boat. Her father pushed it out into the water and climbed in beside her. Then he took up the oars and began rowing out to sea.

Jackie shivered and pulled the blanket around her, looking about her as they went. And then suddenly, she thought she understood.

He grinned at her. "I found it, Jacqueline. Have you guessed yet?"

She looked around in wonder as the mist closed around them. It was like something out of Brigadoon. She nodded slowly.

"It's where the ocean meets the sky! But the mist is the portal. It's the only way to get here. I realized it last night when I was watching the weather forecast."

"It's amazing." She looked at her father, pure adoration welling up inside her. "Like being in a dream. You're brilliant!"

He grinned and didn't deny it.

They rowed for several minutes, admiring the way the sea beneath them seemed to climb the air on misty limbs and disappear into the gray above.

It hadn't been long enough when they reached the shore again, but she was shivering, and her toes were numb, so she supposed it would have to be. He bought them both some hot cocoa at the DoubleDip to help warm them up and then drove her home.

"Thank you," she said several minutes later when he pulled into the driveway. "That was so beautiful! Good night."

"Good night."

She started to get out of the car, then suddenly changed her mind and threw her arms around him. He hugged her back, but she could feel the surprise in his hesitant arms. Then he lightly stroked her hair.

"I'm so glad you came," she said. "I've missed you. All my life I've missed you and Mom."

"I've missed you, too," he said. "I just didn't know it until I met you." He ruffled her curls. "Take care, kiddo." He nodded toward the house. "I think Shonnie's watching out the window, so you'd better not keep her waiting."

She smiled. "I won't. Thanks again... Dad."

His smile seemed to bring the sunshine back through the clouds. How could Shonda not completely adore him? She turned and waved from the front step, then hurried inside. *I've missed you, too.* She replayed his words over and over again and imagined what it would have been like growing up if he had stayed. And suddenly she knew exactly what to give him for Christmas.

"Hey, we missed you last week." The voice jerked her out of her thoughts, and she looked up to see Alicia sliding into the chair next to her as they had line checks the following week. "Where'd you go? One minute you were there, and the next no one could find you."

"Oh... yeah, I... well, my dad is in town visiting and..."

"That's great!"

"Yeah, he's really..."

"So, listen, I've been meaning to ask you—how long have you and Montgomery been... you know," Alicia asked.

Jackie stared at her blankly.

"You make an adorable couple."

"We're not a couple!"

"You're not going out with him?"

"*No!*" It came out louder and more forceful than she intended. "I mean, we're just friends."

"Really? But he's so cute!"

Cute? She'd never really thought of Montgomery as cute. He wasn't offensive to look at or anything. But she saw him more as being aesthetically pleasing than *cute*. Like a nice painting.

Alicia was watching her curiously.

"I guess he's too much like a brother to think of that way," Jackie said finally.

Alicia nodded. "Well. That's really cool. I'll spread the word."

Spread what word? Jackie was beginning to suspect she was the most clueless person on the planet. Boys made fun of her, and girls seemed to speak another language entirely.

Alicia grinned mischievously. "But if you're going to change your mind about the whole 'just friends' thing, you'd better do it fast."

"What do you mean?"

She shrugged. "Just that there are a lot of girls who have their eyes on him. My little sister included."

"Oh." Jackie didn't know what else to say, so she didn't say anything. Montgomery wasn't the gushy type anyway. He wouldn't notice those girls anymore than she did. But over the next few days, she started noticing. A lot of the girls in their class would eagerly say hi to him in the morning and often would try to sit near him in classes where they didn't have assigned seats. And they stared at him a lot. Particularly Amy, Heather, Sarah and Jennifer.

"What are you doing?!" Montgomery finally demanded in an exasperated tone one afternoon as Jackie craned her neck around him during study hall to see if the giggle girls were staring at him again.

"Nothing."

He looked around. "What are you staring at? Honestly, Jax, you've been acting so weird lately! What's up?"

"Nothing," she said again, feeling incredibly dumb. Then she saw Amy leaning forward and whispering to Heather. They both looked over at Montgomery and giggled. "They sure don't think of him as a brother," she murmured.

Montgomery gave her a look that said he thought she was clearly insane, then buried himself in his science book and ignored her the rest of study hall.

Jackie opened her eyes, trying to figure out what had awakened her. It was still dark out. She rolled over and glanced at the clock on her nightstand. It was one o'clock in the morning.

And then she heard it. Something clattering against her window.

She got out of bed and tiptoed to the window, peeking out warily.

A handful of pebbles suddenly pelted the glass in front of her nose, and she jumped back. Then she quickly opened the window and leaned out, praying she wouldn't get brained. She peered into the darkness and then saw someone emerge from the shadows of the old maple. She shook her head in amazement as her father grinned up at her.

"What are you doing?" she whispered as loudly as she dared.

"Come on!" he said softly. "There's something I want to show you!"

She deliberated for a second, then nodded and closed the window. She pulled some warm clothes on—knowing her father, it would certainly be outside, whatever it was—and then slipped downstairs and out the door, silent as a ghost.

He had parked a short distance down the lane so as not to awaken Shonda and Kyle. They drove to the shore, where they had gone out in the little boat before. Stars glimmered coldly in the night sky, and the dark sea beneath barely rippled in the sway of the gentle current. The boat was still there.

He pushed the little skiff to the water's edge and told her to climb in. Then he tucked a blanket around her and put a hot thermos in her hands.

"Hot chocolate?" she asked.

"Vanilla chai. You'll love it. Now, close your eyes," he said.

She obeyed.

She felt the movement of the boat sliding through the water and gripped the sides to steady herself.

Her father rowed for several minutes, the oars making a soft splashing sound every time they plunged into the water anew.

Then they stopped.

"Okay," he said, his voice hushed almost reverently.

She opened her eyes and gazed in wonder.

The whole world was black and silver. The ocean was calm, the water quiet and still, mirroring the heavenly lights overhead in their black depths so that she felt like she was floating in a sea of stars.

"It's so beautiful," she whispered, taking it all in with wide eyes. "Like a dream."

At the other end of the boat, Mason nodded, his features illumined by starlight. "Mother Nature is one of God's best witnesses," he said.

"'When I consider the heavens, the works of thy fingers, the moon and the stars which thou hast ordained, what is man that thou are mindful of him?'" Jackie quoted softly.

"That's a good one," Mason said. "I always wished I'd memorized more Bible verses. They can be so poetic, you know?"

Jackie glanced over at him. Was that his only motivation for memorizing God's Word? "A lot of them are poetry," she said. "And it's never too late to learn more verses."

"Mmm-hmm," he murmured noncommittally. "We should go to Europe," he announced unexpectedly.

"What?" Jackie wasn't sure she'd heard him right, though it did seem the sort of thing he'd propose.

"Europe. We should go. You'd love it! We could paint pictures along the Seine in Paris, attend the opera in Italy, stake out Windsor Castle in England and see if we can catch a glimpse of royalty."

Jackie watched him. He wasn't looking at her. He was gazing out at the stars, real and reflected. Was he serious? Or was this another dream? Although, she thought, his dreams seemed to come true more often than hers.

"What do you think?" he asked.

"I'd love to, of course," she said. "But…"

"Great! I was thinking maybe after your graduation, before you go to college. We could spend the summer abroad."

Jackie's heart was hammering in her chest. Three years was a long time to wait, but such a dream had never felt so close!

"Really?" she asked, hating the quaver in her voice.

"Yeah! It will be fantastic!"

The cold soon drove them back to the shore, but even when she was back in bed, warm under a pile of blankets, she felt like she was still drifting among the stars. Visions of castles and bridges and the Eiffel Tower danced in her head until she fell asleep. ☺

chapter nineteen

Mason and the rental car were waiting for her outside the school at the end of the day.

"They have specials at the DoubleDip today," he said by way of greeting.

"Sounds great!"

"I've been thinking," he said as they drove. "Remember what I said last night about going to Europe?"

"Yes." Her throat tightened. This was it. He was going to tell her that of course they couldn't go.

"I think three years is too long to wait."

"What?"

"So we'll have to find a way to tide us over, 'til you graduate. I heard you have a Christmas break coming up?"

"Yeah. School gets out this Thursday."

"Great! So how about doing something special?"

"Sure!" Jackie said, excited already at the prospect of something different. "Like what?"

"I was thinking New York City?"

She stared at him. "Are you serious?"

"Well, *Aida*'s playing. I thought maybe it was time for your first opera experience."

He was joking. He had to be. "Really?"

"Of course. We can go down Friday, spend Saturday, come back Sunday or even Monday. Give you a chance to see the City a bit. Maybe do some Christmas shopping."

She felt as though someone had just put the moon on a chain and handed it to her. And for some ridiculous reason, she thought she might start crying.

"How does that sound?"

What started out as a smile stretched out of control until her whole face was beaming. "Like a dream."

Now she just had to tell Shonda.

"How was your day?" Jackie sweetly asked her sister, later that afternoon after Mason had dropped her off.

"Oh, it was okay," Shonda said, as she skimmed through the newspaper. "How was yours?"

"Excellent!"

"Really? You look tired."

Her late night excursion had made it a struggle to stay awake in classes today, but it was easily worth every minute.

"Oh, and next time you sneak out, you might want to skip the squeaky stair," Shonda said casually.

Jackie bit her lip. "I didn't sneak—" she began.

"Well, what would you call it?"

"I was just trying to be quiet so I wouldn't wake you. Dad stopped by and wanted to show me something. Shonda, it was so incredibly cool! He took me out in this little boat—"

"Where did he get a boat?"

"I don't know; I think he rented it. But it was so beautiful! I've never been actually out on the water at night. The ocean was calm, and the sky was clear, and it felt just like we were swimming through stars!"

Her sister didn't look impressed. "You could have at least asked."

"I don't ask to go to the cove unless there are chores or something to be done. My grades are better, the room is finished, my homework is always done on time—"

"You shouldn't be out at night."

"We used to take midnight walks before you married Kyle. What's the difference?"

"That was to wake me up so I could finish the homework for my college classes that I was fitting in around my full-time job. I had to take you with me because I couldn't afford a babysitter."

Jackie stared at her, stung. "Oh," she said quietly. "Well, I always loved them."

A flicker of regret appeared in Shonda's eyes.

"Anyway, this probably isn't the best time, but Dad wants to take me to New York City for a few days during Christmas vaca—"

"No," she said instantly.

"Oh, Shonda, come on! It's Christmas! Look, he just wanted to know me. Now I want to know him. This is my chance."

"Jackie, *no*."

"Why? Because you don't like him? Because you love hating him so much that you want me to hate him too? Where's your godliness now? What about forgiving those who've sinned against us? He made a mistake, Shonda. A big one. But maybe he's changed. Don't we owe it to him and to ourselves to find out?"

"We don't owe him anything," Shonda said icily.

Jackie's resolved hardened. "I'm going."

"You'll do as I say. I'm your guardian."

"He's my *father*! And since you took no legal action to keep him out of our lives, there's no reason why I can't go."

She stormed out of the house and slammed the door. She was so angry, her fingers shook as she buttoned her coat.

Montgomery was at the cove, as still as the rock on which he sat.

Jackie smiled in spite of herself. No doubt he was still trying to get Sam to come out and talk to him.

He glanced over as she approached.

"I just had it out with Shonda," she said, plopping down next to him.

"Yeah?"

"She won't let me go with Dad to New York. So I told her I was going anyway."

"Ah."

She was still angry, but she was already beginning to feel a twinge of guilt. "I shouldn't have, should I?"

Montgomery said nothing.

"I mean, I don't think there's any reason why I shouldn't go with Dad. But Shonda *is* my guardian." Jackie sighed. "Oh, why does life have to be so complicated?! What do I do?"

Montgomery frowned. "Well, I mean, *honestly*, you can get to know your Dad right here. You don't *have* to go to New York. It gets a little tricky when they want you to do different things, but since Shonda's been letting you see him here, maybe you should just forget the trip to the City—for now anyway. That way, you'll still be spending time with your Dad, and you won't be disobeying Shonda."

Jackie grimaced. "There you go, making sense again." She tossed a pebble into the water and then shoved her hands back into her pockets, wishing she'd brought gloves. "I know it shouldn't be a big deal, and maybe my motivation is wrong. But I want to go *so* desperately."

"There will be other chances to see the opera. You'll get to the city someday. I promise."

She sighed and turned her face to the sun shining weakly through the trees. "But that means I have to go back to apologize."

He grinned. "Absolutely."

She groaned. "I hate this part. I should be good at it by now, though." She waited until the last rays of sunlight had vanished behind the forest and then slowly got to her feet. "Okay. Wish me luck."

Montgomery looked up at her seriously. "No. But I'll pray for you."

She smiled. "Thanks."

Kyle's car was in the driveway when she reached home. "Here

we go," she muttered, took a deep breath, and went in. She found them both sitting at the kitchen table. Shonda looked like she'd been crying.

Jackie bit her lip. "Shonda…?"

They both looked up.

"I—I'm sorry. I shouldn't have…" she wasn't even sure exactly what to say. "I'm sorry."

Shonda sighed. "I'm sorry too."

"No—"

"Wait," she held up her hand. "I need to say this. You were right. I don't want you to go because he hurt me terribly… and because I don't want you to get hurt too. But…" she glanced at Kyle. He nodded and squeezed her hand. "If you really want to go, you can go."

Jackie stared at her, open-mouthed.

"I don't know if he's changed. I haven't really tried to find out. To be honest, I don't really care. But I think you're old enough that… well, I think this needs to be your decision. So, if you want to go," she said again, "it's okay with us."

Jackie looked from one to the other, her mind spinning. She had been expecting something more along the lines of being grounded and had already resigned herself to the fact that she wasn't going. "You really mean that?"

Shonda nodded.

Christmas vacation was there before she knew it, and Friday evening, she and her father arrived at the Big Apple. She pinched herself as she looked up at the Empire State Building, dazzling with lights, just to make sure she was awake.

The following day was like a dream from the moment she woke up. They saw the Statue of Liberty, walked through the city streets and peered in the windows at Tiffany's. They had frozen hot chocolate at a sidewalk café, browsed through old book shops and even went ice skating in Central Park. As an early Christmas gift, Mason bought her a dress for the opera that night and paid for her to get her hair done at the hotel salon.

She dressed quickly for the opera and then went doubtfully to stand in front of mirror. She stared at her reflection in awe. She hardly recognized herself. Her hair was up in a crown of curls with a few ringlets trailing loose around her face and against her neck, and the elegant evening gown of green silk brought out the pale green of her eyes in a striking contrast. She looked different. Taller. More mature. And maybe it was just every girl's fantasy, but she thought she might even look a bit sophisticated.

When she came out to join her father, he grinned broadly. "You're going to steal the show."

She smiled shyly. "The lady at the salon said putting my hair up made me look older."

He nodded. "Just don't grow up too quickly." For a brief instant, he looked almost sad, but then the moment passed, and the grin was back. He offered her his arm. "Shall we?"

The opera was everything she'd ever dreamed it would be. The sets were resplendent, and the costumes dazzling. The music seemed to get inside her veins and surged and swelled with her blood. By the time the curtain fell on the last act, tears were streaming down her cheeks.

Mason handed her a handkerchief.

"Thank you," she sobbed. The curtain lifted again, and the entire cast ensemble appeared onstage to thunderous applause from the audience. Jackie clapped so hard her hands began to sting. The performers who played Aida and Radames received standing ovations.

"That was so beautiful!" she exclaimed, as they filed out of the hall. "I loved Radames! And the woman who played Aida was amazing!" She thumbed through the program as they walked to find the performer's name. The evening was brisk but not too cold, so they walked the couple of blocks to the restaurant where Mason had made reservations.

The inside was quiet and elegant with plush burgundy chairs around polished tables and a dark carpet that muted everyone's footsteps. Classical music played softly in the background.

The maitre d' seated them, and they perused their menus.

Jackie looked it over carefully, then cleared her throat. "Um—Dad?"

"Mmm-hmm?"

She lowered her menu. "It's in French."

He grinned. "I'll order for you, if you like."

She sighed in relief. "That would be great."

When the server came, Mason placed their orders in fluent French. The young man nodded, took their menus and disappeared.

"Where did you learn French?" Jackie asked while they waited for their appetizers.

"I lived in the south of France for a couple of months, outside of Nice. I met this great couple who had a farm, and they gave me a room and meals in exchange for help around the place. That was a great time. And I lived in Paris for a year before I married your mother."

"Really?"

He nodded. "In fact, that's where we met."

Jackie's heartbeat picked up speed. She knew so little about her mother and nothing about the time she and Mason had been together. "What happened?"

"I was out of college one year and living off the interest of an investment my father had made. She was there as part of a mission team."

Jackie listened, entranced.

"The first time I saw that golden-red hair and looked into those blue eyes, I was sunk." He smiled to himself. "She was so beautiful. And sweet. I followed her back to the States, got converted and joined her church. Seven months later we were married."

Jackie waited, then asked quietly. "What happened?"

His green eyes found hers. "Sometimes things just don't work out." He sighed. "I miss her, though."

"Miss her?" Jackie echoed, the words flying out of her mouth before she could stop them. "How can you say that when you never even really loved her?"

"I did love her." He looked surprised. "I love her still."

She stared at him.

He was quiet for a moment, then said gently, "Did you know I went to your mother's funeral?"

She looked at him in surprise and shook her head wordlessly.

"Shonda saw me. But she wouldn't speak to me. I caught just a glimpse of you—this precious, toddling, beautiful little girl. I wanted to scoop you up and take you away with me. But I knew you were better off with her. I knew Shonnie would give you a stability that I would never have."

Jackie was silent. She wondered what would have happened if he had taken her with him. Would it be a life like this? Fancy restaurants and lots of travel? Would God be in her life at all? Or would she wake up one morning, like Shonda had all those years ago, and find herself without a father.

The first course came soon after, and he brightened. "Great! I'm starving." He started to take a bite.

"Do you mind if I pray?" Jackie asked.

"Oh—sure. Go ahead." He bowed his head and closed his eyes expectantly.

Jackie was tempted to offer up a long, drawn out prayer begging for God to grab hold of her father's life and make him grow up and become the man he could be. But instead she quickly blessed the food and then they ate.

Each course of the meal was better than the last, and by the time dessert came, she was sure she would have to be rolled out of the restaurant. They talked about the opera—which character they liked best; which musical piece had moved them the most.

"I think what I love most is that none of them were stupid," Jackie said and took a bite of her chocolate mousse.

Mason raised one eyebrow.

"Well, you know, so many times one or both of the lovers are kind of dumb. Like in *Two Gentlemen of Verona*. Proteus is a complete jerk! He's unfaithful to his love, Julia, betrays his friend Valentine and gets him banished, tries to steal Valentine's girl, and in the end he has a change of heart and goes back to Julia, and both couples get married and live happily ever after. That's absurd! Why would Julia marry him after all that? And I read a synopsis of *Rigoletto*, and it's even worse. The girl falls in love with this really awful guy and ends up dying for him! What an idiot! And even in the stories where the romantic leads are a little more on the ball intellectually, they almost always give up everything for 'love.' In the tragedies especially. But in *Aida*, they remain true to each other, and then in spite of the great love they share, they sacrifice their happiness for the good of their countries. That just seems so much bigger than Romeo and Juliet running off and getting married and then going out with a double suicide."

There was a twinkle in Mason's eye, and his mouth twitched.

"Well? Don't you agree?"

He nodded slowly and chuckled. "You come off as such a romantic, but when it comes right down to some of the most famous love stories, you're surprisingly well-grounded."

She wasn't sure if that was a compliment or not, but she smiled anyway.

When they had finished, she went out into the lobby to wait while Mason paid the check. A boy her age was standing there. Something about him looked vaguely familiar. Then her eyes widened in surprise. It was Kris Cappencella.

He looked just as surprised to see her and took in the fancy dress and hair with an open stare. "Hi," he said stiffly after a moment of awkward silence.

"Hi." She wasn't sure if she should smile or say anything else. So far, this was the friendliest exchange they had ever had. "What are you doing in New York?" she asked.

"Visiting my dad," he replied.

"Oh. Me too."

He nodded.

A handsome man in a three piece suit with a neatly trimmed beard and warm brown eyes appeared and settled a hand on Kris's shoulder. "They're waiting for us." His gaze flitted over Jackie and then moved past her, eyes widening slightly. "Mason!" he called and smiled broadly.

Jackie's father appeared behind her. "Reg! Good to see you!" The men shook hands.

Jackie felt her eyebrows climbing toward her hairline, but couldn't mask her surprise.

Mr. Cappencella looked from Mason to Jackie and back again, surprise showing in his own features. "I didn't know you had a daughter."

"Sure! Reg, meet Jacqueline."

"Nice to meet you," he said with a nod and a friendly smile.

She smiled back, but there was a strange sinking feeling in her stomach. Her father's friend didn't even know she existed. She glanced at Kris. A funny expression flickered across his face, almost as if he understood how she felt. But then it vanished, and he and his father were gone, and Mason was leading her outside and hailing a taxi.

"So, how do you know Mr. Cappencella?" she asked on the way back to the hotel.

"Reg? We played golf a couple times while I was living here. And he helped me out of a situation."

"Situation?"

"Oh, nothing serious," he assured her quickly. "Just a little bit of a legal jam. He's a great guy."

Legal jam? Jackie decided she didn't want to know. She saw again the surprise in the face of her father's friend and realized how much she and Mason were not a part of each other's lives.

"You okay?"

She nodded. "I think I ate too much."

She was silent the rest of the way. ☺

chapter twenty

Kyle and Shonda were waiting up for her when she returned late Sunday evening. Shonda looked like she hadn't slept all weekend.

Jackie set her bags down and smiled at them wearily.

"Did you have a good time?" Kyle asked, putting his arm around her and squeezing.

"Oh, it was wonderful!" She looked at them both. "But it's even more wonderful to be home."

Shonda didn't say anything, but wrapped her arms around Jackie in a fierce embrace. "It's good to have you back," she said finally and Jackie thought she saw a tear in her sister's eye.

"You didn't have to wait up for me," Jackie said when Shonda had released her. "I mean, I appreciate it but...."

"Oh, don't be so self-absorbed," Kyle said with a grin. "We didn't wait up because we were worried. We waited up because we wanted to see your face when you found your early Christmas present."

Jackie stared at them puzzled. "Early Christmas present...?"

Kyle's grin widened, and a smile softened the lines of fatigue in Shonda's face.

Jackie glanced around the living room but didn't see anything out of place. "Are you going to tell me where to look?"

"Nope," Kyle said cheerfully.

Jackie glanced in the kitchen and then headed for the stairs to her attic room, her sister and brother-in-law on her heels. The door at the top of the stairs was closed, though she was sure she had left it open. She turned the knob and pushed.

The room looked the same at a first glance, though it seemed to be awfully light for the middle of the night.... She looked up. Moonlight poured through a large skylight over her bed. She could still smell the fresh paint on the trim around the window.

She gasped. "You guys!" She spun around and hugged them both at the same time. "Thank you so much! It's perfect!" She ran to the other side of the room and threw herself onto her bed, staring upward at the stars.

"Merry Christmas," they told her and quietly left her alone with her piece of sky.

The next morning, she awoke to light pouring down on her from the skylight. Branches curled about the skylight as if they were real. She smiled and stretched lazily and then looked around the room. It had been a lot of work, but it was so worth it. Her gaze drifted over the mural—and then stopped abruptly. Something was different. She sat up. A tiny face was peeking at her through the branches of the painted trees. And nearby was another. But this one was grinning impishly and hovering over a leaf by means of a pair of translucent wings. *Faeries.*

She jumped out of bed and began studying the mural more closely. They were everywhere—peering out between branches, sitting on leaves, fluttering behind trees with glittering wings. Shadowy figures lurked in the background of the painted forest and as she looked closer, she recognized them as creatures out of Greek mythology—centaurs, gryphons, unicorns, pegasuses—dark and vague in the deep shadows. By the door, she found a stocky leprechaun sitting next to a pot of shining gold and holding out a scroll. It looked like there was writing on it. She bent closer and read, *Jax, Merry Christmas. Montgomery.*

She was still beaming when she went downstairs for breakfast.

"He is so cool!" she exclaimed to her sister.

Shonda smiled. "I take it you found Montgomery's Christmas present."

"Yes! It's amazing! I don't even know if I've found them all yet!"

"He was up there for two days straight. He even came back after supper and worked on it in the evenings."

"Wow," she said as she chomped on her corn flakes. She stopped abruptly. "Shonda, is it all right if I go see him?"

"Right now?"

"I won't be long. I just want to say thank you."

"I guess so..." Shonda said, but Jackie was already running to the hall closet to get her boots. She was struggling into her coat when Shonda caught up to her and handed her a hat and a pair of thick mittens. "Here. It's cold out."

Jackie thanked her and went tromping off happily through the snow. She cut through the woods and knocked at the back door when she reached the Dawson house.

Montgomery pulled the door open, dressed in a tee shirt and flannel pants, his white-blond hair disheveled and his eyes blinking sleepily, a half-peeled orange in one hand.

"You're amazing!" she shouted and threw her arms around him in a bear hug.

His cheeks turned pink, but he smiled as he disentangled himself from her.

"Thank you! Thank you so much! It's unbelievable! It really is! How many are there?"

He ran a hand through his hair and shrugged. "Uh—I didn't count them." He closed the door behind her and went back to peeling his orange while she removed her coat and winter paraphernalia.

"How was New York?" he asked and tossed her an orange.

"Incredible! We saw *Aida* and went skating in Central Park. It was just marvelous! The opera was so beautiful, and Dad bought me a dress, and we ate at fancy restaurants and…" she sighed, "…it was just a dream!"

He ate his breakfast while she talked non-stop, and then, after he'd dressed, they went outside and had a snowball fight. It ended rather abruptly, though, when one of Montgomery's snowballs hit Jackie in the face like a missile and knocked her flat on her back.

"Are you okay?" His face swam fuzzily into focus beyond her snow clumped eyelashes.

"Yeah." She struggled to sit up, rubbing the snow from her face.

"I'm sorry!" he said. But she could tell he was having a hard time keeping the grin from his face.

She shook her head to clear it and shot him a sideways glare. "Go ahead. Laugh."

And he did. He laughed long and hard. "You should have seen your face!" he shouted.

"I couldn't *see* anything," she said dryly, mustering every last shred of dignity she could summon. She looked down at her soggy mittens and wet jeans. "I'm soaked."

He grinned and helped her to her feet. "You can come inside and dry out by the stove."

She shook her head. "I promised Shonda I wouldn't be long, so I should go home." She smiled. "Thanks again. You really did an amazing job with the mural."

"You're welcome. Merry Christmas."

She smiled. "Are you doing anything fun this week?"

He nodded. "Dad's taking a few of us from the soccer team snow boarding tomorrow."

"Wow. Does your dad snow board?"

"Yeah. He likes skiing better, though."

She suddenly thought of Kris with his father at the restaurant in New York City. "Is Kris going?"

He looked at her in surprise and nodded. "Yeah. Why?"

She shrugged. "I was just wondering. I bumped into him in New York."

"Really?"

"Yeah. He was with his dad."

"Wow. Well, you don't seem steamed up about anything. Was there a civil conversation involved?"

She smiled. "We just said hi. But, yeah, he was nice. And I was, too," she added, recognizing the question in his eyes before he asked it.

He grinned. "So, maybe there's hope after all."

"Don't hold your breath," she said with a dry smile. "Have fun tomorrow."

"We will."

She met her father that afternoon and showed him the mural. He was fascinated by the vague shapes of mythological creatures in the forest shadows and deeply impressed with Montgomery's talent.

The week passed quickly. Jackie went to the cove twice to see if Sam was around but saw no sign of him. "What do you suppose Sam does in the winter?" she mused one afternoon as she and Montgomery played a board game by the fireplace in the Dawson's den.

Montgomery shrugged. "Maybe he hibernates."

"No seriously. It's so cold."

"I don't know. He must have some place he goes if he's been living here for so many years. How long has he been here?"

Jackie thought about it. "I don't know. As long as I can remember. I wonder if anyone knows."

Christmas morning Jackie awoke early and reached for her bedside lamp. She rubbed her eyes and looked up. Her skylight was solid white. It must have snowed again.

She quickly pulled on jeans and a big wool sweater and then sank into the beanbag by the window with her Bible. She read each account of the Christmas story from the Gospels in place of her usual morning devotions and then spent a long time in prayer. She prayed for her father and for Shonda and Kyle and for the Dawsons and Sam as well.

She prayed for herself too, for growth and guidance. Sometimes she just felt so lost. As if her existence was some kind of mistake. If not for her, who knows where Shonda and Kyle would be. The Academy tuition wasn't exactly cheap, and she was another mouth to feed and a body to clothe. No matter what they told her, she was certain they would have started a family of their own if not for her. There was a plan for her life. Pastor was always saying that. But sometimes it didn't feel that way.

Shonda had fixed a beautiful breakfast, and later, after reading the second chapter of Luke and spending a few minutes in prayer, they exchanged their gifts.

Mason came over in the afternoon. He had not come over for a real visit since the disastrous first dinner, but Jackie had begged Shonda until she had relented and agreed he could come as long as he didn't stay long.

They sat stiffly in the living room, eating chocolate cheesecake, and Jackie couldn't suppress a smile as she watched her father be painstakingly polite. He had assured her he would be on his best behavior.

When they had finished, Jackie pulled a carefully wrapped present out from behind the tree and handed it to him.

He grinned like a little boy, and his eyes shone as he eagerly tore it open. Jackie wondered how often he received gifts.

She watched anxiously as he pulled a small photo album from the shreds of tissue paper and flipped through it slowly. She had spent hours meticulously selecting pictures from every stage of her childhood and assembling them into a little album. She had included a couple of pictures of Shonda as well. His smile faded as he looked through each page and after he closed it, he brushed his hand across his eyes. Then the grin was back in place, and he hugged her tightly. "Thanks, kiddo. That was great. The only better gift would be a trip back in time." Then he pulled three packages from the depths of his long winter coat and gave one to each of them.

Her sister and brother-in-law looked surprised, but received them graciously enough.

Kyle's was an antique pocket watch.

"It was my grandfather's," Mason said. "I thought it should stay in the family."

Kyle nodded. "Thank you." He didn't say anything more, but Jackie could tell he was impressed because he kept fingering the heirloom gently and opening it to examine the face and the inscription. When he put it down, it went safely into his pocket.

Shonda's gift was a fragile silk shawl of Mediterranean blue.

"Shonda, that's gorgeous!" Jackie exclaimed, fingering the delicate fringe. "It brings out your eyes."

Shonda thanked him and put the shawl back in the box.

To cover the awkward silence, Jackie quickly opened hers. It was a beautifully framed picture of her father and she at the opera in New York City.

"To help you remember the trip," he said.

"It was unforgettable even without pictures, but thank you. This is beautiful."

He left soon after. Once the gifts had been opened, there didn't seem to be much reason for him to stay around.

Christmas break ended all too quickly, and before she knew it, she was back in school, up to her ears in homework and play rehearsals.

The first *Tempest* practice of the term was a big one, because it was the first real rehearsal. So far, the practices had been mostly meetings, discussions, line checks and things like that. Now, they were actually starting to act. Everything was memorized by now, so they weren't allowed to have their copies with them while onstage.

Before her scenes, Jackie was terrified, but as soon as she stepped onto the stage, her fears were left behind, and she became Miranda. Montgomery was fun to act with, and Josh was easy going. She couldn't have asked for a better Ferdinand. His performance may not have been award-winning, but at least he didn't make her feel stupid when she had to tell him she loved him and wanted to marry him.

She stopped by the cove on her way home. It was too cold to stay, but if she went too long without seeing the ocean, she felt a strange kind of ache in her chest, like she was missing a close friend. She walked out to her boulder and sat for a few minutes, closing her eyes and enjoying the soothing lullaby of the waves. But then her toes and fingers went numb, and she decided it was time to leave.

She made her way back along the rocks to the shore. As she stepped down off the last rock, her foot jerked backward, and she stumbled to the ground, landing ungracefully on her backside with a loud "Ooof!" She glared down at her boot, fingering the broken remains of her shoelace. The other half of the wretched thing was still stuck in the rocks. She muttered to herself as she stood up, dusting herself off, then groaned. Loose papers flew from her unzipped bag and fluttered haphazardly on the wind. She snatched for one and caught it. Another she pulled from the water. The last floated tantalizingly close, then was whisked away on a vigorous gust. She charged after it, grabbing as it zigzagged through the air and then slipped through a chasm in the rocks. She heaved a sigh and squinted into the darkness. It probably hadn't gone that far. She should be able to find it, if she went quickly. She wouldn't have bothered, but it was her science worksheet—already finished, naturally—and with her history of delinquent homework, she didn't think the-wind-blew-my-paper-away would cut it. She squeezed through the opening into the darkness beyond and waited for her eyes to adjust. Suddenly the bulge in her coat pocket bumping against her leg made her remember Montgomery's flashlight. She had never given it back. She pulled out the small light and turned it on. The narrow beam sliced through the darkness for a few feet before fading away into the shadows. She walked forward several steps. The cleft was barely more than a narrow defile. It disappeared around a corner into what appeared to be a tunnel, presumably intersecting the rest of the labyrinth of caves.

She glanced around for her fugitive homework.

Suddenly a sound reached her ears. She froze.

It was coming from the tunnel at the back of the cave.

A faint humming noise echoed through the fissure, rising and falling in pitch, snaking its way through the darkness. She held her breath, every ghost story she'd ever heard in her entire life haunting her memory. It was eerie.

And it was getting louder.

A rectangular patch of white at the edge of the flashlight's range caught her eye, and she lunged for the paper, her heart crashing against her ribs like a jackhammer.

Then, abruptly, the sound died away.

She should have been relieved, but the sudden silence was more terrifying than the strange keening had been.

She fled from the cave, her science worksheet clutched tightly in her fist.

Back in the daylight and fresh air, her heart rate slowed, and her breathing became more regular. It was just the wind, of course. Just the wind, wailing through the stone.

This town has enough ghosts, she heard Mrs. Harrison say. She looked back at the black crevice. Just the wind.... ☺

chapter twenty-one

She told Montgomery about the strange noise the next day at lunch. Predictably, he was fascinated and eager to start the cave exploration anew.

"I knew I shouldn't have told you," she said.

"Oh, come on! You don't believe all that ghost stuff, do you?"

"No," she said slowly. Her fears seemed ridiculous over chicken noodle soup and peanut butter sandwiches. But the memory of the soft wailing was clear enough to keep her from wanting to spend several hours crawling along the dark stone tunnels.

"Have you ever heard it before?"

She shook her head, though something tugged at her memory in disagreement. In a strange sort of delayed déjà vu, she felt as if she should have known the sound, belatedly sensing an odd familiarity... like a phrase of a story or a fragment of a dream.

But that was absurd. She shook off the feeling and agreed to meet Montgomery there that afternoon, armed with flashlights.

They entered the caves with high spirits on Montgomery's part and determination on Jackie's, but after two hours of skulking around, they achieved nothing more than stiff muscles and tired eyes.

In the days that followed, they entered the caves several more times, but never heard a sound out of place. And after a while—much to Jackie's relief—Montgomery seemed to lose interest.

The play was progressing nicely. Jackie came to look forward to rehearsals as much as she did visits with her father. And was it her imagination or was school even more bearable now? The change was slight—barely noticeable—but any jokes at her expense seemed more teasing and less malicious. Even her personal devotions seemed to be quickened. She prayed unceasingly for a reconciliation between Shonda and their father and felt a tremendous burden for Sam.

She started carrying around an old study Bible that Kyle had been willing to part with, just in case she ran into the homeless man, but when she finally did see him one afternoon, coming out of the tent in the church parking lot that housed Pastor Hallowell's soup kitchen, she suffered an attack of nerves like she had never felt before. Her heart seemed to be jumping around in her chest, and she was terrified she was going to get things all wrong. How did you witness to someone who couldn't talk? How would she know for sure if he understood?

He smiled when he saw her, and she greeted him with a nervous hello.

"Listen, I was wondering—I mean, I—I don't know how you came to be... where you are... and I don't know what faith you hold to, but I... well, I brought you this." She held out the leather Bible.

Sam smiled and touched it gently. Then he reached inside his coat and pulled out a worn, pocket-sized Bible.

"Oh!" she exclaimed. "You have one! That's wonderful! I believe in Christ—in salvation through Jesus Christ. What faith are you?"

He thumbed through his Bible and handed it to her, pointing to an underlined verse.

She peered down at the fine print and smiled. "John 3:16."

He nodded.

"Well, that's wonderful! I've been praying for you."

His eyes shone softly, and his smile was gentle.

She glanced down at the Bible in her hand and held it out to him again. "This is a study Bible. It was my brother-in-law's, and he gave it to me, but I already have one. So if you're interested in it, you're more than welcome. I'd love to know it was getting some use."

He nodded and took it, a grateful smile lighting up his face.

"Well, I'll see you later, I guess," she said, turning to leave. "Oh! And if you're ever interesting in coming to church, we'd love to have you. Pastor Hallowell is an amazing servant of God." She glanced at the soup kitchen tent. "But I guess you probably already know that."

Sam nodded.

"Well, bye."

He waved.

She walked to Montgomery's after that, eager to tell her friend what had happened.

She found him outside, playing soccer in the snow with Kris. Her heart sank when she saw him.

Montgomery saw her and waved. "Hey!" he called.

Kris was staring at her. She couldn't tell if he was irritated with her presence or just bored, so she ignored him.

"What's up?" Montgomery asked.

"I wanted to tell you, I just saw Sam, and I was trying to witness—and failing miserably," she added with a laugh, "and then he took out this little Bible that he always carries with him. When I asked him what he believed, he showed me John 3:16! Isn't that incredible? He's a Christian!"

"That's awesome!" he exclaimed, catching some of her spiritual high. "I wonder why he doesn't come to church."

"I invited him."

"Great. So are you going to stick around?"

She glanced at Kris and shook her head. "Nah. I've gotta be going. I just wanted to share."

"I'm glad you did," he said, spinning the soccer ball in his gloved hand. "Now I can pray more specifically."

She nodded. "Okay, well, bye." She looked at Kris again, uncertain if she should say anything or not. "Bye," she said.

"See ya," he said.

She hurried home. She was freezing by now, even though the sun shone down warmly from a bright winter blue sky.

She was retelling her story to Shonda as she helped her fix dinner, when the doorbell rang.

Shonda glanced up in surprise. "I wonder who that is."

"I'll go," Jackie offered, and quickly went to the door. She gasped in surprise when she looked outside.

A few feet from the front step, Mason Randall sat astride a shaggy paint mare, and held the reins to a second horse.

"Is Shonnie here?" he asked with a grin.

Jackie nodded, speechless, then called to her sister.

Shonda came to the door, but froze when she saw her father and the horses.

"Hey, Shonnie," he said with an easy smile. "I owe you a pony ride. Remember?"

Jackie nearly broke down into tears of happiness. What a brilliant idea! Just the sort of thing she'd been praying for to bring Shonda around! Just the sort of perfect gesture on her father's part to… she looked at her sister and the thought died.

Shonda didn't smile. Not a trace of warmth softened her icy expression. When she spoke, her words were clipped and cold. "I can't. I'm making dinner. You're about twenty years too late." And she disappeared back down the hall.

Jackie stood there. She didn't know what to do and stared at her father helplessly.

The confident smile was gone, replaced by a look of defeat. The expression looked foreign on his features. It made him look old.

"I know it's not the same," she said slowly. "But if you'd like, I'd love to go for a ride with you."

He nodded slowly, and the smile gradually returned. "That would be great."

"Okay. I'll be just a second."

She hadn't fully warmed up yet, but grabbed her coat and boots and hurried outside. She had never ridden before and climbed clumsily into the saddle, but the stocky bay was sturdy and gentle, and with the exception of a vaguely worried look over his shoulder when she was flopping around, trying to get her feet in the stirrups, he ignored her and was content to follow Mason's mount as they headed out.

Her father was unusually quiet as they rode. He gave her a few pointers and commented on the weather, but most of the time, he rode in silence. They plodded through fields of silver and white and under evergreens with branches weighed down from the heavy snow. The beauty left Jackie breathless. The world looked different from the back of a horse.

She was practically numb all the way through when they got back. "Thank you," she said softly, handing the reins back to her father.

Mason nodded. "I'm glad you came."

"Me too."

"You'd better get inside. You must be frozen."

She nodded and went inside, then watched through the window until he had ridden out of sight. She peeled off her winter clothes and stood in front of the fire for several minutes.

Shonda and Kyle were in the kitchen finishing up their dinner.

Jackie helped herself to some macaroni and cheese, and noticed in surprise the faint acrid smell in the air and the dark brown edges of the dish as she scooped. Shonda never burned things.

She sat down and silently blessed her food, then ate ravenously.

Her sister and brother-in-law were silent, and she wondered faintly if they'd been arguing. She glanced at Shonda. Her sister's pretty face was set in an ugly frown and, remembering the heartbroken look on her father's face, she was suddenly angry.

"Why wouldn't you go with him?" she demanded. "He's trying so hard—"

"It would take a lot more than a pony ride to fix things," Shonda said angrily. "He hasn't changed a bit. He messes up and wants to put a BandAid on your heart. It doesn't work that way, Jackie."

"Shonda, if you would just give him a chance."

"How many chances does a father get?"

"I don't know," Jackie answered evenly. "Seventy times seven?"

Shonda shot her a icy glare, then stood up abruptly and began clearing the table.

Jackie stood up too and dumped the rest of her burnt dinner in the trash.

Kyle was buried in his newspaper when she left, and she was forced to resist the sudden urge to whack him over the head with it. He was head of the household. When was he going to tell his wife to grow up?

She stomped upstairs and started her homework. "Be ye angry and sin not. Let not the sun go down upon your wrath," her verse-a-day flip calendar preached at her. She turned it around and began laboring over her algebra.

She was just finishing when there was a knock at her door.

"What?" she snapped.

The door opened, and her brother-in-law stood framed in the doorway.

"Hi," he said.

"Hi."

He wandered over to the window and sank down into her bean bag, looking perfectly ridiculous in the squashy purple vinyl.

She put down her pencil and waited.

"I'm not going to bother with small talk tonight because I'm just too tired," he said. "I just came up to ask you a question."

That wasn't what she expected.

"You remember those letters that she hid? From your dad?"

Of course she remembered them. She nodded shortly.

"Did you ever stop to think about why she kept them?"

"What?"

"If she had really wanted to eliminate him from both your lives, she would have just destroyed the letters, Jax. But she kept them."

Jackie looked down. That had never occurred to her. "Why would she do that?"

"Because she loves him."

Jackie stared at him. "Kyle, she *hates* him."

He glanced out the window and fiddled with the sash from the curtain. "Sometimes the line between love and hate can be pretty fine."

"What do you mean?"

He shrugged. "She's angry at him for leaving her. And broken hearted. But she's also angry at herself because she loves him so much and wants so badly to have her father in her life again."

Jackie was silent. She had never really stopped to try to understand her sister's feelings. Could Shonda really love their father? She looked up at Kyle. "She told you that?"

He smiled. "No. She didn't have to."

She was in a better mood when she awoke, and Shonda was civil at breakfast, calmly acting as if nothing at all had happened.

The temperature had climbed drastically over night and all day the air was filled with the sounds of dripping as the snow banks shrank and the icicles melted. The sun poured down determinedly through gaps in heavy clouds. When school got out, Jackie and Montgomery walked to the cove to rehearse one of their scenes together. The water was high, and melting chunks of snow and ice swirled sluggishly.

They were halfway through the scene when the shadow of a thick mass of clouds darkened the cove, and a sudden downpour caught them by surprise.

"Quick!" Montgomery shouted, shoving his book inside his jacket. They dashed to the nearest crack in the rock and took shelter from the driving rain. Montgomery pulled out his flashlight from his bag—he never went anywhere without one anymore—and examined their surroundings. "We can wait here til the rain stops." Suddenly his eyes lit up with a glow Jackie was beginning to associate with crawling and dark and sore limbs. "Hey! Remember that cavern—the big one—that we found the first time we really explored?"

She nodded reluctantly.

"We should go there and practice our lines! Think how cool they'll sound, echoing like that!"

It was a good idea, she had to admit, but she didn't relish the idea of actually getting there. "But by the time we get there, the rain will most likely have stopped. We only have the one flashlight. And anyway, we probably won't be able to find it again."

Montgomery grinned. "It's a straight shot. I'm sure we can."

She sighed. "Okay. Why not?"

Five minutes later as they crawled along through the long low tunnel, she could think of plenty of reasons why not. But it was too late to turn back now, and it would be really cool to practice their lines in a stone auditorium crafted by the hand of God Himself.

Suddenly, Montgomery stopped dead in front of her.

"What?"

"Shh!"

She tried to listen above the sudden noisy increase of her pulse. And then she heard it. The strange humming, like some kind of eerie music, echoing down the passageway. She wanted to turn and run, but Montgomery was stealthily moving ahead.

They emerged from the low-ceilinged tunnel into a small chamber. The echoing hum was louder here, but the echo was gradually decreasing and the melody becoming clearer.

Jackie's heart was beating annoyingly fast. This was no wind or rocky reverberation. She swallowed nervously.

Someone was singing.

Montgomery put his finger to his lips, and they moved silently across the stone floor, his flashlight pointed downward to make the beam of light less noticeable.

Jackie's heart skipped a beat. Was that a light? She tugged at the back of Montgomery's jacket and pointed. A faint glow flickered from a narrow opening at the left side of the chamber.

They walked on cat's feet to the tunnel entrance. It stretched straight and smooth before them. They eased their way down the passageway toward the beckoning light.

The singing was growing louder.

Montgomery switched off the flashlight.

Jackie held her breath.

The words were distinguishable now, but she couldn't understand them. It sounded like another language.

They reached the end of the tunnel, and the giant cavern yawned ahead of them. Montgomery glanced back, and in the gloom, she saw him give her a brief nod, which she supposed was to encourage her that they weren't doing something incredibly stupid. *Too late,* she thought. She took a deep breath.

They peeked around the corner.

A lantern several yards in painted the chamber in a leopard's coat of light and shadow.

And bobbing above the lantern was a pale face.

Jackie nearly screamed, but Montgomery suddenly grabbed her arm.

She looked closer and gasped.

It was Sam. ✇

chapter twenty-two

Jackie and Montgomery stared in astonishment.

He hadn't seen them yet. He was looking down and fiddling with something in his lap, singing softly to himself all the while.

Jackie listened, enchanted. The haunting melody rang clearly off the rock, resounding through the chamber and piercing all the way to her soul. It was beautiful. She could almost be in an ancient monastery, listening to a monk singing psalms.

And then the music stopped.

Sam looked up, his penetrating blue eyes fixing them in the lantern light.

The moment seemed to last forever. Then, finally, Jackie choked out, "Sam?"

The shattered silence seemed to spur him into action. He nodded briefly and turned and walked away.

"Sam!" she called after him, but he had vanished into one of the far passageways.

They were quiet as they crept back through the tunnels, remembering the one they had found before that led to the shelf overlooking the cove.

"What language was that?" Jackie asked, as they stepped out into the fresh air.

"I don't know," Montgomery said. "I've never heard it before."

"Me, either. But… it does seem vaguely familiar for some reason."

Montgomery shrugged. He seemed more irritated than anything else. "I just don't understand why he would lie about it all these years."

"Maybe he didn't," Jackie said.

"What do you mean?"

"I don't think he ever communicated that he could not speak. I think he just simply chose not to talk."

"What difference does it make? It was still deceitful, wasn't it?"

"I suppose. I don't know. I don't think he ever tried to make anyone believe anything. I think all he was trying to do was be invisible."

Montgomery shrugged again. "Whatever. If you say so."

They had reached the edge of the woods.

"Well, goodnight."

"Goodnight."

She walked home slowly, deep in thought. She hummed a fragment of the melody Sam had been singing and wished she could have caught some of the words. Then she could ask someone what language they were.

Over the next few days, she hummed the song often; on the way to school, coming back from *Tempest* meetings, sometimes even between classes. Sam didn't show himself. If his wish was to be invisible, he was certainly succeeding now.

A week passed. Then two.

The weather had turned bitterly cold and drove them inside on even the sunniest days. They spent many afternoons in the Dawson's den or in beanbags in front of Jackie's window, working on their lines as they sipped hot cocoa.

Jackie spent three afternoons a week with her father, and he was even starting to join them at church on Sundays too. And at least once a week, he treated both she and Montgomery to a dessert at the DoubleDip and listened to their lines. He was an excellent coach, full of advice but never nagging. He offered Montgomery tips on how to lower his voice to sound older without making it sound forced. And when they had practiced enough, Jackie loved nothing better than to hear him launch into a story about actors he had known or plays he had seen on his travels.

On a particularly cold afternoon after a fresh snowfall, Jackie trudged through the drifts on her way home from visiting with her father, enjoying the crunch the snow made under her boots. She hummed Sam's song into her scarf as she walked. She had given up on trying to remember the foreign words. It was such a pretty melody. She wished she knew more of it.

Suddenly she stopped.

Of course. *Of course!* It wasn't the words at all that had seemed familiar. It was the melody! She started running, kicking up snow as she went. She was completely out of breath by the time she reached home, but she pulled off her boots and coat and charged up the stairs, narrowly missing Shonda and a basket full of laundry.

"Sorry!" she called back, without slowing. When she got upstairs, she began digging through her CDs until at last she found the one she had been looking for. She hadn't listened to it in over a year. It was a poor quality compilation of world music she had found in a clearance bin at the mall. She'd listened to it only once, and then it had quickly sunk to the bottom of her compact disc collection. But there was one....

She skipped through the disc, listening to just the intros as they wavered cheaply from her speakers. And then she found it.

She scanned the back of the cover for the title, and her eyes flew over the foreign jumble of letters without even attempting to pronounce it. But it answered her question.

The song was Irish.

Jackie overslept the next morning and barely made it to school before the first bell rang. She had been awake until the wee hours of the morning, musing over her discovery... and her suspicions. She kept her theories to herself, and when school was out, she shouted a goodbye to Montgomery and ran for the library.

To her relief, Mrs. Jamison was there, dressed in what looked like an Indian woman's sari.

"Why, hello," she said pleasantly. "Back again, are you?"

"I came to ask you more about the Mulqueens."

Mrs. Jamison smiled. "Goodness, you are persistent, aren't you? Well, have a chair and see if you can't put that tree together. It's completely eluded me."

Jackie sat down. "What I wanted to ask you, Mrs. Jamison—"

"Call me Zoe. If I'm going to be your research assistant, we should be on a first name basis, don't you think?"

Jackie smiled and nodded.

"Now, what did you want to ask me?" Zoe asked, as she neatly fitted two pieces together.

"I wanted to know about the boys... about how they died."

A cloud flitted across her violet eyes. "Well... that's not the sort of conversation suited for a day like today, is it? Can't you think of a more pleasant question to ask?"

Jackie shook her head. "I'm sorry. It's just terribly important to me." She hesitated. "They drowned, didn't they?"

Zoe nodded slowly.

"At Winds Cove?"

Zoe put down the puzzle piece she had been fingering. "What's in the past should stay there, and the dead should stay buried, don't you think?"

Jackie bit her lip. "I—I suppose so..."

Zoe shook her head. "How they doted on those boys." She glanced up at Jackie and smiled, but her bright eyes shone with sadness. "They were from Ireland, you know. Jamison took me to Ireland for our seventh anniversary."

"It must have been lovely," Jackie said automatically, trying to think of how to persuade Zoe to tell her.

"Yes. Yes, it was. We went to County Kerry—where they were from. Of course, I didn't tell Jamison that. He might have thought it odd...." She shrugged. "Anyway, it was a lovely time."

Jackie glanced up. "How well did you know them?"

"Not as well as I would have liked," she said softly, then looked over. "They were very shy. Dylan was young and full of fun. Ian was more serious. I used to think he carried the weight of the world on his shoulders." Her violet eyes misted over. "He had such beautiful blue eyes... like the ocean in the summer." She shook her head, as if to banish the memory, and looked up. "Well, I think that's enough for today," she said quietly. "I'm quite tired, actually."

"But—"

"There's enough sorrow in this world already, Jacqueline, without dredging up past tragedies. This town had seen a lot of sorrow. Don't make us relive it."

Jackie nodded slowly and got up to leave. After a few steps, she glanced back.

Zoe Jamison was staring sadly at the puzzle before her.

"Zoe?"

She looked up, and Jackie watched in surprise as she wiped away a tear. "Yes?"

"Um... my school is putting on a play... and I'm in it. Shakespeare's *Tempest*. I'd love it if you could come."

She smiled faintly. "Oh, no, dear. I never attend social functions. But thank you so much for the invitation. You're a dear girl. I'd invite you to my house, but I don't entertain anymore. Not since Jamison's passing."

"Oh. Well, thank you for all your help."

"Of course. Come and see me again sometime."

Jackie nodded and left.

She kicked a stone as she walked. She hadn't even been able to ask her question. But the more Jackie thought about what Zoe had said, the more she began to suspect that Mrs. Jamison had revealed a lot more than was initially apparent. She referred to her husband by his surname and admitted that she had not married him for love. And yet she spoke so tenderly of two boys who had been dead half a century and whom she claimed to barely know. Especially the one called Ian. She saw again Zoe's misty eyes and the telltale tear trickling down her cheek. She had no proof. Only her own unfounded theories. But she was suddenly and unequivocally certain that Zoe had been in love with Ian Mulqueen.

She hadn't gone far when a car pulled up beside her, and her father grinned through the window.

"Hey! Need a ride?"

She smiled and climbed in.

"So how was the library? Did you get some good books or was it business instead of pleasure? I worked in a library once. It was great. When it was busy, I was hoppin', but when it was quiet, I got to read for hours."

"I've sort of been doing some research on some local family history," Jackie explained.

"Excellent. Who's the family?"

"The Mulqueens. The inn you're staying at used to be their house."

"Really? It's always interesting to check up on local history. You can find amazing stuff."

She nodded. "So what are you doing this afternoon?"

"Actually, I was coming to look for you to say goodbye."

Jackie's heart nearly stopped. "What do you mean goodbye?"

"Not a permanent one," he assured her with a little laugh. "I've finished up some articles and thought I'd take them down to that magazine in New York and give them to the editor."

"Can't you just email them?"

"Yeah. Yeah, I can do that. But um... I just thought a change of scenery would be good. Just for a few days," he added quickly.

Jackie felt her stomach sinking down toward her toes.

"There's not a whole lot to do around here," Mason continued, "so I thought I'd take off for a little while and take care of some business while I'm at it. Maybe dig up some more free lance jobs."

She tried to look enthusiastic.

"Hey," her father said, reaching over and lightly touching her cheek. "I'm coming back. I promise."

She looked at him, scarcely daring to hope. "Really?"

"Sure! You can't get rid of me that easily." He grinned and winked at her.

She smiled and felt a wave of relief wash over her. Of course he would need to get out a bit. Of course.

"He's a free spirit," she told Shonda a half hour later, after Mason had dropped her off, and they'd said their goodbyes. "You can't expect him to be content in a little town like this when he's used to cities and friends. He just needs to get out. He'll be back," she finished certainly. "I know he will be."

Shonda's initial lash of anger was gone by now, and she was watching Jackie with a sad look in her eyes. But she only said, "Of course he will be."

The next day, she and Montgomery went in search of Sam.

They checked all the usual places in town and ended up at the cove.

"If he's in the caves, we'll never find him," Montgomery said, looking around.

Suddenly Jackie gasped in surprise. "We don't have to," she said in wonder. "Look!"

And there was Sam, standing under the willow tree. As usual, he had found them.

When they reached the willow, the three of them stood awkwardly for a moment. Then Sam said, "Come with me."

They exchanged glances and followed him, saving their questions for when they reached their destination. He led them through the narrow split in the rock through which Jackie had chased her homework weeks earlier and, after pulling a lantern from behind a loose rock high up on the wall, followed the winding passageway for several minutes.

Jackie watched the dancing shadows nervously. He could lose them in here all too easily, and they could wander around in the dark for days without ever finding their way out.

At last, they stopped. Sam pushed on a solid looking slab of rock, and Jackie watched in surprised when it moved aside. Then the older man ducked through the opening and disappeared inside. Jackie took a deep breath and followed with Montgomery.

Whatever she had been expecting, it wasn't this.

She looked around in amazement. It was a fair-sized round chamber, the walls worn smooth. Sam had set the lantern down on a crudely made table, but there was much more light than you could possibly get from a flame. She looked up. A hole high up in the rocky ceiling allowed a single beam of sunlight to wash the dark away, and the fine screen of plant life visible through the opening cast delicate leafy patterns across the rock.

A couple of chairs huddled around the table, one rough hewn like the table, the other a slightly rusty metal folding chair. There was a lifetime of accumulation here. A scarred bookcase held dozens of discarded library books. A moth eaten rug covered half the floor, and a low bed heaped with old blankets sat in the corner near a fire pit.

"Welcome," he said, leaning against the wall.

"Sam!" Jackie exclaimed. "You can't have lived here all this time! What about the winter?!"

"Well, between this and a couple of shelters and lots of warm clothing, I manage." He had a lilting accent. Every word seemed musical.

Jackie shook her head. "There's so much I want to ask you."

He shrugged. "What do you want to know?"

"Well... who are you?" Montgomery demanded. "What's your name?"

"What's in a name?" he responded. "Sam has worked for the past twenty years. It seems silly to change it now." He smiled faintly, and his brilliant blue eyes glowed like the sea on a summer day.

And suddenly, she knew.

"Except that it isn't your name, is it?" Jackie asked. "Ian?"

He blinked in surprise, and Montgomery gaped at her.

"Ian Mulqueen," she said softly.

"How did you know?" he asked, his voice no more than a whisper.

"Zoe Jamison. When I figured out that you were singing in Irish, I went to ask her if they ever found the bodies of those poor boys. But she wouldn't tell me. She did, however, mention, how blue Ian's eyes were." She shook her head. "Why?" she asked.

He looked at her steadily for a long moment, and when at last he answered, his voice was low and flat, his face cold and empty. "Because my brother was the only thing I had left."

His eyes took on a faraway look, and he seemed to be gazing back through time. "It was really windy that day. A hurricane had swept up the coast. The water was mad. Just crazy. Waves like I'd never seen on the Atlantic. It was the three of us there at the cove. Dylan and me. And our friend Hal. We thought it would be fun to go swimming... " he shook his head as if he was seeing it all over again. "Dylan dove in first. He was always first. But he didn't come back up. At first, we thought it was some kind of joke. But then a minute passed. And another. I jumped in after him and sent Hal for help. But as soon as I felt that current, I knew..."

"I hid in the caves while the divers searched," he said. His voice sounded like gravel. "I knew they would make me go home if they saw me, and I was determined to stay until Dylan was found. I waited for Hal. But he never came back after that day. I sometimes think... if he had come... alone... that maybe I... " He sighed. "That maybe things would have been very different.

"After a while, the townspeople stopped looking. But I couldn't give up. I suppose deep down I knew that he was dead. But I couldn't just leave him. He was my little brother—my responsibility. I spent a year looking for him. I searched every single day. It became my purpose."

"What made you decide to give it up?"

"I didn't give it up." His fierce blue eyes met hers. "I found him."

Jackie felt a chill run through her body at the thought. "Oh," she whispered.

Montgomery glanced at her, and she saw the horror mirrored in his eyes. "What did you do then?" he asked.

Ian's eyes fell to the floor. "I buried him."

He sighed, then turned back to them. "I thought of returning to my uncle's house. But by then, everyone thought I was dead of course. And it was easier to just stay dead. As dead as he was."

Jackie and Montgomery stared at him, speechless.

"But the people had been searching for you too," Jackie said. "It would have spared the Mulqueens so much grief if you had just gone home. They thought you were dead." She thought of Zoe. "They all thought you were dead."

He nodded. "I know that now. At the time, quite honestly, I never even thought on it. My only thought was for Dylan. But as much as I would wish things had transpired differently, it won't change anything. I am where I am and content to be there."

"So what happens now?" Montgomery asked, after a long pause.

"Nothing."

"Don't you want people to know who you are?"

"If I'd wanted anyone to know, I would have told them decades ago." He gave them a meaningful look.

Jackie and Montgomery were silent. There didn't seem to be anything left to say. So at length, they said goodbye, feeling distinctly unsettled when the man known throughout the town as "Silent Sam" said goodbye back.

"Shouldn't we tell someone?" Montgomery asked as they walked home.

Jackie had been pondering the same thing. "I don't know. I mean, it's not our secret to tell. And I'm not sure it's really any of our business. His relatives are dead. There's no reason for everyone to know; nothing to be gained."

"Except the Mulqueen's old estate and family fortune."

Jackie stopped. "I hadn't thought of that."

"What happened to it?"

"There was no next of kin," she said, recalling her research. "I think everything just went to the town."

"Oh."

They started walking again.

"Well, if he was interested in any of that, he could have come forward a long time ago," Montgomery said.

"Yeah. I guess we can just wait it out and see what happens."

He nodded. "Yeah."

They reached the road and parted company.

"See you tomorrow."

"Bye," Jackie called back as she turned down the road. If he had only come forward. If he had only gone for help with his friend Hal. If only... How different things might have been. But as Sam—no, Ian—had said, he was where he was. They couldn't change the past. They could only live with the present and try to make a better future. But what was a better future for Ian Mulqueen? Living down the infamy of fifty dead years or existing in the quiet, peaceful lifestyle he had chosen?

Early Saturday morning, Jackie left for the cove, but instead of turning off at the path, she kept walking until she was in the middle of downtown. She didn't stop until she was at the common, staring up at the marble fountain. The angel faces looked less angelic and more like teenage boys. She walked around the edge until she found the writing Montgomery had stumbled across. She gently pulled back the vines and started scraping at the moss, finishing the job her friend had started. Slowly, painstakingly, she uncovered the names.

Ian and Dylan Mulqueen. In Loving Memory.

She thought of Desmond and Brigit Mulqueen, dying alone and childless. Then Zoe Jamison flashed across her mind, married to a man she didn't love. How different things could have been for everyone. ☺

chapter twenty-three

In the days that followed, Jackie and Montgomery became more accustomed to a talking Sam and gradually grew comfortable calling him Ian, though they were careful to refer to him as Sam when there were people around.

Mason Randall returned as he had promised, showing up at school to pick her up one mild afternoon and grinning in pleasant surprise when Jackie unceremoniously threw her arms around him.

Soon the play was looming up before them.

Jackie and Montgomery pooled their pennies and bought a ticket for Ian. He was hesitant at first, but then finally agreed to attend. Mr. and Mrs. Dawson even offered to give him a ride and assured them they would take care of him.

With the increased rehearsals and costume fittings, Jackie saw less and less of her father. He was busy freelancing articles for a magazine, so he didn't seem to mind the additional free time. In fact, Jackie thought distractedly one evening after a phone conversation with him, he seemed almost relieved. But that was absurd. He was as excited about the play as she was.

The day of the performance arrived with a storm of butterflies in the pit of Jackie's stomach. The students involved in the play were a lost cause to the teachers.

At lunch break, Jackie went outside, nervously gnawing on her sandwich. She didn't even know what was in it. Her taste buds seemed to have gone defunct. She watched as a group of high school boys played basketball on the parking lot pavement. She ran over her lines in her head as she watched Josh go up for a lay-up. The words were clumping together in her mind, and she struggled to untangle them. A senior boy had the ball and was driving toward the hoop. Was it "rather like a dream than an assurance"? Or "rather like an assurance than a dream"? Josh jumped up to block as the other boy jumped up to shoot, and they collided in mid air, then landed on the asphalt with a bone-jarring thud. "'Tis far off and rather like a dream," she said. Students crowded around the fallen boys, and with a start, she realized Josh had not gotten up. She ran to join the huddle of concerned and curious classmates and shoved through the group. The other boy was on his feet, but Josh was groaning and gripping his ankle, his face ashen. Oh no...

A couple of guys helped him to his feet, and the teacher on duty sent him to the nurse's office. Jackie's first thought was for the play, though a stab of guilt reminded her to feel sorry for poor Josh. What were they going to do?

Almost as one, everyone turned to Kris Cappencella.

Jackie swallowed. Oh great.

Several hours later, Jackie stepped out of the makeshift dressing room and headed for the auditorium. Josh had been taken to the hospital the next town over. The sprain wasn't too serious, but it was enough to keep him off his feet for several days.

She had gotten over the shock and disappointment by now, though it had taken a couple of hours. Kris's usual cool exterior had been shattered when he learned he was going to have fulfill his role as understudy and perform for a large audience with only half a day's notice.

Students stared at her as she rustled down the hall in her gown. She had to admit, the volunteers had done an amazing job with the costumes. Her dress was pale and simple, but fluttered and flowed with every move she made. Mrs. Lewis, Alicia's mother, was in charge of hair and makeup and twisted Jackie's curls into a meticulously arranged style that somehow looked both free and flowing.

"Jackie, you look gorgeous!" Alicia exclaimed, when Jackie joined the other cast members backstage.

"Thank you," Jackie said, too nervous to be embarrassed by the compliment. Her heart was pounding.

Montgomery smiled at her, cool as ice.

Kris looked like he was going to be sick.

"I don't think I can do this," he murmured to no one in particular.

"You're going to be fine," she whispered automatically.

He looked at her as if he'd never seen her before, and in that moment, as she gazed into his panic-stricken eyes, the animosity fell away. "I'm not even supposed to be up here," he hissed. "My costume is all wrong because it was fitted for Josh. The pants are too short, the shirt is too tight—"

"You look fine."

"—I'm going to forget all my lines."

"Look at me," she said, grabbing his shoulders. "Look into my eyes." He shoved his hair out of his face and did as she said.

"You are going to be just fine. Now take a deep breath."

He did.

"Good. Now let it out slowly. Good. Now do it again." She coached him through some breathing exercises and then, when the audience on the other side of the curtain had fallen silent while the principal introduced the play, she prayed with him. It was a quick prayer—a simple plea for God to calm their nerves and help them all to do their best, glorifying Him with their efforts. When she said "Amen," he opened his eyes, and met her gaze calmly. There was a bit of the old Kris back in those eyes and he watched her in surprise.

"Thanks," he said.

And then the curtain rose.

After an initial fumble with the curtain early on in the production, the play went off without a hitch. There was a gasp from the audience as the first set was revealed, and Jackie smiled as she watched from the sidelines, waiting for her cue to go on. The sets were beautiful. The students and volunteers had really outdone themselves and if everything continued to go well, this would be by far their best fund raiser yet.

When her cue came, she swept onto the stage with Montgomery beside her. Her heart was racing, and she could feel the adrenaline flowing through her. Her lines came fluently; her voice was steady and clear. Kris rose to the occasion and was brilliant. He put a fresh spin on his character, and much to her surprise, they played off each other even better than Josh and she had.

Montgomery was sensational. He was so convincing as an aging duke with the elements at his command, Jackie half expected the wind to blow all the windows in the school open. During the rehearsals, the play had seemed to go on forever, but that night, time took wing. She looked for Mason while she was onstage, but the spotlights glared in her eyes and turned the audience into a darkened mass. Before she fully realized she was actually acting in front of a large audience, the curtain was falling on the last act.

The applause was deafening in the school auditorium. The cast milled behind the curtain excitedly.

Jackie was absolutely glowing. She could feel her cheeks flushed with excitement and the blood pounding through her veins. She turned to Kris standing next to her and smiled. He was staring at her intently, his brown eyes solemn.

"I'm sorry," he whispered.

Her smile faltered. "Sorry for what?"

"Everything. For being a jerk all our lives. I'm really sorry."

She stared at him in amazement, and then slowly a smile spread over her face.

This time he smiled back.

Out of the corner of her eye, she saw Montgomery watching them. She glanced over. He was grinning behind his gray beard.

The cast joined hands as the curtain rose and bowed to the audience. The thunder of applause echoed in her ears long after she had left the stage.

When she came out of the classroom the girls were using as a dressing room, Kris was standing in the hallway, leaning against the wall. He straightened when he saw her.

"Hey," he said.

"Hi."

"I just wanted to thank you. I mean, you really helped me out a lot. And I wanted to tell you that uh… you did a really good job."

"Thanks," she said in surprise. "You did too."

"Thanks."

They stood awkwardly for a moment, then Kris said, "Well, I'll see you tomorrow."

"Yeah. Bye."

Jackie turned and walked away, her heart beating oddly fast for having just had a brief exchange with someone she couldn't stand. She wanted to glance back at him, but had the strangest feeling that he would be doing the same thing. So she kept walking until she turned the corner and was swallowed up in the crowd of students and parents milling around the school auditorium.

Shonda and Kyle found her at once. Kyle was grinning broadly, and her sister threw her arms around her. "You were amazing!"

Jackie beamed. "Thanks!" She glanced around for Mason, but there was no sign of him.

"Where's Dad?"

Shonda's face tightened angrily, and Kyle shook his head. "He couldn't make it," Kyle said.

"Oh..." Jackie felt as if the floor had suddenly fallen out from under her, but she tried to keep the disappointment from her face.

"He called right before we left."

"Sure. I understand."

"But you really were unbelievable! Everyone is saying so!"

Jackie forced a smile. "Thanks."

Suddenly the crowd seemed to turn and surge around her, and she was caught up in a sea of admirers. "Congratulations!" she heard over and over again. "You were wonderful!"

She thanked the countless parents and students, blushing at their praise.

Mr. and Mrs. Dawson jostled their way through the crowd, and Mrs. Dawson enveloped her in a hug. "You were perfect," she said into her hair. "Just perfect." Mr. Dawson beamed his approval.

Jackie smiled and for a moment forgot the disappointment of her father's absence and basked in the admiration.

Then a man appeared before her, his white hair short and neatly combed, his suit pressed and creased. For a moment she didn't know him, but then she looked into his brilliant blue eyes. "Sam!" she exclaimed.

"We told you we'd take care of him," Mr. Dawson said with a smile.

Ian smiled down at her and winked.

She winked back.

Montgomery appeared soon after. He clapped her on the back in congratulations and shook Ian's hand. "Sam! You look great, man!"

Jackie wanted the evening to last forever, but all too soon it was over, and she was packed into Kyle's car and heading home.

It wasn't until she was in her own room, with soft piano music drifting from her CD player, that she allowed herself to think again about her father. He hadn't come. The most important moment of her life, and he hadn't come. She gazed at the stars through her skylight until they blurred into pale streaks of light. Then she curled up into a ball and cried herself to sleep.

At school the next day, the students continued to congratulate her. She tried to push her father from her mind and enjoy the attention, but as the day progressed, she found she was just playing a role. Not even the exceptional review in the local newspaper could lift her spirits. She oohed and ahhed and blushed appreciatively when Mrs. Cox read it aloud in class, but her mind was somewhere else. On a boat on the ocean, floating through stars; skating in New York City; drinking vanilla chai at two o'clock in the morning. Had it all been a lie? Had he meant any of it? She couldn't believe she had been so wrong about him.

At lunch break, Mrs. Cox called her aside. "I just wanted to tell you that you did a phenomenal job," she said. "I'm very proud of you."

For a moment, Jackie rose from her despondency and felt her face grow warm. "It was a good experience." She managed a grin. "But I still think I would have enjoyed playing Ariel more."

Mrs. Cox smiled. "Actually, the other teachers wanted to give you that role. But I thought playing Miranda might be better for you."

Jackie's brow furrowed in confusion. "What do you mean?"

"Miranda is the popular princess role," her teacher explained. "The beautiful maiden who enchants all who meet her. Ariel is a spirit—a mysterious and magical fairy creature who accomplishes much, but who is invisible to almost everyone around her."

As the words sank in, Jackie began to understand.

"It would have been tempting to allow art to imitate life," Mrs. Cox said as she reached out and gently touched Jackie's hair. "But where's the adventure in that?" Her eyes twinkled warmly.

Jackie gazed up at her teacher, gratitude and horror warring within her. "But it could have ruined the play!"

"It was a gamble, I admit. But one that paid off."

A group of girls from her class walked by. Heather called out, "Hey, Jackie, a bunch of us are going to the DoubleDip after school. See you there?"

"Sure," Jackie answered, still unaccustomed to the popular-girl treatment.

Mrs. Cox smiled. "And now it seems that life is imitating art."

Jackie smiled back.

When school was out, she joined the other students at the ice cream parlor. The kids were nice, but she still felt out of place. She was beginning to wish she hadn't come when Montgomery and Kris walked in and joined them.

"Hey," they greeted everyone and then dragged a small couch over to the group and sat near Jackie.

Kris smiled. "Hey."

"Hey," she returned with what she hoped was a genuine smile.

Montgomery leaned over. "Are you okay?"

"Sure."

"I'm sorry about your dad," he said softly.

She shrugged. "I should have known. Everyone warned me. Even you. It's my own fault."

"You don't have anything to blame yourself for," Kris suddenly spoke up.

She glanced over in surprise.

"I know it's none of my business," he said quickly. "But it doesn't do any good to beat yourself up every time he doesn't follow through on a promise." He grinned faintly. "Trust me. I should know."

She met his gaze for a long moment, then her face relaxed into a smile. A real smile. "Thanks."

He nodded. "Anytime."

She glanced at Montgomery. "Sam sure cleaned up nicely, didn't he?"

"Yeah. I hardly recognized him."

"So what is it with you guys and that homeless dude?" Kris asked. "I've seen you talking to him. What's the deal?"

Jackie and Montgomery exchanged glances.

"He's a really nice guy," Jackie said.

"But he can't even talk. What do you do? Hold staring contests?"

"You can communicate a lot without words," Jackie said. "He loves to read. Sometimes I just bring books for him to borrow. And you should see him when the library puts books in the discard box. He's like a kid at Christmas."

"So what do you think his story is?" Kris asked.

"Whatever it is," Montgomery said, "I'm sure it's a good one."

Later that night, Mason called.

It was odd. Jackie wasn't at all surprised. As soon as the phone had rung, she'd had the strangest feeling that it was him.

"Hello?"

"Hey, kiddo, how are you?"

She didn't answer. Could he really be that insensitive?

"Yeah, sorry I missed the play. I'll bet you were fantastic!"

"Why couldn't you come?" she asked, trying to keep her voice steady.

He was quiet for a moment. "It was just… time to leave. There's a time for everything, you know? It says it in the Bible."

Jackie was silent.

"Oh, c'mon, Jax, you know me. I can't stay in any one place for too long."

"Yes. I know," Jackie answered coldly.

There was an uncomfortable silence.

"Yeah, so anyway, I'll uh… try to swing by again sometime."

She wanted to cry. She wanted to hit something. She wanted to yell angrily, "Don't bother!" But instead she said stiffly, "Okay."

"Great! Well, I'll talk to you later then! Bye!"

"Bye," she said, but he had already hung up.

She replaced the receiver and turned to see Shonda standing in the doorway.

"If you want to sing a chorus of I-told-you-so, feel free," she told her sister bitterly.

Shonda didn't say anything. She just wrapped her arms around her in a fierce embrace. "We'll never say another word about it. Just forget him."

Jackie nodded into her sister's shoulder, but deep down she knew she never would. You just couldn't forget someone like that. He was everything she'd ever dreamed of in a father. Except for one important thing, she thought. *He's not here.* ෴

chapter twenty-four

She walked to the book shop after school the next day and browsed the shelves in the used book section. She ran her fingers over the worn bindings but then left without buying anything. She wandered back through the center of town and paused by the common, where several students from the Academy lingered. Alicia and Kris both waved. She waved back and continued on. She didn't trust herself to talk to anyone just now. The wind was picking up speed, and the overcast skies threatened the storm the weatherman had been promising, but the temperatures hadn't yet dropped from the unseasonable warmth. She left the town center behind and followed the road toward home, her gaze fixed on the ground a few yards in front of her feet. There was a funny ache in her chest, and her pretty little town was suddenly stifling and unbearably small. She wanted to be somewhere else. Someone else. She rounded the bend in the road and came upon Pastor Hallowell's small white cottage.

Pastor Hallowell was outside raking old leaves and debris from his lawn in preparation for Maine's brief summer, and wearing a tee shirt with a picture of the Eiffel Tower on the front of it and "I love Paris" scrawled over it in loopy letters. He glanced up as she approached, and smiled.

"Hi, Pastor."

"Hello, Jackie," he called. "I'm just trying to get these leaves raked up before the storm comes and turns them to mush. *Trying* being the key word," he added with a rueful grin as a gust of wind scattered the leaves, strewing them all across the lawn again.

He stopped raking and walked toward her, brushing crumbled bits of dry leaves from his tee shirt and chuckling. "I could never wear this while I was in France without being branded as a tourist." He looked up at her, his eyes twinkling. "How are you this afternoon?"

"Okay," she said, hoping she didn't sound as down as she felt.

He studied her for a moment. His sharp gray eyes never missed a thing. "Is everything all right?"

She shrugged and forced a smile.

He tilted his head, a knowing look on his seamed face.

The strained smile disintegrated, and her gaze fell to the dry brown carpet of last autumn's leaves.

He leaned on his rake and waited.

"He didn't come," she said softly. She looked up. "My dad. He didn't come to the play."

Understanding swept his features, and he nodded slowly. "I see."

"Well, I don't!" The words came out in a torrent, and she didn't even try to stop them. "Why would he do this? How could he do this? He knew how important this was!"

"Perhaps he had a good reason."

Jackie met his eyes coldly. "It was *time*. That's all he said. It was *time* to leave." She shook her head and smiled bitterly. "Well, he's had a lot of practice with that, hasn't he."

He watched her with an expression that reminded her of Kyle, halfway between sympathy and rebuke. "Let's sit," he said, nodding toward the front steps of his tiny house.

She sat on the top step and sighed heavily. The anger was draining out of her, and she suddenly felt very tired. "Why can't I just have a normal family like everyone else?"

"Because there are no normal families, Jackie." The wind ruffled his iron gray hair. "Because normal in many people's eyes means perfect. My parents were married for fifty-seven years and by all accounts were a great marital success, and I loved them dearly. But my father was often inconsiderate, cruel even, and he had a temper that he never fully learned to control. My best friend in college had a textbook all-American family, if one were to judge by appearances. But his mother had a plethora of emotional problems and was extremely self-absorbed. Look at your friend Montgomery. He lost his brother to cancer. Kris's parents are divorced. Alicia's are separated. Brent's older brother has a history of drug problems, and his parents are heartbroken because of it. Each family, whether two parents or one or none, has its problems. Because families are made of up people. And people sin."

"I know," Jackie whispered. "And I love Kyle and Shonda, I really do. And I'm very thankful for them. But it's just not fair. All I've ever wanted was to have a mother and a father, together, who love me. What's wrong with that?"

"Nothing. But, Jackie, let me ask you something. Do you believe God makes mistakes?"

"No, but—"

"Ah..." He held up his finger. "There is no 'but' with God. He has given you the family you have for a reason. I don't know that reason. You may never know it while you're on this earth. But it's His reason. And sometimes, unsatisfactory as that may sound, that must be enough. This life is but a prelude of what is yet to come. And the challenges God places before us are to strengthen us and make us more like Him. Our chief end is to glorify Him, regardless of our parents or our children or our classmates or our own sinful selves."

Jackie stared at the ground, absorbing his words, recognizing their truth even though she wanted to ignore it. It wasn't a mistake that Mason Randall was her father. It was no accident that she was raised by her sister. God had a reason for it, and that was really all she needed to know. She nodded slowly and stood up, Pastor Hallowell rising with her.

He patted her shoulder gently. "It may not be what you wanted to hear."

She sighed. "But it's what I needed to hear." She looked up at him and smiled, her first real smile all day. "Thank you, Pastor."

"You'd better get on home before this storm breaks."

She nodded and said good bye, then crossed his lawn and headed for home. She glanced up at the heavy gray skies, growing darker every minute. The storm would be here soon. On an impulse, she turned off at the trail that led to the cove. The ocean was always spectacular right before a storm.

She made her way out over the rocks to her usual boulder and sat down. She scanned the area, wondering if Ian was around, but saw no sign of him. She would stay until the first rain drop fell. The sea air felt blissfully cool on her face. Between play rehearsals and visiting with her father, she hadn't come for the sunrise in over a week, and the cove seemed angry at her desertion. The winds buffeted her, and foaming waves surged higher and higher, spraying her face with a cool mist. The water churned in the cove as if in a great cauldron, and the leaves and twigs that had been blown into the water were pulled down into the dark depths. She looked up at the low-hanging heavens. The rain would come any moment.

Her mind turned Pastor Hallowell's words over and over again. No mistakes. No accidents. She was who she was and where she was for some purpose. But that didn't excuse Mason. The fact that she was meant to learn something from being around him didn't mean it was okay for him to shirk his God-given responsibility of being a father. "I worked so hard on that play...." she whispered. Anger welled up inside her again, and she reached inside her bag and jerked the picture of her parents out from her Shakespeare volume. If he didn't want to be a part of her life, he didn't have to be. Furiously, she tore the photo down the middle and hurled her father's half into the water. She put the remaining half with her mother's smiling face back into the book and slammed it shut, stuffing it back into her backpack. The little half picture of her father skimmed across the water as it swirled around the edge of the cove. A funny ache pierced her chest as she watched it whirl and twirl with the current. Her throat constricted, and a single tear trickled down one cheek. The picture swept by again, this time a little farther away.

She scooted closer to the edge of the rock and reached out toward the picture as it circled around again. She snatched at it, but it was too far away. She lay down on her stomach and stretched out as far as she could. The picture danced by, just out of reach.

A drop of rain fell from the sky and landed with a splash on the end of her nose.

She stretched farther. If that was all she could have of her father, it would be enough. She would make it be enough. The water swirled, and the picture glided tantalizingly close. She made a desperate lunge, and for a fraction of a second, she thought she felt paper beneath her fingers. Then a wave broke over her and swept her from the boulder.

The shock of cold water closing over her head numbed her senses. She bobbed back to the surface, coughing and spluttering. The waves rose around her so high that for a moment she couldn't see anything but water. Then she glimpsed her rock.

Thunder rumbled ominously, barely audible above the roar of the sea. She tried to swim toward the boulder, but the current drove her back, and she found herself fighting just to keep her head above water. The waves pummeled her, and the harder she struggled to reach the edge of the cove, the farther away she seemed to drift.

Treading water frantically, she brushed the brine from her eyes and tried not to panic. Her clothes were so heavy. Her shoes felt like they'd been pumped full of lead. If she could just stay afloat, maybe someone would come. Desperately she prayed—for energy, for calm seas, for a rescuer. If she could just stay afloat…

A giant wave overwhelmed her, plunging her beneath the surface. She kicked madly and gulped the air when she emerged. Her strength was nearly gone. She wondered faintly what would happen when she could no longer tread water. How would it end? What would she feel? And she marveled at the irony that the place she loved most in the world would be the place that destroyed her. How much time had passed? Seconds? Minutes? Hours? With her last reserve of energy, she tried one last time to reach the shore, but the current caught her up and swept her along in a whirling rush. The boulder flashed by. Her arms and legs ached from keeping her head above water. A jagged edge grazed her arm, and she dizzily realized she was on the far side of the cove, near the steepest of the rock walls. Her leg struck something sharp and hard and went numb; then her whole body was slammed into a cluster of almost entirely submersed rocks. She scrabbled for something to hang on to, breaking her fingernails and scraping her hands until they bled, but the water tore her away. She wondered dully if sharks ever ventured here. She had never seen one, but the cove was deep. The water flung her past her boulder again, and she realized dimly that she was going in circles. Images flickered in her memory. The leaf. The picture. Ian's odd gesticulations. Dylan. *Dylan.*

Another wave forced her under and this time, she couldn't seem to get back to the surface. The current wrenched her this way and that and she felt as if the water was trying to tear her to pieces. Her lungs screamed for air. She tried desperately to kick, but a flood of panic engulfed her as she realized she didn't know which way was up.

She stopped struggling and let the water drag her along, waiting for it all to finally end. A strange sort of peace settled over her, and in a far away voice, she heard Pastor Hallowell saying *no mistakes, no accidents* as the cove pulled her down and claimed her for its own. ☺

chapter twenty-five

*Yea, though I walk through the valley of the shadow of death... Where
the ocean meets the sky... If by your art my dearest father, you have put the
wild waters in this roar, allay them... What time I am afraid... We are such
stuff as dreams are made on... I will trust in thee... You've been making our
lives more beautiful every year... Had I been any God of power, I would have
sunk the sea within the earth... I will fear no evil... I didn't know you had
a daughter... Flights of angels sing thee to thy rest... There is no but with
God... And he arose and rebuked the wind... Don't grow up too quickly...
And said unto the sea, Peace, be still... I knew you were better off with her,
anyway... What manner of man is this that even the winds and the sea obey
him... For thou art with me...*

She drifted... through time and space... and the only sound in
her ears was the gentle rhythm of the ocean. Where was she? Was
she anywhere? Was she even alive? She could imagine she was at the
shore during summer break, napping in the sun. She could almost feel
the sand beneath her. Perhaps this was some sort of way station on the
way to heaven. Her fingers dug into the powdery earth. It really did
feel remarkably like a beach.

Jackie opened her eyes.

The scenery didn't change.

It was as if the world had been plunged into deepest night. Or maybe it was night. Where was she? And how did she get here? A flood of images flashed through her memory, and the last thing she remembered was hitting her head on something hard.

Her whole body ached. Pain stabbed through her right leg. Her left temple throbbed. She tried to pull herself into a sitting position but her wrist gave out under her weight, and she fell back again. She lay there silently for a while—she didn't know how long—and waited for the pain to ease. After a while, her eyes began to adjust, and the black divided itself into varying shades of gray. Murky light filtered down from somewhere far above her. No, not really light, she thought. More a lessening of the darkness.

A brilliant flash scared her to death and momentarily blinded her, leaving her in darkness more complete than before. What was that? She waited for her heartbeat to slow. A blood clot putting pressure on some part of her brain? Divine mugshots?

A rumble of thunder answered her.

Lightning. It was still storming.

Her eyes adjusted more quickly this time, and when the lightning flashed again, she was ready. She squinched up her eyes to protect them from the painful flare of light and looked around as quickly as she could, taking in her surroundings.

She didn't see much, but it was enough. Stone walls rose around her and disappeared into the blackness above her. She must be in some kind of a cave. But how did she get here?

Gradually, as her eyes continued to adjust, the lightning no longer blinded her, and she was able to see more of the cave. The walls themselves were lost in shadow, but the cavern floor was soft and sandy, and a pool of water lay at her feet. The water didn't seem to have a source but moved with the rhythm of the surf.

The entrance to the cave must be under water! It was too dark to see through the water, but even as she sat there, the current carried the water up over her feet and splashed her knees.

She was starting to shiver. She had to get warm soon. And dry.

The water surged in again, this time up past her knees.

The tide must be coming in.

She froze. The tide… She looked around, straining her eyes to see through the darkness. The sand stretched away toward the walls.

She forced herself into a crouching position and then slowly stood up. Her right leg could barely support her, and she shifted most of her weight to her left. Then, slowly, she began hobbling away from the water. The back wall of the cave rose up before her, as shadowy and forbidding as the other three. The sand ended, and the stone floor sloped steeply up as she neared the back of the cave. She couldn't see much of anything. But she reached out, and the touch of it told her all she needed to know. The rock was smooth and slippery. Worn from centuries of water beating against it. The familiar trappings of panic began to rise within her.

She had survived the whirlpool only to drown in a black cave.

The shivering was growing uncontrollable. She was just so cold. She rubbed her arms briskly, in spite of her throbbing wrist. She lowered herself gingerly onto the sloping rock floor and gently ran her hands over her injured leg, trying to assess the damage. It wasn't broken or she wouldn't have been able to put any weight on it at all. Her pant leg was torn at the thigh, and the fabric was stiff and sticky. A wave of nausea nearly overwhelmed her as her exploring fingers found the gash in her leg. She couldn't tell how deep it went and wasn't sure she even wanted to know. She felt dizzy and weak and wondered how much blood she'd lost. She wished Montgomery was there to tell her she wasn't really bleeding.

The crash of thunder echoed through the cave, and another flash of lightning revealed the rising water level.

She was wearing a button down short sleeved shirt over a tank top and quickly peeled off the outer layer and tied it around her leg above the cut. She wasn't sure the little shirt would be enough stop the blood flow even if she was still bleeding, but it was the only thing she could think of to do.

Then, slowly, agonizingly, she began to climb. She didn't know if she was climbing toward anything. All her tired mind could think of was *up*. She had to stay above water. Maybe the cave wouldn't fill to the top. Maybe she would find a way out. Maybe...

She prayed as she climbed, forcing her lips to move, as much to focus on the words as to try to drown out the pain of her screaming wrist.

She had reached the wall itself. Not quite as slick as the sloping floor, it was nevertheless much steeper and she knew she would not be able to climb it. But she had to try. "Please, Father," she whispered, and ran her fingers up the stone until she found a handhold. "Help me." She took a deep breath and shifted her weight to her bad leg, then hauled herself up, her good leg scrambling until it found a narrow lip to balance on. She was nearly sick from the pain, but instead of waiting, she forced herself to repeat the process, groping for another place to grab, another foothold.

"Yea, though I walk through the valley of the shadow of death... " She eased her way higher, dragging her hurt leg. "I will fear no evil, for thou art with me."

Her foot slipped and she suddenly slid back down to the bottom.

She sat there for several minutes, trying to breathe, trying to pray. She barely even noticed the tears flooding over her cheeks.

Lightning flashed. The water had reached the rock.

She wanted to scream. Perhaps she did. She was nearly numb from cold and exhaustion. Even the pain was beginning to dull, but she was too scared to be thankful. It wasn't supposed to end this way. She was only fourteen.

Dylan had been fifteen. His life had been snuffed out so easily.

It was different when it was someone else—removed and far away. Things like that happened to other people. They happened in books and movies and plays. They didn't happen to you.

She prayed. She didn't know what else to do. She begged for a miracle. For mercy. For anything. She thought of Shonda and Kyle. Did they even know she was gone yet? How long had it been? She hoped they would have a baby soon. And then cried because she wouldn't be there to see him. She thought of the Dawsons and wondered if they would miss her. She hoped Montgomery would keep drawing. She thought of her father and wished she had his torn picture to keep her company. She had to forgive him. And then she realized in mild surprise that she already had.

Another burst of lightning illuminated the cave, and for the first time, she noticed that the far corner was not as steep as the rest of the walls. Maybe... just maybe... she could drag herself up it. It felt like it took an eternity just to cross the cavern to the other side. She splashed through ankle deep water as she edged around the cave, clinging to the walls for support. She finally reached the corner and realized that rather than the wall being less steep, what had looked like a more gradual climb was actually a rock pile, reaching toward the ceiling. There must have been some sort of rock slide long ago. These rocks too were worn smooth and slippery by the surf, but as she cautiously began to climb, she found them easier than scaling the walls. She dragged her right leg over the rocks behind her. Some of them felt alarmingly unsteady, but at this point, she didn't feel she had much to lose. It was by the grace of God alone that she finally reached the top, the water only inches below her feet. She sighed. She had made it. Her relief lasted only seconds as she looked around and realized there was nowhere else to go. She squinted in the shadows but saw nothing that looked like an escape route.

She shifted her position, and the rock beneath her started to slide. She cried out and grabbed for anything. Another rock began to wobble. Her fingers caught hold of something—it felt like a skinny strip of leather. She jerked on it to see if it would hold but it slipped free of the rock. She studied the back wall, running her fingers over the rough edges. The piled stone wavered beneath her. To steady herself, she reached out to the adjoining wall that formed the right side of the cave and snatched at the nearest rocky projection.

She gasped in astonishment. A whole chunk of the rock came free in her hand.

She eagerly thrust her hand into the cavity it left behind, and the surrounding rock loosened at her touch. She pawed at the crumbling stone, her heartbeat quickening as it fell away, and then stuffed her fist through the hole into the space on the other side. She had found a way out! Now if she could just widen the opening... She wrenched at the stones, tearing off what remained of her fingernails and scraping her fingers. More rock slid away. And more. But was it big enough? She could feel the water around her knees now. She glanced back and peered into the gloom at the swelling flood.

A flare of lightning lit up the cavern and something caught her eye. She froze. What was that? She waited. When the lightning blazed again, she saw it.

A flash of silver.

It vanished as quickly as it had appeared. She stared into the darkness as the seconds slipped by.

The captured ocean surged around her waist. The water was rising faster and faster. There was no more time. She shoved her arms into the narrow opening ahead of her and then squeezed through.

Blackness swallowed her as she tumbled into the adjacent cavern. She scrambled away from the opening, following the rocky floor as it climbed upward to higher ground. "Thank you, Father," she gasped. "Thank you."

Cold, pain and fatigue merged until she felt only numbness. All she wanted to do was sleep. She forced herself to her feet. She had to keep moving. She groped slowly through the darkness, limping painfully.

Suddenly she stumbled over something large and before she could stop herself, fell to the ground in a sprawling heap, crying out in agony at the spasm that shot through her wrist when she tried to break her fall. She sat up slowly and for a moment didn't move, waiting for the nauseating waves of pain to pass. She reached out with her other hand to find what she'd tripped over. Just a pile of rocks. She was drawing her hand away when something brushed it. Something sticking out of the rocks. She touched it hesitantly. It felt like wood. She let her fingers slide up the slender rod until they came to something else. It seemed to be another stick but this one was horizontally across the first one, held in place, it seemed, by some kind of cord with a pointed rock dangling off of it.

Suddenly she jerked her hand back, and a chill raced through her body as she realized what it was.

A cross.

She had stumbled across Dylan's grave.

From then on she crawled. She didn't know for how long, or how far she had gone. She was weak with exhaustion, and maybe she was only imagining it, but after finding the grave, even the air seemed to feel like death.

At last she found a break in the chamber wall and crawled through it. A few feet beyond the opening, she collapsed.

Stay awake. She knew she had to stay awake.

She rolled onto her back and then pulled herself into a sitting position, resting her back against the cold stone.

"Don't sleep," she whispered.

She quoted Bible verses in her head, straining to recall the words that normally came so easily.

She realized dimly that the narrow strip of leather she had pulled from the rocks was still clenched in her hand. Had she been holding it the whole time? She ran her fingers over it. There was some kind of a sharp rock hanging off it that felt strangely familiar.

"Just stay awake."

She was still mumbling when she saw it. A tiny blur of light bobbing along in the darkness, growing larger with each passing moment.

And then it was there in front of her, dazzling her eyes. A pair of strong arms were gently lifting her from the cold, hard floor. A rough low voice murmured soothingly, "There, there. It'll be all right, lass. It'll be all right."

And with a faint smile playing on her lips, she knew that it would be.

No accidents. No coincidences.

Thank you, Father. ☙

chapter twenty-six

She was warm.

She could feel sunlight on her face.

Slowly, she opened her eyes.

The hospital room glowed in the morning light. Or was it afternoon?

She remembered only snatches of Ian carrying her through the woods to the Dawson's house and banging on the back door. What happened after that was reduced to a succession of images and sounds. Mrs. Dawson on the phone; Mr. Dawson taking her from Ian and putting her in the back of the car with Montgomery. Through a heavy fog she saw her friend's worried face peering down at her and heard Mr. Dawson saying distractedly to Ian as he ran red light after red light, "I thought you couldn't talk." By the time they reached the nearest hospital, she was unconscious.

Sore and stiff, she tried to sit up, careful not to put any pressure on her wrapped wrist, but sank back against her pillow. Laying down felt good for right now.

She glanced about the room. There was no one there now, but the flowers and cards covering the window sill and table suggested that she'd had visitors. There were so many flowers… She gazed at them in awe. Daisies, roses, wild flowers. A medical cart near her bed was crowned with fresh-cut lilacs. She breathed in their fragrance. She loved lilacs. Shonda and Kyle must have brought them.

She tried again to sit up, and this time succeeded. She sat for a few moments and then gingerly swung her legs over the side of the bed. The room tilted a little, so she sat like that for several minutes until the dizziness passed. Then, cautiously, she got to her feet. Her right leg was bandaged and refused to hold her up, so after a couple of deep breaths, she hopped awkwardly to the window.

"You get back into bed, young lady!"

Jackie turned as a nurse bustled into the room. "I just wanted—"

"At least you had sense enough to stay off that leg." She grabbed Jackie firmly by the shoulders and steered her back to the bed, helping support her as she hopped. The effort was exhausting, and she sank gratefully down onto the bed.

"I just wanted to see who the flowers were from." She looked longingly at the brightly colored bunches.

"About every person you've ever met and all their fourth cousins, I imagine," she said briskly, checking bandages and instruments, but she smiled kindly as she gave Jackie a small cup of liquid to drink, followed by a glass of water. "Drink this, and I'll see about getting you some supper."

"Supper? Is it evening?"

"If I hadn't come in when I had, no doubt you would have enjoyed a splendid sunset."

Jackie noted the white walls had gone from cheery gold to a soft red. "I'm enjoying it anyway," she said with a smile.

The nurse paused and took in the red walls, and a slow smile spread across her plain features. She pressed an intercom button and ordered a dinner tray, then said to Jackie, "Now let's find out who all your admirers are."

She brought the flowers and gifts over one by one in a vibrant parade of color. Jackie buried her nose in the blossoms. The daisies were from Mrs. Cox. An arrangement of lilies and orchids was from the Academy, and another of irises, carnations, bluebells and a few species Jackie couldn't identify was from the church. A dozen roses of varied colors were from the Dawsons, and there were cards from church members and classmates and even parents. By the chair was an orange tree lodged in a meticulously painted pot with *Tempest* quotes scrawled around it. She smiled. Montgomery, of course. A framed black and white photograph from the play was signed by all the cast members, and in a corner by itself was a single yellow rose with a note that simply said, "Get well. Kris."

The news that she was awake spread quickly, and soon Shonda, Kyle and the Dawsons were crowding into her room. Mrs. Dawson was particularly gushy while Shonda just hugged her and cried. Kyle and Mr. Dawson each hugged her too. After several minutes, they left her to rest, but Montgomery lingered behind.

His face was pale and drawn. He looked like he hadn't closed his eyes once the whole time she'd been sleeping.

"I love my tree," she said as he drew close to the bed.

He was silent at first, his eyes fixed on her face. "You really scared me, you know."

And she was amazed to see tears in his eyes.

She smiled and threw her arms around him, ignoring her protesting ribs. He hugged her back.

Over the next few days she did little more than sleep. The slightest exertion seemed to exhaust her, but as the days passed, she felt her strength gradually return. Shonda and Kyle came to see her every day. Her sister brought her some of her own pajamas so she didn't have to wear the awful hospital gown and took the clothes she'd been found in home to be washed.

"Oh," Shonda said, before she left one afternoon. "I almost forgot. This was in your jeans pocket." She held out an arrowhead on a long leather cord.

Jackie took it in surprise and turned it over curiously, running her fingers over it. The feel of the pointed stone and the grain of the leather cord recalled a vague memory. She dimly remembered pulling it loose from the rocks as she climbed. She caressed the worn edges, and suddenly it all made sense. Such perfect sense that she wondered why she hadn't realized it long before.

She awoke the next afternoon to find Montgomery sitting at the little table by the window, sketching.

"Hi!" he said cheerfully when he saw she was awake.

She smiled and pushed the button on her bed until she was in a sitting position. "Hi." She looked around, but there was no one else in the room. "How'd you get here?"

"Kyle dropped me off. He had to run some errands. I'm not alone, either." He glanced toward the door.

She looked over and smiled.

Ian stood in the doorway.

"Hello, lass," he said. "You're feeling better?"

She nodded. "Stronger every day."

"That's good."

"I've been hoping you'd come to see me."

His eyes twinkled. "Well, it's a long walk, isn't it."

"Hey, have you seen this?" Montgomery asked, handing her a newspaper.

She looked at it curiously. The front page was plastered with two large pictures—one of her and the other of Ian. A double headline screamed, "Local Girl Rescued—Missing Heir Found."

"Wow." She scanned the article. "How did it get out?"

Ian sat down in the other chair and said nothing, so Montgomery told her. "Well, the reporters all wanted a story on your rescuer, and their radar about went off the charts when they found out it was a homeless man whom everyone thought was mute. But it was the Irish accent that really got them asking questions."

"So what happens now?"

"I don't know. I guess the owners of the inn are in a bit of a panic. But Ian's not even trying to reclaim his land, so…" He shrugged. "I guess we'll see."

She nodded, and they were quiet for a moment. "I'm glad you're both here," she said at last. "There's something I want to show you."

They watched expectantly as she reached into the nightstand drawer and pulled out the arrowhead.

Ian blinked in surprise.

Montgomery's eyes widened. "But that looks just like…" He reached inside his shirt and pulled out his own.

They approached the bed, and Ian gently took it from her hand and held it out next to Montgomery's. They were nearly identical. Montgomery stared at them. "Then Hal…?"

"My friend Hal was Henry Dawson, your grandfather."

Montgomery looked at him in confusion. "Why didn't you ever tell me?"

Ian's features arranged themselves into an expression somewhere between regret and indifference. "Hal thinks I'm dead," he said simply. "It's been so long now, I don't know if he'd care one way or the other. But I thought that if you knew your grandfather was a part of all this…" He shook his head. "I just didn't want you to feel stuck in the middle, that's all."

Montgomery nodded slowly. After a moment of silence, he asked if anyone wanted anything to drink and went down to the cafeteria to get a soda.

Jackie plumped the pillows behind her and then turned to Ian. "You know, I never got a chance to say thank you. How did you know to come looking for me?"

Ian's weathered cheeks turned pink. "I saw your bag out on your rock. I knew you wouldn't leave it." He shrugged modestly. "Lucky I was there is all."

She smiled. "There is no luck. I shouldn't be alive. But I am. And it's no accident."

"Maybe the cove wanted to share its secrets with you," he said with a grin.

"Maybe God wanted the world to see Sam for who he really is."

"And who would that be? An Irish aristocrat who dines at soup kitchens and wears cast off clothes?"

She smiled. "A hero."

"I'm no hero, lass. I'm a coward. There's some who might say I've disgraced my family name and thrown away my life."

"Maybe. But you saved mine." She met his gaze steadily. "The path you chose may not have been the ideal one. But perhaps God allowed it so you'd be there when I needed you. No one else could have found me, Ian. No one else would have known where to look."

He nodded and looked down at the arrowhead in his hand. "Where did you find this?" he asked softly.

"In the cavern where I woke up. The one the water washed me into. It was caught in the rocks." She hesitated. "Where did you find Dylan? Was it in that cavern?"

He nodded slowly.

"You know, I found another arrowhead while I was down there."

He looked up. There seemed to be no end to the depths of his brilliant eyes.

"It was attached to a cross."

He sighed. "When I found him, he was missing his. I knew how much he loved it. In fact, they were his idea. So I left mine at his resting place." He looked down again at the arrowhead and squeezed his fingers over it. "You've returned something to me that belonged to my brother. And I thank you for it. I could ask for no greater gift."

She nodded and smiled. "I can't say the act was consciously

deliberate, but I'm glad I could bring it back to you."

"Well, I'd better let you get back to sleep," he said. "Your brother-in-law will be here soon to collect us."

Suddenly she remembered the flash of silver she had seen and called after him. "Before you go, there's one other thing I'd like to ask you."

He paused.

"That cavern where you found Dylan—where I woke up—I thought I saw..." she hesitated.

He smiled. "I told you the cove wanted to show you her secrets."

She stared at him, and her heart started pounding. "Is it really—? The legend, I mean, of the silver cave—"

He grinned. "Remember now—a secret is a secret." He winked. "I'll round up Montgomery."

"Good night, Ian," she said, and she couldn't keep from smiling. "Thank you for coming."

He ducked his head in a quick nod, then left the room.

The hospital discharged her the following day with a pair of crutches and a warning to take it easy. Her leg was healing quickly, but they wanted her to keep her weight off of it for at least another week.

Shonda fixed up the couch for her to sleep on until she could handle the stairs to her room and insisted she take another day off from school, so Jackie hobbled about the house until she thought she would go out of her mind.

"Pleeease, Shonda, let me go to school tomorrow," she pleaded that evening. "Being cooped up like this is driving me absolutely insane!"

And so for the first time in three years, Jackie stood out at the end of the driveway and waited for the school bus. The driver knew to stop for her because Shonda had called the school, but the students stared in surprise.

"Jackie!"

She looked down the length of the bus and saw Alicia Lewis waving to her.

"There's room back here."

She awkwardly made her way down the narrow aisle to the back of the bus.

"Right here, Jackie. You can sit with me." It was one of the giggle girls. Jackie thought her name was Amy.

"Thanks." She sat down gratefully and struggled out of her backpack, so she could lean back.

One of the boys quickly took her crutches and stowed them under his seat.

As soon as she was settled, everyone began talking to her at once, asking how she was feeling and telling her how glad they were to have her back.

School was more of the same, and the teachers were almost as enthusiastic as the students.

"Hey!" Montgomery said, when she finally had a moment to herself. "I would have come to see you yesterday, but Mom thought it would be best if you had some peace and quiet."

"I wish you had come," she said. "I was bored to tears." She glanced around at all the friendly, concerned faces. "I sure didn't expect this, though. I feel almost like a…"

"Celebrity?" he finished with a grin. "You should. After you made the front page of all the local newspapers, I wouldn't be surprised if people started asking for your autograph."

She smiled. "Well, I hope it doesn't go that far."

The day passed quickly, and she was never alone for a moment. Every time she turned around there was someone offering to help her, and if Montgomery wasn't at her side at the moment class ended, one of the other guys would grab her books and carry them to the next class for her.

Before she knew it, the final bell had rung, and she was packing up her bag for home.

"Here, let me take that for you."

She glanced up and found herself looking into Kris Cappencella's brown eyes. "Uh—sure. Thanks," she stammered as he took her backpack and slung it over his shoulder. "By the way," she said, as they walked down the hall, "I never thanked you for the rose. It's really beautiful."

"Yeah, sure." He shrugged lightly and glanced away, but she caught a glimpse of a smile on his lips and thought his cheeks might have turned a little red.

By the end of the week, Kris had become her self-appointed bodyguard, carrying her books between classes and making sure she always had a clear path through which to walk.

Montgomery didn't comment on it, but every now and then she would catch sight of an infuriating grin on his face when he saw her limping through the halls with Kris at her side.

After a full week had passed since she'd returned home, the doctors gave her the okay to start using her leg more, and she was able to sleep in her own bedroom again, though they urged her to continue using the crutches for at least another week, if not two.

It was a few days later before she had worked up the nerve to ask Shonda to drive her to Winds Cove.

"What?" Shonda asked. "You want to go back there? Why?"

"No, I don't really want to go back. And that's why I need to."

She was more than a little nervous about returning to the cove. Her sister drove to the path and then parked the car as far off the road as she could get it. Then, they slowly made their way down the mossy lane until they reached the edge of the forest. Shonda looked out over the playful waves as they frolicked around the rocks.

"Are you sure about this?" she asked, doubtfully.

"I have to do this," Jackie said. "Or I'll never go out there again."

"Is that such a bad thing?" Shonda asked.

"Yes. I need this."

They hobbled cautiously down to the water's edge and sat on a rock beneath the willow tree. Jackie sighed. She hadn't told anyone, but her dreams were haunted by waves and whirlpools and dark, damp caves. But now, gazing at the glittering water through the trailing willow boughs, she thought she could finally put the incident behind her.

They didn't stay very long, and Shonda seemed relieved when they were back in the car again.

Jackie didn't return to the cove again until she was rid of the clumsy crutches. Her days were mostly occupied with catching up on schoolwork.

The day she left her crutches and cast behind at the hospital was a day of tremendous celebration. Kyle, of course, suggested ice cream, and Shonda assured him they had some at home. So as soon as they reached the house, Shonda headed for the kitchen to get the ice cream and Jackie went upstairs to her room to fetch a book Kyle wanted to borrow.

She swung open the door and flicked on the light switch.

"SURPRISE!!"

She staggered back against the doorway as teenagers from church and school popped out from every corner of her room. She glanced down the stairs and saw her sister and brother-in-law grinning up at her.

A card table had been set up and was covered with nachos, raw veggies, and soda, and soon Shonda and Kyle came up, lugging an enormous ice cream cake. Music was playing on her little stereo, and voices raised in laughter resounded throughout every corner of the house. Twinkle lights were everywhere, around the windows, in her orange tree and strung along the slanted ceiling so that at first glance, the lights seemed to be wound through the painted tree branches. A balloon bouquet next to the bean bag marked it as her temporary throne.

"This is the coolest room I've ever seen!" Alicia exclaimed, examining every inch of the mural, and several others nodded in agreement.

The party raged for a solid three hours, everyone talking, laughing and eating much more than they should. Kris and Brent were even persuaded to bumble through their old duet comedy routine and by the time they were done, everyone was laughing so hard, they were in tears. Jackie wiped at her eyes and marveled that she hadn't found it funny before.

On a sudden stroke of inspiration, Jackie asked everyone to sign the wall beside the door before they left and within minutes the area that had looked like a meadow and a stretch of blue sky was transformed into a giant greeting card.

When everyone was finally gone, Montgomery stayed behind to help clean up.

She left the lights up. Their soft glow added to the feeling of the enchanted wood.

"Thank you," she said to the three of them when they were done. She tied up the last bag of garbage, and Kyle took it outside and then drove Montgomery home.

She was exhausted, and Shonda sent her off to bed. She'd never had a party—not one like this—and as tired as she was, she lay in bed reliving the night into the wee hours of the morning. ♌

chapter twenty-seven

Jackie sat out on her rock. The water was still and calm and reflected the forest and rocks around it in its mirror-like surface. A faint breeze ruffled her curls. She heard footsteps behind her and turned, expecting to see Montgomery or Ian. Her heart skipped a beat.

"Hello, Jacqueline." Mason Randall smiled, but it wasn't his usual grin, oozing with charm and self-assurance. He looked nervous.

The shock slowly faded, and she felt the hurt and anger rekindling inside her, but tried to shove the feelings aside.

"I heard you... ah... had a bit of a spill out here." He glanced at the water. "You okay?"

She nodded. It didn't matter. Nothing he said or did could matter.

"Do you mind if... would it be all right if I joined you?"

She hesitated, then shrugged and turned her gaze back out to the water. He would say his piece, and then he would leave. Just like he always did. And that was fine. Because Shonda and Kyle were her family.

He sat down next to her. She waited for him to speak, but he didn't. They sat in silence for several long minutes.

"I don't blame you for hating me," he said at last.

She sighed. "I don't hate you, Dad."

"Well, I do. I know I let you down. And I know there's no excuse for it. But if—if I could just explain what I felt... maybe you would understand more. Shonnie's done an amazing job raising you. The two of you have something special. When I was here, that relationship was gone. Wasn't it?"

She nodded slowly.

"That's why I left. I had caused so much damage already, I didn't want to shatter what you had with her."

"If you hadn't left the first time, you wouldn't have had to worry about all that damage," Jackie said coldly.

"I know," he whispered. "But don't you see?" He stared at her earnestly, his eyes pleading with her to understand. "I just wasn't ready to be a father. There was still so much to do and see! It wasn't time for me yet."

"So you left us."

"It's not quite that simple."

"Then complicate it for me."

He ran his hands through his dark hair. "I'm a free spirit, Jacqueline, just like you. I couldn't be chained to a house and family—I needed freedom. Not a wife and a dog and two-point-three kids in a suburban house. I wasn't meant for that life." He sighed. "But I know that's no excuse." He smiled bitterly. "I've never been good with responsibility. I can't even keep house plants," he added with a rueful laugh.

"What I'm trying to say is, I know I'm not perfect." He met her eyes, then looked away. "Okay, that's the understatement of the decade. I'm a complete failure as a father. And as a husband. I know that. To tell you the truth, there were so many times that I wanted to come back. But I knew my shortcomings as well as my attributes. I knew I would leave again. And I knew that I wouldn't make your life any better for being in it." He paused. "So when I came back and met you…" He shook his head helplessly. "I was scared.

"When you open your heart up to love and be loved, you risk the possibility of disappointment. I don't mean being disappointed, though that's true, too. I mean setting yourself up for disappointing others. I guess, I shouldn't be afraid of that anymore… not after I've disappointed so many. But, it still scares me. I was putting myself in a vulnerable position, and I was destroying your relationship with Shonnie. So I did what I always do. I ran."

"But I don't want to run anymore," he whispered.

Jackie looked up in surprise.

"It's not like we'd be living together. I'll probably be in New York, but we could see each other on weekends. And talk during the week. And maybe eventually, I could move out here. Or maybe, you could come to New York. I can't promise that I'll be the ideal father from here on out. But I do promise to really try… that is… if you still want me in your life."

She was silent. She wanted to believe him. Never had she connected with somebody so completely. Never in her life had she known such a kindred spirit as the man who sat beside her. But how could she trust him, he who had betrayed his wedding vows and the trust of his two daughters?

"So, now, I need to ask your forgiveness. Not just for missing your play. For everything. For everything I did… and didn't do. I figured it was too late for Shonnie, but that maybe there was still a chance for us…"

She could feel him watching her intently.

"Is there? Still a chance? I know I've messed things up—it's something I'm really good at—but in spite of all my faults, I really think that it's the right thing to do. I even talked to your pastor, and he agrees… and… I think it's what your mother would want."

She didn't say anything. Her fists were clenched so tightly, her fingernails were digging into the skin of her palms. She had forgiven him already. But did she really want to risk being brokenhearted all over again? There's the rub, she thought ruefully. Love requires risk. It always has.

He held out a square package. "I was going to mail this, but…"

"What is it?" She glanced at it a little suspiciously. It looked like a bribe.

He shrugged. "Just something I've had for a while. I picked it up a year ago when I was traveling. I bought it with you in mind, actually, and then realized I didn't know you enough to... to know if you'd even like it. I guess you could say this was sort of the catalyst for coming up here in the first place."

Curious in spite of herself, she took it and slowly unwrapped the brown paper.

In the soft folds of a length of blue silk, lay a leather bound journal, its pages edged in silver. Each page displayed a painting or sketch from a play along with an accompanying quote. Most of the selections were from Shakespeare, but as she flipped through she saw some from Marlow and Johnson as well.

"It's so beautiful!" she whispered, touching the pages gently.

"It's from England," he told her. "I know it doesn't make up for missing your play, but..."

She looked up at him. He said nothing else, but his eyes were pleading.

She hesitated for a brief second, then smiled and nodded, and a gentle sense of peace flowed over her. "It's perfect. Thank you."

"You're welcome." His features relaxed into a grateful smile. "I can't stick around this visit. I've got a job in New York working on a newspaper. It's mostly freelance type of stuff, but it's steady. I need to start saving if we're still going to do Europe." His smile was anxious.

She nodded. "Yeah. Guess I'd better start saving, too."

He grinned and stood up. "Yeah. Well... Goodbye." He stood there uncertainly for a moment.

She smiled again as she stood up and then hugged him tightly. She felt the tension leave his body as his arms wrapped around her fiercely.

"I love you," he said softly. "Whatever mistakes I've made, whatever mistakes I'll make in the future, I love you. And I love Shonda. I don't deserve either one of you, but God gave us to each other, so we'd better make the best of it, right?"

She looked up at him. "I love you, Dad."

He beamed.

She carried his smile with her all the way home.

Shonda was not impressed with Mason's return. "He shows up when it's convenient for him. That's the way it's always been and that's the way it will always be. And if I were you, I wouldn't hold my breath about Europe, either."

"I'm not holding my breath," Jackie said quietly, some of her enthusiasm fading away. She excused herself from the table and went to her room. She flopped down on her bed and pulled out the journal her father had given her. She flipped absently through the pages, reading the quotes and admiring the illustrations. She came to a beautiful painting of Miranda and paused to read the quote, but was surprised to find not only a line from the play, but an inscription penned by her father.

To my beautiful daughter, May you always live in the place where the ocean meets the sky. With love, dreams and memories of starry places, Dad.

She smiled and read it again. And again. She fell asleep with the words dancing across her memory.

It was still dark when she awoke and a quick glance at her alarm clock told her she'd only been asleep for a few hours. Her throat felt parched and she slipped out of bed and down the stairs to get a glass of water. She was padding quietly toward the kitchen in stocking feet when the sound of voices coming from Shonda and Kyle's bedroom reached her ears.

"Shonda, I love you, and I know what your father did was wrong and that it hurt you terribly. But you have got to let this go. You must forgive him. And turn it over to God."

"I can't."

"You have to. Shon, forgiveness is necessary for life. And it is *required by God.*" He paused.

Shonda said nothing.

"You know that I'm here for you. I will support you. I will help you in any way I can. But you *have* to take care of this. For yourself, for your father. Especially for Jackie—she needs to come to terms with this, and she needs your example. But mostly because it is *right*. It is what God wants and what He commands."

Jackie slipped quietly away as she heard her sister start to cry, the glass of water forgotten.

The weekend at last! Jackie sighed in relief as she stepped outside into the sunlight. There were only a few weeks left of school. Then the summer would stretch before her in long lazy days filled with sunshine, reading and working at the store with Shonda. She took her time as she walked home.

When she walked in to the house, she found her sister sitting in the overstuffed armchair in the living room, scribbling away on a sheet of paper. Jackie flopped down on the couch. "What are you writing?"

"A letter to Dad," her sister replied without looking up.

Shonda must have felt her staring because she glanced up and smiled. "I know. Crazy, huh?"

"Why…?"

"Because I need to."

"You mean you've forgiven him?"

She nodded. "And I'm asking for his forgiveness too. It's time I put this behind me, wouldn't you say?"

Jackie didn't answer, but watched her sister carefully as she returned to her letter. The lines around her mouth were gone. The tightness of her face and rigidity of her posture had vanished.

Shonda looked up and met her gaze.

"You seem different," Jackie said at last.

Shonda smiled. "I am." She twirled the pen between her fingers. "Yesterday I was a wreck. I cried all day long. Poor Kyle," she added softly with a remorseful grin. "Then finally, after a *very* long sleepless night, I just... gave it up. Turned it over to God. I couldn't handle it anymore, so I let it go. And today I feel the most amazing *freedom*."

She turned her gaze to the scene beyond the living room window. "You know, it's funny. I've been so angry with him for so long, that now I..." she shook her head. "I wish you could have known him the way he was when I was little. We had so much fun! He taught me to read. He taught me to ride a horse. I know I always made it seem like Mom loved to get up early and watch the sunrise—and she did—but it was because of Dad. He used to drag us out from under the blankets so we could watch the sun come up with him. He hated to sleep. He felt like he was wasting time. He had so much passion. So much life. Like you." She smiled faintly. "I don't suppose he's really changed much. But back then, I didn't know the way things would turn out. It's hard to see him in the same light now." She sighed. "Now I just feel... burdened for him. You know, I don't even know if he knows Christ." She glanced down at the paper before her. "That's what this is about. Asking for his forgiveness, putting this behind us and looking forward. I know things won't change overnight. But it's a beginning." She studied Jackie briefly. "I know I haven't been the best example in all this." Her eyes met Jackie's. "I'm so sorry."

Jackie quickly crossed the room and threw her arms around her sister.

Shonda smiled and hugged her back. "Do me a favor and learn my lesson with me, so you won't have to go through this yourself." She pulled back so she could look into Jackie's eyes. "Don't hold on to bitterness the way I have. It makes you unhappy and old and puts you in a cage of your own making. The chief end of man is to glorify God. It's hard to do that when you've locked yourself behind bars." She smiled again. "And before you run off with William Shakespeare, I have something for you."

"For me?"

She nodded. "I found this while I was doing your laundry." She pulled out the torn picture of their mother. "And I thought that maybe you might like to have this." From under the stationary, she pulled another photograph and handed it to Jackie.

Jackie stared in amazement. It was the same picture, except this one was whole.

"Where did you…?"

"I've had it for years," Shonda said. "In my Bible. I think for a long time, I used it to keep the hate burning. But deep down, I always loved him." She smiled. "I'd like you to have it now."

Jackie thanked her, trying desperately not to get all teary-eyed.

Shonda hugged her again and then said, "Now why don't you get started on your homework, so I can finish up mine." She patted Jackie's arm and turned back to the letter. ◡

chapter twenty-eight

The days turned balmy as the wind whispered of the coming summer. To avoid a legal battle, the hotel owners had agreed to give Ian the guest house from the estate, along with a couple of acres bordering Winds Cove. They even moved the cottage there for him. When he was all settled in, he extended an invitation to Jackie and Montgomery for tea.

"Why do you suppose they were so generous?" Montgomery asked, as they walked down the path toward his new home. "I mean, if it went to court, they wouldn't necessarily lose. He chose to stay away and let everyone think he was dead."

"I asked Kyle that," Jackie answered. "He does their accounting. He said they figured that it was better to give him a little than risk losing everything. The courts could possibly rule in his favor because he was the victim of such trauma. They might decide he wasn't capable of rational thought at the time or something. And I guess they gain a lot of good will from the townspeople—you know, being nice to the town founder's only descendant who's basically come back from the dead in a made-for-television sort of drama—and they're getting some good publicity. They'll probably have a good season with the tourists this year."

They approached the cheery little white cottage on the newly cleared lot near the cove.

Ian opened the door and beamed at them. "Come in! Come in!" He motioned them in eagerly.

They stepped into a fair-sized room crammed with a small kitchenette, a table and chairs, a wood stove, a couch, an overstuffed chair and *lots* of books. There was a bookcase on every wall and stacks of books everywhere. Two doors at the back wall opened into a tiny bedroom and bathroom.

Jackie sat down on the sofa and took the tea Ian offered her. She sipped it and then set it on a small coffee table crowded in front of the couch. She smiled. The table was no more than a framed piece of glass balanced on four piles of books.

It wasn't much by most people's standards, but it was cute and cozy and compared to where Ian had been living for nearly half a century, it was a palace. Candles and lanterns cluttered any available surface, and Jackie smiled again. The guest house was fully wired, but Ian only used the little generator for hot water and plumbing and continued to rely on sunshine and candles for light.

Ian sat down across from them, a smile creasing his weathered face, and pulled out two carefully wrapped packages and handed one to each of them.

"What's this?" Montgomery asked in surprise.

"Belated Christmas gifts," Ian said, a twinkle in his bright blue eyes.

Montgomery's package was wrapped in newspaper, but hers was swathed in pale green fabric with an intricate design spiraling across it in a duet of dark green and silver thread. Jackie touched it gently. It felt like silk.

She looked up at Ian. He was watching her intently.

"It's so beautiful," she said.

"It was my mother's. I found it when I looking through the stuff in the attic at the inn. Dylan had brought it with him when we came to the States." He smiled. "As soon as I saw it, I thought that it was the exact color of your eyes. If she had known you, I believe she would have wanted you to have it."

"Thank you." She felt wretchedly like a typical girl as tears sprang to her eyes, but she blinked them back and opened the package with care. A black and white photograph in a silver frame lay in the delicate jade colored folds. Her breath caught as she studied the picture. Three boys perched on a large boulder in the water, all smiling into the camera. Two were dark haired, and the third was blond with a mischievous lopsided grin. Around each of their necks was an arrowhead on a long cord.

Montgomery also had a picture, but in his the boys were playing soccer in a wide field.

She shook her head sadly. Three boys who would travel three very different roads. Three lives forever altered by one windy day.

She rose and squeezed around the makeshift coffee table and hugged Ian tightly. "Thank you," she whispered.

Montgomery shook his hand and thanked him as well.

When she got home later that day, she went quickly up to her room and removed the picture from the folds of the scarf. Something on the back of the frame caught her eye. There was something written. She squinted to read the fine scrolling print.

For Jackie. With much love, Ian. May the wind be ever at your back and may God hold you in the palm of His hand.

She smiled and set the picture on her bookcase next to the other photographs of her parents, the *Tempest* cast, and her father and her in New York City. She knew the wind wouldn't always be at her back, for trials and struggles were what forced you to grow. But for the moment, it was.

"I smell roast duck," Montgomery announced as they walked through the back door into the kitchen.

Jackie sniffed the air. "I've never smelled duck before. Didn't your mom say we were having manicotti?"

He nodded. "I can't understand it. The only person in my family who likes duck is…" He stopped suddenly.

"What?"

"Shhh!"

Suddenly he ran from the kitchen.

Jackie followed, bewildered. What on earth was going on?

Montgomery charged into the living room, Jackie trailing behind.

"Gramps!" he yelled.

An older man with white hair and dark eyes sat in an arm chair, talking with Mr. and Mrs. Dawson. His lined face crinkled into a smile as he stood and enveloped his grandson in a hug.

"I didn't know you were coming! What are you doing here?"

"I thought I'd surprise everyone."

"Well, mission accomplished," Montgomery said with a grin. "Oh, this is Jackie."

He smiled down at her. "I've heard a lot about you, Jackie. It's a pleasure to finally meet you."

She smiled and shook his hand, but his intense eyes shifted back to his grandson.

"I want you to take me to this friend of yours you call Sam."

Montgomery's smile wavered. "Oh. Okay. Why?" He glanced at Jackie nervously.

The elder Mr. Dawson simply smiled. "Let's go tomorrow. Early. Maybe we'll even catch the sunrise."

The dawn was cold and fierce, the colors blazing across the sky and turning the water to fire.

Jackie watched the colors fade as the sun rose higher. She glanced over at Ian and smiled. He had come silently out to join her soon after she'd arrived. He didn't know that Hal was coming. She knew she hadn't done anything wrong, but she still felt a bit like a traitor.

Ian's smile suddenly faded, and his bright blue eyes narrowed.

Jackie turned. Montgomery and his grandfather were standing at the edge of the forest.

Ian gave her a searching look, but watched silently as the two approached. Henry Dawson didn't hesitate when he came to the little peninsula of rocks and walked out with certainty. When he was just a few feet away, he stopped.

Ian slowly rose to his feet.

Hal stared at him, disbelief and anger, hurt and betrayal warring in his dark eyes. His gaze lingered on the arrowhead Ian wore around his neck. When he spoke, his voice was barely more than a whisper. "All these years... I thought you were dead."

"I was dead," Ian said softly. "Let's leave it at that."

The minutes seemed to stretch out as the two men stood silently, eyes locked on one another, filled with an emotion Jackie couldn't define. Anger? Guilt? Were they blaming each other? Or was this some sort of strange reconciliation?

After what felt like forever, Ian held out his hand.

Hal stared at it, but didn't offer to accept.

"Would you... will you forgive me?" Ian asked.

Hal stood there for a long, long time, his gaze steady and dark. "I don't understand why you did this," he said at last. "I'm not even going to try. But the fact that you and I are still alive means one thing: that Dylan's work here was done. And yours and mine is not." He slowly extended his hand and clasped Ian's formally. "I'm going home in the morning. I want to leave with a clear conscience."

Ian nodded slowly. "Must you go so soon?"

"We have both moved on since that day. We just chose different roads. Kilree holds nothing for me anymore. Only ghosts."

"I'm not a ghost," Ian said softly.

"You might as well be one." Hal's sweeping gesture encompassed the cove. "Haunting the place where you died."

"You don't understand," Ian said, "You've never lost a brother."

"No," Hal agreed, fixing him with a meaningful look. "I lost two."

Ian was silent. "So you're leaving. And all is forgiven?"

Hal was quiet, and for a moment Jackie didn't think he was going to answer. He seemed so cold. Not angry or sad... just detached. Indifferent. Then he looked away, and she couldn't see his face.

"Only if you will also forgive me."

Ian looked as surprised as Jackie felt. "For what?"

"For leaving. Dylan may have been beyond our help, but if I had stayed, we might not have lost you too."

Ian slowly shook his head and said earnestly, "There is nothing to forgive."

Hal nodded and turned to leave. But before he'd taken two steps, he paused and glanced back, and for a moment, the cool façade cracked, and he seemed young and vulnerable. "Just tell me one thing: if I had returned, by myself, after... when the others had gone away, would you have come out? Would you have come home?" There was a tormented look in his eyes, and Jackie wanted to cry at the pain and the guilt she saw there. She remembered what Ian had told her. If Hal had only come back... things might have been very different.

She watched him almost fearfully and then saw that Hal did too.

But Ian smiled. "I think I had already chosen my road by then."

Hal nodded, and years seem to lift from his face. A ghost of the old grin appeared. "You hid in caves. I hid in crowds. Maybe we're not so different after all."

Montgomery caught her eye and nodded slightly toward the shore. He quietly started back, and Jackie reluctantly followed, slipping past the two men.

"I just think maybe they should be alone. Now that we know Gramps isn't going to kill him," he added with a grin.

Jackie glanced wistfully back. She wanted to hear every word that was said as the two old friends started a new friendship, in the place where everything had shattered. Perhaps that's why things had happened the way they had, she thought, watching Ian and Hal sitting on the boulder. Through seemingly unrelated tragedies, so many people had been brought together in this tiny, insignificant part of the world. But not by coincidence. They were all part of a master plan in the tapestry of life, each of them an individual thread in the pattern. For the first time in her life, she felt as though she truly had a specific purpose, even though she wasn't sure yet what that was. She didn't have to know why. She only had to know Who. She smiled as she left the cove behind and obediently followed Montgomery into the forest.

The wind whipped the water into a frothy swirl of blue and white and blew back her long tangle of dark curls. She reached up to feel for the scarf, neatly braided through her hair, to make sure it wasn't coming loose. Montgomery sat beside her, his eyes closed against the dazzling sun, his legs dangling off the edge of the boulder.

Her gaze swept the cove.

On a blanket a few feet from the water's edge, Kyle, Shonda and Mr. and Mrs. Dawson gathered around a picnic lunch. Several feet away under the weeping willow, Ian and Hal lounged in canvas folding chairs.

The sea shimmered in the bright light. It looked like silver.

She smiled to herself.

"What?" Montgomery asked lazily. "You have a secret?"

Jackie laughed softly. "Maybe someday I'll share it with you."

The water gently tickled the bottoms of her bare feet, and the cool breeze caressed her face. *Don't worry, Wind*, she thought. *The cove's secret is safe with me.* And through the emerald leaves of the forest, she heard the wind breathe a soft sigh of relief. ◡